The Nightmare Machine

The Nightmare Machine

an *Anyway Books*® Novel by

John Nicholas Datesh

Published by

Loiseau Media

The Nightmare Machine

An Anyway Books® Novel by

John Nicholas Datesh

Third Print Edition published by
Loiseau Media/Anyway Books 2016
ISBN 978-1-940227-14-6

Publishing history:
e-Editions - John Nicholas Datesh, Jr. 2009
First Print Edition - Tower Publications, Inc. 1979
Second Print Edition – Loiseau Development 2013

Cover based on the painting
The Gates of Hell **by**
Julie Kimball

The Nightmare Machine

CHAPTER ONE

Thomas Jordan knew he could be dead before the week was out.

He was not too young to die. That did not worry him. He had no desire to live forever, either, but, if he were right, living out the week would be a triumph.

It was a simple question he pondered. Should men serving the same institution coincidentally die in their sleep? No, he was sure enough of that. Yet, unless he could fathom the logic of it, Jordan would join his long-time associates any day.

Just thinking about it made him uneasy. Hence, the walk outside his grounds. He leaned back against the cool, damp wall that confined his town estate and scanned Kingsfield Place as if it held some clues.

Jordan dreaded the timing, not the fact, of the threat. To end incomplete, that was what Thomas Jordan feared.

Kingsfield Place had a sense of completeness that always made him feel comfortable. The unlit, cul-de-sac ran for a quarter of a mile along the wall of his estate, ending where the ten foot barrier jutted out to accommodate useless stables. The street ran its course to a dead-end admittedly, but it went so far as, and in the direction, it had been intended to go. Could he say so much for himself?

Not of his work, certainly. He had taken his uncle Harley Talbot's engineering company and parlayed it into a multinational conglomerate monster with its own mind and will. Jordan and Talbot Incorporated was not his life, though it had, he knew, kept him out of World War II. In return, J & T had, as his wife so often claimed, consumed most of the life it had preserved.

His family, such as it had become, was hardly a complete anything, except a mess.

Hadn't he intended to be a surgeon saving lives on a daily basis, to have his own close family? That had been his naive plan before 1931 came and swept the foundation of those hopes away with his and his father's savings. Working for his uncle, Harley Talbot, had only been a temporary thing, a detour from that carefully plotted course.

He had done well enough with Talbot Engineering, parlaying his uncle's firm into the multinational Jordan & Talbot Incorporated. His immediate successes in radar innovation had made him important, preserving him from the ravages of a war that claimed a dozen of his friends. The wealth it brought him made him an attractive catch for Carolyn and gave his family all of the advantages, including the big house he now hated. In return he had exchanged his dreams. Such small dreams, a family, a medical career.

He had gotten a start on a family with Carolyn, a son and a daughter, a nice place to live, but those components never quite fit together. Carolyn had finally opted for a separation in 1972 after thirty years of trying. The children had been lost along the way. Johnny, who was never really his anyway, had reconciled himself to his inadequacies through drink and a token position in J & T's French subsidiary. It was Madelaine, the once affectionate little girl turned brilliant and emotionless as a young woman, who he had truly lost. If he could somehow reclaim her, Jordan would have enough of the family he had wanted.

Like Madelaine, there was another child that he hoped would restore his original plans. He had founded the Talbot Research Hospital as a vehicle to belatedly join a profession he had deserted. If he had spent his life creating electronic gadgetry and generating unspendable wealth, he would channel both toward the advancement of medical science.

The computer-medical research center, the Talbot, as it was usually called, had progressed well in its first five years, only to be squeezed by the recent recession. Operating on sharply curtailed income, the Talbot had been forced to dismember the carefully assembled staff of researchers. It had not recovered yet from the "Talbot Purge" and might never become what he had intended it to be. He had to live long enough to see that the Talbot fulfilled its goal.

It came down to that. He needed time. For God's sake, he needed time. Time to restore Madelaine and the Talbot to him. And something about the grim "Coincidences" of the past five weeks warned Jordan that he would not have that time. Not unless he could make some sense out of it.

Determined that his life not end until it could terminate as he intended, Tom Jordan strode through the shadows of Kingsfield Place toward Fifth Avenue and the gated entrance to his largely deserted estate.

Beyond the graceful sloping lawn, the looming mansion seemed ominously dark. The only light he could see was that in his study, where his work lay waiting, where his dreams lay unfinished.

~ ~ ~

The young man wiped the perspiration from his forehead and jumped out of the rear of the Volkswagen bus. Inside, it was suffocating. Once outside the close confines of the van, he could at least breath. He stretched his five foot five inch frame, working out the stiffness that had accumulated over the hour and half of installation work.

Satisfied, without even looking, that everything was in its proper place, he latched the rear doors and locked them. It wouldn't do for some nosy passerby to break into his expensive equipment. He only had so much money, or rather so little money, and he did not want to keep Jordan waiting any longer. The old bastard had already gotten six weeks more than he deserved. Glancing at his watch, he noted that it was still too early to head to Jordan's gaudy mansion. He had gone over the grounds once before to no avail, but the failure was now an advantage. This time he would have no difficulty setting up. He had confidence in his techniques even if Jordan did not.

Still, he resolved to get to Jordan's place earlier than usual. He wanted to watch the old fool spend his last waking hours–and make sure that he drank that last cup of coffee. Jordan wouldn't appreciate Ray Carleton's work then, either, but later, only a few hours later, he would. For a brief moment, just before he died.

~ ~ ~

The somber chimes of an antique brass clock reminded George Bestral that it was ten o'clock. Forty minutes earlier, George's employer had returned from his evening stroll and, as usual, had retired directly to his study. Mr. Jordan had barely spoken when he had shed his lightweight jacket and cap. The butler had received only a quick "Thank you" for taking them from him. Settled behind his desk, Jordan had indicated that he had an hour's more work to finish before coffee.

George did not expect Mr. Jordan to work that long. The days of Jordan's extraordinary concentration had faded in the prior several years. It seemed, in fact, that it was the very absence of the distractions of a household that made concentration more difficult. Since the discouraging days of the past winter, even an hour of uninterrupted work had become increasingly rare.

The weight of events bothering George's employer had intensified during the month of June and Mr. Jordan barely spent any time at all at the house. There was, of course, no longer much point to being in the rambling, empty mansion. Carolyn had left three years before, Johnny and Madelaine many years before that. Even George got a bit lonely, with the once large staff reduced to himself, Kelly, the gardener, and two inefficient, prematurely senile housemaids. As Mr. Jordan no longer ate his meals at home, in favor of the University Club, the cook had been "let go". What little things that needed done in the kitchen, the housemaids did during the day and George managed himself in the evening.

The coffee, for example. Of course, George had always served the coffee, at ten, but only recently had taken the job of preparing it as well. It was not the least bit difficult. George rather wished it were more complicated, as it had been. Not too many years ago, Mr. Jordan's evening coffee had been carefully brewed to his taste. Ten o'clock had been the routine hour, when Carolyn and the children had lived there. He had taken his coffee at ten, always in the study, always alone, a haven from the angry tumult of the household.

In Jordan's younger days, the coffee had served to extend his waking and, therefore, his working hours beyond one o'clock. The ritual had evolved, however, into a decaffeinated ceremony divorced from its original meaning. An ardent coffee drinker all his life, Jordan now drank Dennison Decaffeinated, a freeze-dried product of J & T's Dennison Foods subsidiary. He no longer drank coffee to keep him awake, but not to keep him awake.

With the coffee steaming in an antique pewter pot, George measured amounts of the "additives", as he labeled them, which Jordan demanded. After Jordan's doctor had insisted that he avoid both sugar and cream in his diet, Dennison Foods had embarked on a crash program to develop an artificial CafeCream and an artificial sweetener to flavor their artificial coffee. George, reluctantly, followed his orders to use nothing else in preparing Jordan's evening coffee.

Jordan had even shipped a ton of the new sweetener, "Sweet Tooth", from its Chicago test market directly to the Talbot in January. From its basement storage, "Sweet

Tooth" was available to anyone fool enough to want it. The limited supply George allowed in the kitchen was secreted away in a special cabinet reserved for Dennison's "uncivilized" products, in order to avoid inadvertently "poisoning" either himself or some innocent guest.

Having added the proper amounts, George noted that the Dennison Decaffeinated and the CafeCream were both in dangerously short supply. The new box of "Sweet Tooth", used only once before by Jordan's doting assistant at Talbot, Jean Skeffington, for the baking of his birthday cake, could be safely returned to the special cupboard. To aid his failing memory, George left the other two ingredients on the counter until he could order more.

That chore completed, George balanced the tray on one hand and backed through the kitchen door to the service hallway. Though he had never once spilled a drop of coffee, George preferred that less expensively carpeted route to the study. Training had always led him to the least conspicuous course. Indeed, that characteristic had induced Harley Talbot to hire him away from a fine London household in which Talbot spent an entire week without noticing the butler once. Training had become reflex over his years with Mr. Talbot and his nephew.

Without knocking, George slipped into the room, automatically closing the double doors behind him. As much of the first floor, the study had elaborate oak doors and a two-story ceiling. Unlike the other rooms, however, the study lacked the feel of spacious elegance usually imparted by high ceilings. Small and cramped, it conformed to Tom Jordan's own taste. Shelves of imposing volumes lined the darkly stained walls, crowding worn overstuffed chairs into a cozy huddle.

Behind the presiding, polished Mahogany desk, George found Thomas Jordan staring out one of the high windows.

"Your coffee, Mr. Jordan," George said softly, setting the tray on a small table adjacent to the desk.

Jordan sighed, but did not stir. "I was beginning to wonder what had happened to you, George," he said wearily.

Pouring the coffee, George chuckled. "I've been here a bit too long to get lost between the kitchen and the study, Mr. Jordan."

With a wan smile, Jordan took the cup and put it tentatively to his lips. Having tested the concoction he shook his head. "A little shy on the sweets, George. Are you still trying to ease me off the 'Sweet Tooth?'"

Without changing expression, George declared, "For your own good, Sir. It will poison your system if the CafeCream has not already."

Ironically, Jordan replied, "My poor 'Sweet Tooth' will not be responsible for whatever happens to me."

The silence that followed lasted only so long as Jordan did not see the slice of birthday cake hiding behind the coffee pot. "For God's sake, Bestral," Jordan cried," Is that what I think it is?"

Prepared for the reaction, George said, "I thought that you might be hungry."

"Not for a reminder that I am 65 years old," Jordan retorted. "You have spent the last three days making me feel each lousy one of them." Innocently, George insisted, "It must be that I envy you your youth. I am two years your senior, Mr. Jordan."

Tom Jordan laughed out loud. "Then why don't you feel them?" he demanded. "Christ, you're better off than when I inherited you from Uncle Harley in '43. That's 32 years, George."

"So it is," George agreed cheerfully.

"I'm glad you're still here, George," Jordan said. He glared at the birthday cake mocking him from three feet away. His 65th birthday was three days old. "I didn't get a chance to check the mail today."

George had hoped to avoid the subject. "Nothing serious, bills primarily."

It had not helped, then, his consciously avoiding the phone call to check. He had depended on the mail to provide him with a lift. His birthday card had not come. Madelaine could not have forgotten. Even Carolyn had not forgotten and she had reason enough to try. "I'm sure it will come tomorrow," George said offhandedly.

Though he appreciated George's feigned confidence, Tom Jordan did not share in it. He had last heard from Madelaine in early June, when she had forwarded her concise report on the revised capital improvement program for Talbot Instruments. Madelaine's increasingly little use of him was devastating. Her few attentions somehow only depressed him, perhaps because she attended only to his business needs. Maybe those were the only ones she thought he had.

He sighed and sipped some coffee. Adding more "Sweet Tooth" made it more bitter than usual. He shrugged off the difference as a fitting derivative of his sour attitude.

"George," he said, "I got her preliminary statements today." He watched the butler fix his eyes on the sheath of report resting serenely in Jordan's brief case. "She is a marvel. Talbot Instruments turned a record profit for the first half, despite lower volume."

Impressed, George took a seat in the deep cushioned chair opposite his employer. He felt that the conversation might go on for a time. "That's very helpful," George commented.

"Helpful, Hell!" Jordan croaked, "J & T needed a profit somewhere. Even our friend Einberg let me down this last quarter. They made peanuts over there at Tylton." A memory made him grimace. "Jesus, if Tylton had been on LIFO accounting, as Maddy suggested, they'd've been swimming in red. God damn, the world is going to hell. She's the only one who doesn't know it."

"Madelaine made the cover of another magazine yesterday," George informed him. "MS, I think."

"That rag again," Jordan said with a shake of the head. "She's been on it three times. Or is that four now?" He tried to catalog the magazine covers on which he had seen her in the last year, but gave up after the first dozen. "I love her dearly, but even I am getting tired of seeing the faces she puts on for those covers. Has she forgotten how to bend that mouth of hers?"

George had less difficulty conjuring the numerous images of his employer's daughter. He spent much of his time keeping Mr. Jordan current on the many articles recently printed about Madelaine. "She is a remarkable girl, Mr. Jordan. You've always known that."

Frowning deeply, Jordan glowered down at the pale frosting of the cake. "Remarkable?" he asked rhetorically. "Yes, that was easy to see. But for God's sake, George, I had greater hopes for her than this. An MBA for her wall and a balance sheet for her bed. I obviously did something wrong."

"Madelaine has chosen her own life, Mr. Jordan," George commented. "You should not ask for more than that."

"You mean I'd better not," he snapped.

"That is another way of looking at it," George agreed calmly.

Jordan lowered his eyes, only to see the list laying before him. It reminded him how little time he might have. "I'm sorry, George," he apologized glumly. "I'm not in very good shape today. I've been working on this thing too long. It makes me dwell on all the wrong things."

So it had. He thought about his heart.

Tony Morex, his physician, had assured him his heart was strong, its arteries in good shape and that his overall health was excellent. Jordan had evidence that Tony was wrong. It had happened in the middle of the night, as it did later, with the other four. He had awakened in the midst of a sound sleep, his heart pounding hard enough to explode. Ironically, a small dream had turned into a nightmare, one playing out his death. It had been too real, too immediate, too certain. He had awakened abruptly, cold, soaking wet and shaking.

That event, maybe even a minor heart attack, had made him realize that he would not live forever. The harrowing sequence of death that took four of his closest associates convinced him that he had been supposed to die.

Too soon.

George interrupted his thoughts by placing the cake on top of the list of suspects he had compiled, the list he hoped might tell him how to avoid death. Jordan looked up, revealing his tired, reddened eyes. George, his only companion, the only one left in the house with him, smiled and nodded, indicating Skeffington's cake.

"Alright," Jordan said, capitulating. "I'll eat the damned cake. And every bitter bite will remind me of every time you bullied me into doing what you wanted me to do, George."

"Very good, Sir," George replied. "Shall I leave the coffee?"

Looking into the empty cup, Jordan directed, "No. Just pour me another cup and this time add a dash of 'Sweet Tooth' while you're at it. I'll finish it in bed. I've had it for tonight."

George gave his stiff half bow, learned as an adolescent, and finished his task. He felt uneasy leaving his employer alone, but understood that Mr. Jordan had dismissed him. "Goodnight, Mr. Jordan."

Poised over the cake, Jordan said, "Goodnight, George. I hope you sleep better than I intend to."

"Thank you, Sir."

When George closed the door, Jordan rose and selected a short novel from among his rows of books. He had resorted to reading himself to sleep since early June. He returned to the desk and the slice of cake. He was dissatisfied with the cake, too, he thought. He ate it quickly, however, despite an unusually bitter aftertaste, similar to that prominent in the coffee. Christ almighty, he thought, even the "Sweet Tooth" is turning on me.

Before reading very far into the novel, Thomas Jordan had fallen asleep. Sleep had not come so easily for weeks and some nights not at all. This once, however, he had not even finished the coffee before his eyes closed.

He enjoyed a heavy slumber, as well. By three in the morning, when his last dream began, it seemed that nothing could wake him. He remarked to himself, in his dreams, that he felt he could sleep forever.

~ ~ ~

He was in the conference room of the Talbot Research Hospital. The surroundings, however, looked more like those of a palace, with lofty ceilings and rich, ancient tapestries. He stood in the center of a large ballroom, in which he hosted a military dress ball. All about him, colorfully uniformed men guided elaborately gowned ladies through a blurry dance.

Though Thomas Jordan, inventor and industrialist, was obviously the master of the gala, he stood alone, unnoticed by the whirling crowd. In every direction gallant officers and their partners moved in time to rousing music. He knew that he could change the dance, the tune, even the costumes. It was his dream, not unlike many others that placed him among strangers doing strange things. Though uneasy, Thomas Jordan decided to leave the dream as it was, because it seemed too late to make any difference.

He saw her across the room, her silver ring rapping a different tempo against the low swivel chair, a tall, broad-shouldered young woman. At first her hair was short and, like her dress, a nondescript brown. The next instant her hair unfurled, flowing down to the middle of her back. In the light, her gown glistened white and gold. The transformation so annoyed her that she spun around in a single easy motion. Her eyes, glaring of molten silver, fixed on him with expressionless disapproval. Behind the thin, sharply lined mask, she was angry with him. For some reason she was always angry with him now.

He saw his hand stretched out before him, boldly reaching for her. She tilted her head back slightly, in characteristic hauteur. She recoiled a step, one foot running away from him, the other toward him. Poised to move in either direction, her long narrow body swayed against the rhythm of the music.

Every step he took toward her, induced a corresponding re-treat. When he stopped, she stopped, still tensed to move again. Their movement began to approximate a dance, out of time with the others and the orchestra, but a dance coordinated and electric. As they glided about the hall, still feet apart, creating their own music as they went, Thomas Jordan called gently to her.

Maddy.

Maddy.

She laughed harshly, as she had learned to while still young.

You are all I have, he said.

Then you have nothing, she replied coldly. Only this foolish costume ball.

He promised her he would end it, send them all away, if only she would grant him one, familiar waltz. Her eyes glimmering in the light of a thousand candles, locked onto his. She peered into his soul and found the barren darkness illuminated by a simple, music box waltz. Her thin mouth grew wider, into a smile.

Finally she took his hand and curtsied deeply. He bowed just a little, as George would and her laughter was young again. His hand on her waist, they filled the large elegant chamber with grace unfamiliar to them both. They lost themselves in a lilting waltz played by carved wooden figures on tiny instruments.

Sudden pain shooting through his head made him stumble, but he maintained the dizzying pace somehow. His partner, petticoats swishing, hair flying, swirled with him and he could ignore the strange feeling seizing his forehead. He paid no attention to a shadow descending the staircase, out of costume, out of place.

Dancing until the pain exhausted him, Thomas Jordan lay at the feet of a dark, ill-defined figure. The stranger spoke, intoning something Thomas Jordan could not understand. The face tried to become familiar but remained hazy and unformed. Jordan commanded that he leave. The visitor responded that he would not leave until he had exacted justice, vengeance, death, in the name of Ray Carleton.

You cannot awaken, the twisted mouth said. You will sleep forever. There is no escape but death.

Jordan rose shakily and tried to move away. The stranger stayed with him, cognizant of his every intention, devouring his every thought. Jordan became frightened as the stranger remained always before him no matter where he ran. The light suddenly revealed a club, a huge, heavy automatic rifle, bayonets embedded in the butt.

It became clear that he could not evade this pursuer. Jordan reached into his pockets always so deep and crowded, hurling their contents at the adversary relentlessly bearing in, hefting his club, swinging it in practice. The defenses Jordan called upon had no effect on his oppressor. No one offered aid. The uniformed guests now stood aside, as he once had. When first the club made contact, Jordan did not feel pain, but the continued blows forced him to the ground. Powerless and terrified, Thomas Jordan realized that he had no escape. The horrible truth struck him: He would not, could not awaken. The next swing of the club would undoubtedly kill him.

Vainly he searched his pockets again for something to stop the stranger. They were empty. He searched the crowd for familiar faces, but he saw none. Was she there? He needed time to listen.

Time was over as the weapon bore down again on his throbbing head his life did not have time, not even a second

*to remind him of its errors, disappointments, empty achieve-
ments and loneliness. All he saw was Maddy's picture, faded,
far away and that was enough.*

*He felt the first blade driving into his forehead. A second
found his left eye, rupturing it immediately. Wood smashed
scalp, then blasted bone aside in its quest for the soft tissue
so futilely protected. The parts of the skull not flying into the
room, surged forward with the club into his brain. The
pounding of a huge drum accompanied the pain pulsating
through his body. When the walls began to drip with gray
mush, Thomas Jordan's dream ended.*

~ ~ ~

Thomas Jordan had a great deal of work to do that morning, but George hesitated to deprive him of the luxury of
oversleeping. When Jordan failed to respond to George's
first knock, George considered seriously letting

the exhausted man rest longer. He knew, however, that
Jordan would rather keep to his routine. They both were
men of habit at their age.

Opening the door halfway, George slipped inside. He
gasped and fell back against the door, slamming it with a
loud thump.

A moderate sleeper, Jordan had thrown his bed covers
off, tearing the sheets in several places. One split pillow left
a trail of feathers from the bed to the dresser where it had
knocked the toilet articles to the floor. A digital Talbot Instruments clock had been smashed against the dressing
mirror. His coffee cup had bounced off the wall staining the
paper and carpet.

As George moved unsteadily to rouse the contorted
sleeper, he saw that Jordan's mouth hung open as if in a
scream. The shoulders were hard and stiff, the skin a pasty
gray. George instinctively pulled his hands from the corpse,
repelled by the sensation of death.

He did not remember the phone call he made that brought Dr. Anthony Morex to the house, or sedative injection that helped return him to coherency.

CHAPTER TWO

"No!" Carleton sat bolt upright before awakening. The shadowy, swirling figures had come so abruptly, moved so hauntingly, so familiarly that he could not stand to keep his eyes closed.

Grabbing his ringing clock, he read the time as 8:35. Three good hours of sleep. That was plenty under hypnosis. It was all he had asked for. Three hours of peaceful, dreamless sleep. Only at the end did the nightmare intrude. Stupid Goddamned dream, he thought.

Carleton bounded from his bed, feeling ready for anything. He scurried around the cramped one bedroom apartment gathering his clothes, brushing his teeth meticulously, shaving his sparse whiskers. The thin, light brown hair fell into place without encouragement. Carleton wrinkled his freckled nose in approval. He felt much bigger than his five feet five inches and one hundred and twenty-two pounds. With a tap of his high forehead, he started for the door.

The chatter of his shoes on the bare floor reminded him that his ancient landlady was a light sleeper. Barefoot, he made his descent carefully to the second story landing of the narrow staircase. The groan of the first weight on the step beyond the landing stopped him. There was a stirring below in the shadows.

He despised the ritual. Every morning, he tried to slip by his landlady. She would never dare to come down to his makeshift laboratory in the second level cellar. Rather she lay in wait for him as he came down the stairs each day. The minute she heard a sound she would move to block his ingress to the lab steps. If only he hadn't been forced to move out of his other place.

"Raymond?" the high-pitched, weak-bodied voice called.

Damn, he said to himself. If it hadn't been for Carstairs, Jordan and the others, he wouldn't have to live like a fugitive with an overbearing mother.

"Raymond?" Mrs. Gergorian asked again. "I hope that's you up there and not some burglar."

She knew perfectly well that it was he. He gave up the idea of eluding her by trying to get to the front stairs before she could. She would have a stroke trying and he would have to stop and call an ambulance. He was late enough.

"Close your eyes and you'll never know!" he suggested coming down out of the darkness.

The old woman's eyes grew big. "Oh, Raymond. You forgot your shoes. You'll catch cold." She shook her head disapprovingly. "You really should be more careful. You're not that hearty, you know."

"I didn't want to disturb you," he said truthfully.

"But then it has been warm lately, I suppose. But you'll get grass stains on your socks."

"There's no grass in the cellar."

"Grass stains are so hard to wash out," she added. "Are you going out?"

He had planned to make a run over to the Talbot, to pick up some things from his former project partner, Madjerin, but he had no intention of telling Mrs. Gergorian. She would insist that he pick up some Jell-O for her. "I'm going downstairs to the lab."

"I think you should cut the lawn first, Raymond. It's supposed to rain later. You know how hard it is to cut wet grass." She looked at him with an expression of vacant inquiry. "It's not good for the grass either, is it? Or is that hair?"

Carleton had forgotten about his promise to cut the lawn. He checked the sky for an indication of rain. The usual light summer haze held no threat of precipitation. Mrs. Gergorian had, as usual, conjured information designed to bend him to her whim. He hated that kind of foolish assertion of dominion. He didn't put up with that kind of thing anymore. Still, he would cut her lawn for her. Not because he felt he had to, as she wanted, but because he vaguely liked the idea of yard work. It was menial, of course, but he had never been allowed to do it when young. "Ramie is too small," his mother had always insisted.

Carleton lied, "It's still too damp from the dew. I'll get it after it dries up."

Mrs. Gergorian nodded happily and shuffled through the door that led to her kitchen, where she would make herself some coffee with the Dennison Foods "Sweet Tooth" he had given her. She wouldn't bother him for a while after that.

Freed of her interruptions, he could move the equipment back into his lab, cut the lawn and, perhaps still get to the Talbot before Madjerin, who worked nights, left for the day. He hated the idea of hurrying to conform his schedule to the contemptible Madjerin. She was a source of new cerebral graphs, but, otherwise she was worthless. She had been an impediment when they had worked together. He was better off without her underfoot. Only as long as he needed her would he tolerate her.

It wouldn't be much longer.

But it wouldn't be today. To hell with Madjerin, he was in no hurry. He would pass up the Talbot until tomorrow. He was in a position to determine his own pace. Let them wait, he decided, as he ambled deliberately out to the van. He would wait a little longer, so could they.

~ ~ ~

The incongruity hit Montgomery from the moment his car passed through the gates. The street he had just left,

though residential enough, had a clamorous, frenzied quality. A major avenue, it was too heavily traveled to be attractive even to those who lived along its cracking gray asphalt.
With the smog settling on Pittsburgh that particular morning, Fifth Avenue seemed all the more colorless and urban.

Once his car nosed through the opening in the sandstone
walls, however, the scene flowered into one of pastoral
greens, clean whites and brilliant reds. Instinctively, Montgomery checked the sky above him for phantom blues and
wisps of white. Seeing the usual gray haze, he accepted the
estate as real.

No matter which direction he glanced, the detective
found neither hint of, nor concession to the environs which
he had just left. The spacious lawn rolled gracefully toward
the house, each blade of its grass seemed trimmed to exactly the height recommended by his Lawn-Boy booklet.
The shrubbery, hedges and trees were shaved rather than
cut. Blossoms, flowers, gardens indicated that their late
master had appreciated beauty.

Though unused to splendor, Montgomery knew that
much. Fine things, like people, have their way of revealing,
even to the ignorant, the qualities that make them superior.
Montgomery stood awhile at the door of the Jordan mansion, absorbing sights completely out of place in his world.
The serenity of the place surrounded as it was by a crowded
neighborhood disoriented him.

The disquieting calm ended abruptly with the intrusion
of a large man in a pea-green, white-lettered uniform. Exercising his powerful lungs, the man berated a smaller figure
in soiled khaki dragging a ladder toward a pickup labeled
"Allegheny Window Service." Struggling after the other two
came a third man spilling soapy water from three large
buckets. In a colorful vernacular, striking even to Montgomery, the large workman promised never to wash the Jordan
windows again. The diminutive target of the abuse paid

him no heed, obviously unconcerned with either the warning or the aspersions cast upon his personal habits and family history.

Montgomery swallowed a grin and tried the front door. While on an assignment, Montgomery did not allow himself the luxury of amusement. Death was a serious matter to him. Indeed, it dominated his career and his life. For some, man's dignity served as a common denominator, giving human existence it's meaning; for others, love, suffering, wisdom served as a focus. Montgomery, however, accepted mortality as the essential characteristic binding humanity and natural death as its first right.

As he approached the dead man's room, the detective wondered how Thomas Jordan had faced the realization that men, even great men, were ruled by death, its inevitability, its eternity. Did he, as most others did, seek to forestall it? Or had he tried to hasten it? More importantly, for Montgomery's purposes, had someone else intervened? For if natural death was a right for Montgomery, then murder was the ultimate wrong. When anyone usurped a man's right to die, Montgomery's duty, he believed, lay in setting the balance right. If necessary, he would do the same for Thomas Jordan.

The grim scene that comforted Montgomery as he entered the room, therefore, piqued his professional and personal curiosities. While the rest of the house was ordered, the room was in chaos. Furthermore, it had a strange feel to it. The dimensions of it were not quite those of a grown man's room. The light walnut, clean-lined, Campaign furniture seemed a shade too small, suggesting that the room had been designed for an adolescent. The neutral colors indicated masculinity, yet off in one corner there sat a small, badly scratched, girl's dressing table. The mirror of the dressing table had been shattered. The rest of the room was a mess, as well. Montgomery was certain that no one had disturbed the condition of the ravaged room, but someone had created it. Only a violent struggle could have brought such havoc to a bedroom.

Sitting quietly on the window sill, Greg Bernelli, representing the Coroner's Office, quietly watched Montgomery's entrance. Jordan's personal physician, Antony Morex, stood stiffly facing away from both the bed and Montgomery. Their continued silence annoyed the detective.

"So," he barked, "What's the story?"

Bernelli, as though freed by the sound of Montgomery's voice, replied immediately. "Dr. Morex and I agree, Monty. It was an infarction… a heart attack."

"Definitely," Morex stated flatly.

Morex' tone of voice conveyed a sense of certainty that unsettled Montgomery. He could not accept so simple a cause for a death as violent as Jordan's had obviously been. "Good, then I can go home!" he snapped. "Listen, damn it. You guys got me out here."

Morex's shadowed eyes, set deeply in a broad dark face, did not blink, as they scrutinized Montgomery. "Quite right, Sergeant," he said finally before abruptly leaving the room.

The fatigued mystery in the Doctor's manner warned Monty that he was in for a long frustrating morning. "Come on Bernelli," he demanded. "What is the story? Christ almighty, you know how many cases I've got on."

The assistant coroner nodded sympathetically. "And I've got another one back at the lab for you." He let Montgomery roll his eyes before explaining. "Our friend Morex here is a big shot. He knows my boss pretty well, I guess. The whole damn morgue went stiff this morning when he called."

Monty growled at the prospect of "top level" interference. Politics had its place, but it was not in homicide. He did not like to see procedure ignored as a favor to anyone. Homicide investigations belonged to another order of things, above politics. "Swell," he said. "What is it? Whitewash?"

The question made Bernelli's face take a funny shape. He looked as though he were amused and knew he should not be. "Whitewash? Not with you here," he said. "Uh, uh. He wants a full dress autopsy.

"For what?" Montgomery's confusion displaced his anger.

Bernelli lifted his shoulders and held them. "You'll see in a minute." He did not bother to explain.

Having known Bernelli for several years, Montgomery knew the young man had said all he would say. Trying to extract more information from him would only make Montgomery's ulcer burn. He passed the minutes waiting for Morex's return by looking over the body on his own.

Its expression reminded him too much of one worn by a black kid tortured to death in Philadelphia back in 1958. Bernelli had left the mouth open and that gave the face the same look of conscious horror. A swelling by the hand indicated a broken wrist. Through the cold skin he could feel a shoulder separation as well. If it had been a heart attack, it had been one ugly heart attack.

The corpse disturbed Montgomery enough to make him give up his investigation and retreat to the window. He looked out, watching for any signs of entry. Below, by twenty-five feet, he could see Jordan's gardener still hassling with the window washer. George, the butler, tried to intervene without success. Not until the truck began its retreat, did the controversy cease. The tiny grounds-keeper promptly hopped on a sit-down, electric lawnmower and repaired to his corner, and what appeared to be a small cottage hidden among the trees grouped along the right-hand wall.

The approach of a red Mustang II rolled up the drive as the gardener disappeared. The car stopped beside the butler trudging back toward the house. The driver detained Bestral for sometime. Several times during the conversation, the butler glanced toward the window at which the detective stood.

Before that conversation ended, Montgomery heard Morex reenter the room. In his hand, the doctor held a dull metal coffee cup. He carried it so gently that Montgomery assumed it was filled. When he examined it, however, he found no more evidence of coffee than a few caked drops. Baffled, he looked up at Mores, who only stared back at him from under heavy eyebrows. Montgomery finally lifted the cup and took an inquisitive sniff. Shooting a glance at Bernelli, he returned the cup to him. "Okay. was all he said.

~ ~ ~

George waited at the door for Rick Stapler, catching his breath. The weekly strain of calming the crews from Allegheny Window Service had drained him more than usual. He was too tired to face returning to the house alone and felt the need of Stapler's company before rejoining the doctors and the County detective in Thomas Jordan's room.

Richmond S. Stapler, Tom Jordan's young attorney, left his car in the parking area at the side of the house. He was still a little numb from the news that George had telephoned him earlier. The short walk from his car around the house, with everything looking so normal, gave him time to doubt that Thomas Jordan was dead.

At his office at seven o'clock, mainly because a certain ill mannered redhead had turned him out at 5:30, Stapler had been awaiting the arrival of his secretary. He needed Heloise to make his coffee and sooth his headache. Heloise always made his coffee and soothed his headaches. George had phoned just before her arrival and Rick had not understood him the first two times.

"He's dead, Rick," George had said the third time.

The word 'dead' finally pierced the haze left from the night before. "Jordan?" he had asked loudly enough to aggravate his headache.

"I don't believe it."

Her pretty blue eyes had widened in shock, as she leaned against the desk. "Oh, my God," she had whispered.

"Yeah," Stapler had replied. "I'm on my way out there, now. We'd better start thinking about an emergency meeting of the full Board of Directors at J & T. We'll have Red Melton take over the Talbot for now," he had added preparing to leave. "Better call Jean Skeffington."

Heloise had not responded until he had reached the door of his office. "This is awful!"

If she had started to cry, Stapler had not wanted to know and he had without further comment. The grueling drive through town had forced him to think. He had recalled with uneasiness that four members of Jordan's circle had also died in recent weeks. Rick had known them all, as the Secretary of Talbot's Board of Trustees, but only Thomas Jordan's death had affected him. He had not expected a man like Jordan to die somehow. Jordan had seemed so much greater in stature than the others had and not just because he was Stapler's only major client. Perhaps, he thought as he shook George's hand before entering the house, perhaps he had gotten to know Jordan too well; it was never a good idea to get to know someone too well.

As the two men proceeded up the gently curving staircase, George prepared Stapler for the sight of Jordan's room. He took pains to describe the extent of the convulsions and their effect. Stapler seemed not to be listening, his eyes fixed on the open door down the hall. Rick could hear voices in the room and tried to distinguish them. He recognized one, but it was not the one that belonged there. It brought a reply in a weary graveled voice he also recognized, that of Tony Morex.

"It is too much like the others," Morex was saying when Stapler entered. The attorney started at the scene that opened before him. The usually ordered room of Thomas Jordan had been so completely demolished that even the small portrait of Madelaine has been smashed.

He felt unsteady, slightly dizzy, stepping back into George who had entered after him. Standing in the middle of the disarray Stapler saw three men. Morex, of course, he had known for several years. The young man he had never seen before, but the third, older and more serious, he recognized. The thick hair, ruddy cheeks and intense expression were too familiar. When Stapler saw the smug grin, he remembered the name. "Well, Monty," he said accepting the detective's hand. "It's been awhile."

Montgomery pursed his lips to eliminate the smile. "Probate and police don't mix much, Stapler," he remarked, without disguising his preference that the status continue.

Stapler nodded to Tony Morex and to Bernelli he extended his hand. Montgomery took care of the introduction. "Stapler, this is Greg Bernelli out of the Coroner's Office." He motioned Bernelli to give Stapler the coffee cup the assistant coroner was holding.

Bernelli's move was so coordinated that Rick ended up shaking the cup along with the doctor's hand. "How do you do, Dr. Bernelli?"

Bernelli, embarrassed by his clumsiness, waited until Stapler had the cup. "Fine, Mr. Stapler," he said thinly.

Stapler stood with the empty cut for a moment as the others watched him anxiously. The scrutiny began to annoy the bewildered lawyer. He looked into the cup, but found no explanation for their strange behavior. "I take it I missed the Danish, too."

Montgomery savored Stapler's discomfort a second longer and then suggested, "Take a whiff, Counselor."

hesitating long enough to appear to have ignored the detective's instructions, Rick examined the cup. He detected a light, but distinct, odor mingled with that of the coffee. It meant nothing to him, and he was sure Montgomery knew it.

"Smell anything, Counselor?" Montgomery asked innocently.

Stapler had to shrug ignorance. "Perfumes I can identify for you, Coffee, no," he admitted. "If you really have something this time, Montgomery, let's hear it."

Morex, disquieted by the delay, answered before the detective could speak. "This cup of coffee must have contained a large dosage of a sleeping powder," he explained. "Maybe glutethemide."

With a weak grin, Rick said, "Thanks, Tony." He looked at Montgomery as he continued, "I can always count on you to give me at least a convoluted generic name. Montgomery, on the other hand, will run for me around a week before telling me why the hell he's even here." He did not give the irate cop time to reply. "But that's Okay. I need the exercise. What is it? An overdose?"

Morex shrugged with a kind of fatal helplessness. "I don't think so, but we'll have to wait for a complete autopsy."

"What do you mean by that?" Stapler demanded. "I thought... Christ! Is that really necessary? Jordan's an important man in this town. I don't want only half of him showing up for the funeral."

Bernelli took his turn to explain. "We coroner types don't like doped corpses."

"And neither do I." Montgomery added forcefully.

"This is not the place for a debate," Stapler snapped.

Following George's suggestion the group descended to the study. Stapler brought up the rear, trying to understand what Montgomery was up to. He had run into the irascible cop once before while working as a public defender just out of law school, prior to joining Sinker & Lyne. The detective's mind, he recalled, had a devious twist in it somewhere and a relentlessness that had shaken the fledgling attorney during a cross-examination. He also remembered that Montgomery had the reputation as the best of the state's homicide men. He would never waste his time on something that did not concern homicide.

Only after the five men had settled into the study of the late Thomas Jordan, did Rick pursue his curiosity. "Come on, Monty," he began. "Accidents didn't used to be your line."

Montgomery stared at Stapler blankly. He had no use for lawyers generally and he felt that Stapler was worse than most. As a kid attorney, Stapler had taken away a conviction he had risked his neck to get. Montgomery did not forget that kind of thing easily. He said nothing.

George spoke up to break an awkward silence. "Rick," he stated softly. "Mr. Jordan never used any sleeping medication."

"But surely," Rick objected

"Never," George reiterated. "In the forty years I have known Mr. Jordan he has not once used sleeping pills, powders, anything. There is nothing of that kind in the house."

Jordan used to take pills," Rick reminded him. "There might be some left around."

Montgomery, becoming involved in the idea, forgot his antipathy towards the lawyer. "My people have gone over the place pretty well, Stapler," he said. "I've got some pretty nosy boys, but we didn't turn up a thing."

George grimaced. "They were indiscreetly thorough, Rick. I caught one of them searching the dishwasher."

Montgomery took the comment as a compliment. "And the medicine cabinets, the closets and the dressers. The kitchen too, of course. The coffee is Okay. So is the sugar. And that coffee creamer. Even the dishwater detergent. It isn't here."

"How about J & T?" Rick wondered out loud. "Or the Talbot?"

"To my knowledge," George repeated, "he has never kept it anywhere. He simply does not use it.

Stapler wracked his memory for indications that Jordan would have put in a supply. "He was having a hell of time sleeping lately, George."

From his distant chair, Tony Morex casually dismissed Rick's idea. "I offered him a sedative for that, but Tom abhorred drugs. I could hardly get him to take aspirin."

Unable to deny the truth of Morex's statement, Rick simply nodded and lapsed into silence. He couldn't quite comprehend what others were suggesting. He had known Jordan intimately for almost seven years. The older man had often confided in him, both as attorney and as friend, perhaps even as quasi-son. Suicide was out of the question.

"Had he been depressed or anything lately, Bestral?" Montgomery inquired.

George glared at the detective with a look reserved for apostate. "Things were very difficult for him," George acknowledged. "But Mr. Jordan would never do such a thing," he added answering Montgomery's implication.

"He's right, Monty," Stapler agreed, breaking his pensive silence. "Depression is one thing, suicide is another."

Nodding, Monty said, "You guys make it sound like a dirty word. The guy has a right to commit suicide as far as I'm concerned. I'm not trying to dirty his name, I just want to settle this drug thing." He settled his frame deeper into the comfortable chair. "So why was he depressed?"

"Plenty of reasons," Rick replied. He had cataloged them himself minutes before. "The recession was hurting business. Not just at J & T of course, all over. The income from the endowment of the Talbot was way down. So was the market value. That was his pet project. He had to cut way back on the budget. I suppose that haunted him all spring. And his family..." He did not bother to finish. The less said about the family, the better.

But the thought of the Jordan family and its wretched dissolution reminded Stapler of something that had been bothering him for several days. "Say, George," he asked, "Did Madelaine...?"

George's nod cut him off. "Her card got here this morning," he said sadly. "It came with some samples from TI."

"Third Class!" Rick snarled. "That Goddamn bitch!"

Monty's eyebrows jumped. "Who's Madelaine? Should I know her?"

"If you need an ulcer.", Rick shot back

"Wife?" Monty asked George.

"His daughter," the butler responded quietly.

Venom in his voice, Rick butted in. "A poor facsimile of a daughter. She didn't give a good Goddamn about her poor old man, or anyone else, for that matter!" Agitated, he was out of his chair, pacing the room.

"The worst part of it is that the dumb bastard worshiped her. Christ! It's almost obscene. She'll get everything. Everything. And she couldn't even manage to get a simple birthday card here on time?"

"Rick is a little hard on Maddy," George explained. "It is hard to understand her, but it was not easy for her growing up here. The parents never really got along and were finally separated in 1973. Her brother became something of a drinker at school. Madelaine adapted to the tensions here in her own way.

"To the disadvantage of everyone," Rick added. "Jordan spoiled her bloody rotten. And so did you."

"Perhaps," George conceded, smiling a little.

"When do I meet her?" Montgomery asked. Rich women galled him, but fascinated him as well.

George replied, "I phoned her before you came.

Stapler sighed gratefully. "I was afraid I'd get that chore."

"I felt I should tell her," George said almost proudly.

"How did she react?"

"She said she would fly in tomorrow to take care of things," George replied.

"That's my girl," Rick retorted. "By the way, George, did she ever get that nose fixed?"

Disgusted, Montgomery muttered, "Figures, somehow." The portrait of Madelaine Jordan was taking shape and he didn't even like the frame.

"You left her little choice, Rick," George replied.

"Well," he noted unabashed, "she had it coming."

After Montgomery's questioning glance shifted from Stapler to him, George felt he had better clarify the situation for the sake of both Madelaine Jordan and Stapler. "Madelaine" he explained, "is an amateur boxer, Sergeant. We have a small gym in the basement as a matter of fact."

"She needs a punching bag when she comes to town." Rick said. "I'm usually it."

George continued, suppressing his amusement. "In their last 'engagement' Rick broke her nose."

Stapler grinned proudly. "And never regretted it."

CHAPTER THREE

The Talbot Research Hospital had been a haven for Ray Carleton. The post-doctoral position he had held there had kept him out of the university culture that he simply hated. At the Talbot he had not been expected to teach or to prove that he was learning as he had at first Michigan and then Cal Tech. He did not like sharing his ideas with those who could not appreciate them.

At the Talbot he had not been under pressure to do anything but develop projects within the discipline for which the Talbot was created: The application of computer and electronic technology to medicine. At least, that was supposed to be the case. In April, however, the Board of Trustees betrayed him and dozens of others. That treachery rankled, but what Carleton could not forget was that the Board, or rather six of its nine members, could not see his superiority over the others and especially over Dr. Madjerin, his immediate associate.

Walking through the double glass doors of the Talbot as an outcast, always an outcast, Carleton felt the rage building up again. The guard inside the door took a long look at his card and stopped him. "Sorry, Dr. Carleton," the tall, chubby man said, "Your pass has expired."

He was so stunned that he dropped his briefcase on the tile floor, creating an echo that ran the long corridor and back. "Bull shit!" he retorted and moved to go past.

The massive guard blocked his path and shook his head. "I'll call Miss Skeffington. I'm sure she'll clear you."

Retreating a step, Carleton agreed. He hated being at the mercy of a twit like Skeffington, but he consoled himself with the thought that he had already gotten even with her, though, as usual, she would never realize it.

The guard covered the speaker of the phone. "She asked you to come up to here office, Dr. Carleton. I guess she'll issue you another card."

Carleton nodded and proceeded to the elevators. After a glance at the guard, in case he was watching–the idiot wasn't–Carleton pushed the down button. He would go see that red-headed floozy when he was good and ready. First, he wanted to get some more material from Madjerin. The Talbot had ten above-ground stories and five below-ground. The office Madjerin now had was on the second underground floor, which was something of an indication of what Jordan had thought of her brainwave ID project. Carleton had his own ideas about cerebral mapping, but he shared everyone else's view of Madjerin herself–she did not really have a top level intellect.

The woman from India stood over her desk. Madjerin, who never used her unpronounceable first name, was very small, shorter than Carleton, and excruciatingly thin. The white lab coat she wore looked several sizes too large for her, though it was the smallest available. Her dark little hands were clasped tightly behind her back, the knuckles a light brown.

"Have you been here long, Madj?" Carleton asked loudly.

She jerked around in a motion that should have hurt. When she saw it was Carleton, she smiled. "Ray. You alarmed me."

"I know," he replied, "How's the work?"

The smile disappeared. She lifted her hands slightly and let them drop. "Money problems."

Wickedly, Carleton said, "If you didn't have any money you wouldn't have any problems. Look at me. Carefree and destitute."

Madjerin felt terrible about Carleton's position, but would not have traded places with him. That she couldn't do. Even without a research grant, Carleton was at least able to remain in the United States. She wouldn't. Her money problem arose from the fact that her only remaining source of money, an outside grant, would probably terminate in the fall. She, too, had been a victim of the Talbot Purge, keeping only her office and privileges, not her basic grant.

"We'll have to compare notes one of these days, Madj," he suggested, half-heartedly. He had other plans.

She cheered up immediately. "That would be good. We worked pretty well together."

"That's why they broke up our team. Afraid we'd win a prize or something." Carleton laughed. Without her, he might have. And she was still at the Talbot.

"Listen, Madj, I need some more raw material," he said, changing the subject. He wanted to get what he had come for and then get away from suffocating presence. She was so thick, he could not bear looking at her. "You said a while back that you had mapped a batch of new people. I was wondering if I could borrow some."

Enthused, Madjerin pulled Carleton by the arm over to her file cabinet. "I had the Mayor, the Police Commissioner and some other police people in here two weeks ago. They were very impressed."

Carleton was also impressed. The Mayor? That suggested several interesting possibilities. He had never been very fond of the ubiquitous Mayor of Pittsburgh. Everybody else loved Pete Flaherty. Carleton despised him. "Can I have part of the graph?"

Madjerin lifted the folder out with the name Flaherty on it and carefully tore the computer-drawn graph in half. "I don't need more than this," she said as she returned one half of the sheet to the folder. Do you want the others?"

Biting his lip as he visualized taking on City Hall, Carleton nodded. "Why not. We shouldn't restrict ourselves to top grade minds, now should we?" No, certainly not, he decided. "After all, our work is intended for applications outside walls of the Talbot, right?"

~ ~ ~

From the window stretching across the back wall of his office, Rick stared toward his Mount Washington apartment. Perched up on the ridge, across the rivers, it had a superb view of the city, far better than that from his office. Pittsburgh, he thought, was like a woman: Better seen at night and from a distance. Up close in revealing daylight, one saw its crowded streets, its dilapidated, sooty buildings and the haze hanging in the air. At night, from his lofty apartment, the city glowed like the face of a romantic school girl in candlelight, only its beauty, not its blemishes visible.

The sudden stop of a rusting cab drew his attention from his refuge on Mount Washington. As it pulled to the curb in front of the building, he feared that Madelaine had arrived early. He relaxed when he saw the small people emerge. Besides, he knew she would not take a cab. Absently, he studied the discharged passengers, a man and a woman huddled close together as though it were either winter or midnight. Amused by their affectionate behavior, he wondered if Madelaine Jordan ever snuggled up to anyone for the kind of warmth most people need even in July weather.

Behind him he heard the door open and he waited for Heloise's voice. Heloise Carpenter had the kind of voice one waited for, gentle and warm, as though physically near. From the first time he had heard that voice–how many years ago? Ten, Twelve?–he had waited to hear it again.

"Is she here?" Heloise asked softly.

Though he had been expecting her voice, Stapler started. "What?" he responded, knowing what she had asked. He spun in his chair to face her. "I'm sorry, Hel. I guess I was daydreaming again."

"Uh, huh," she commented with her most understanding smile.

Heloise was, and always had been, the image of woman-liness to Stapler. She had bright blue eyes setting off a slightly upturned nose and a fully developed mouth. The thick hair that framed her oval face waved its way casually to her shoulders. From there down, Heloise improved, though the sedate blue dress did not make it obvious. There were times when she was the only woman he wanted.

"You'd better wake up before Madelaine gets here," she scolded, noting the distant look in his eyes. "You have plenty of time. She was only due in a couple of minutes ago. Not even Madelaine can fly directly into your window."

"Not without a full moon."

Heloise carefully brushed back a lock of hair. "You don't understand women, Ricky, that's your problem."

"My problem is surviving them," he corrected her. He sighed and glanced toward the window again. "I don't know, Hel. She's going to come bulling in here, looking for the usual fight. Somehow, I don't think I'm up to it today."

"You'll be up to it. But if you don't get some work done before she gets here, that will won't be probated in our life-time." She shifted the Jordan Estate master file into the cen-ter of his desk.

Offhandedly opening the file, Stapler groaned. "Oh, shit!"

Used to any level of his language, Heloise peered down from behind him, her hand firmly on his shoulder. It was so natural for her that neither of them noticed it. "What's wrong?"

His finger pointing the way, Stapler explained. "We've only got four trustees over at the Talbot. We don't even have a Goddamned quorum. Son of a bitch."

"Mr. Melton said he'd call an emergency meeting."

"Red?" Rick asked.

"When did you talk to him?"

"About half an hour ago. He was over at the Talbot," she said. "He said that, as vice-chairman of the Board, he had the authority in this case to act as Administrator of the Talbot.

Glum, Stapler added, "Only temporarily. The Jordan Foundation will have to name new trustees. Three guesses who now heads the Foundation."

Unsettled, Heloise asked, "Not Madelaine?"

"Well, that leaves two chances, but you have narrowed it down. I'll give you a hint. The answer is very tall, dislikes yours truly and will be the end of the Talbot as a charitable institution."

"That's three hints."

"Not really. The first two are pretty general."

"Rick," Heloise said earnestly, "Don't worry about it."

"You're right, Hel. It may not be my problem long." Resting his chin on one palm, Stapler reviewed the situation at the Talbot.

He was in trouble. "Without Jordan, I'm cooked. I've done Okay as the Talbot's counsel, but you and I both know I'm no world-beater. Jordan had to ram me down a couple throats over there. Now that he's gone, I'm not sure they'll stomach me very long. And if Maddy really decides to take over, I'll be lucky to be allowed the use of a door on my way out."

It had not hit him until that moment, but in Thomas Jordan, he had had a rare and valuable friend. Without Jordan's help, he'd be hard pressed to remain in business. He had lost his biggest client, Jordan himself, and stood to lose his second largest, the Talbot. Eighty percent of his billings had come directly from those two sources.

He began to wish that he had remained a humble associate with Sinker & Lyne instead of splitting off with the firm's best account. Perhaps he would have made partner by the age of thirty-two rather than being on the verge of starting over again. He could go back to criminal defense work and lose weight.

Her voice cheerless, Heloise tried to console him. And herself. She did not want to have to leave him. "The Jordan Estate will keep us busy. And the trusts could support any lawyer and his efficient, loyal secretary for years, Ricky. In the meantime, we can build up other business."

Her use of "we" buoyed his spirits. "True. Unless, of course, our Madelaine gets one of her bright, newsworthy ideas and thinks she can live without me."

"Never.

"She is the executrix after all. I'm just the simple, well-meaning attorney whose name and address are on the pretty blue wrapper around the instruments. That won't slow Maddy down if she wants to punish us for breaking her nose." That was a real possibility, he knew. "My only hope is that she'll need me to straighten out the mess I created."

Firmly, Heloise suggested, "In that case, Mr. Stapler, I think you might treat her a little more gently than you have in the past. Mr. Jordan was always amused by it. Madelaine is not."

"Dearest Heloise, do you want to tell me how gentle I am supposed to be with a woman who is almost as big as I am, smarter than I ever want to be, and an infinitely better boxer." There was truth to all of that. His admiration for Madelaine was sincere enough. She was the only woman, the only person, who intimidated him both physically and mentally. "I can only absorb so much punishment."

With a toss of her lively hair, Heloise turned to leave. "I'll let you know when she's here," she snapped, annoyed with his description of Madelaine. "You can shadow box until then."

"Keep her in her corner for a minute first, Okay?" he pleaded.

With mock sweetness, she asked, "Do you need time to build your courage?"

"No. My temper."

As Heloise stepped out of the room, he called, "Hey! How much do you want to bet she's not in black, Hel? How much?"

She poked her head around the door without bothering to re-enter. "You surprise me sometimes, you're so old fashioned."

"So is your father's death," he replied. "Ten bucks."

Demurely, Heloise rebuked him. "Gambling breeds immorality." "Which is why I'm trying to get you to bet."

She shook her head. "Sorry. But if she is in black, you owe her an apology."

"Those, my dear, are very high stakes," he said grimly. "Alright. But if I win, you leave JJ and come away with me."

Curious, Heloise asked, "Where?"

"To Harrisburg. To the Probate Convention."

With a forced smile, she shook her head again. "You are gambling now." With that she closed the door.

Staring at the door, Stapler wondered if someday she shouldn't take that gamble. He had come close enough before. Close enough. His eyes focusing on the Jordan file and its extensive asset schedule, Stapler remembered that numbers were safer.

~ ~ ~

Despite the tales of a "Talbot Purge", there were still plenty of people running around the Research Hospital as far as Montgomery was concerned. The atmosphere of the corridors had the intensity of normal hospitals. For that matter, the Talbot looked like any other hospital, its white-jacketed staff hurrying about the sterilized halls with obvious purpose. Numbered doors spotted the immaculate, white-tiled walls. Efficient nurses called everyone "Doctor" and squired feeble-looking patients to obscure destinations. Monty had the same queasy feeling he felt in other hospitals.

Waiting impatiently beside the desk outside Jordan's office, Montgomery recalled Stapler's capsule description of the bustling Talbot Research Hospital. The irreverent attorney had said something like "It is a twelve million dollar inferiority complex; one man's offering to the divinity of medicine."

Stapler's scorn for the purpose of the Talbot seemed, to Montgomery, well placed. He did not like the feel of it. While the Talbot, as everyone associated with it called the institution, did not pretend to be a real hospital, it self-consciously patterned itself after one. Patients, borrowed from the neighboring hospitals for the experiments conducted within its maze of computer labs, were each assigned to a room, a nurse and a "doctor".

The nurses themselves were on leave from the other hospitals while the doctors were more PhD's in psychology, electrical engineering or chemistry than MD's.

The scope of the Talbot's pretension extended beyond merely emulating a medical facility. Its staff seemed dedicated to a goal greater than the mere repairing of individual ills. They all spoke of 'Medicine' as a child, perhaps retarded and certainly not very bright, that they would lead to maturity and greatness. Each individual in the building had pledged his career to Thomas Jordan and that man's purpose, the dream that his money, his computers and his sophisticated instrumentation could revolutionize the science of medicine.

A conversation with Jordan's executive assistant, Jean Skeffington, a well-heeled redhead pirated from Philadelphia's Main Line, gave Montgomery the impression that Jordan had set out less to aid Medicine that to conquer it. Skeffington, imbued with a devotion to her late boss, spoke of Medicine as though it were already a subsidiary field of computer technology. She had so rhapsodized the virtues of Thomas Jordan and his ideal that she had not answered any of his questions.

As she returned from her last attempt to control herself, Montgomery steeled himself for further weeping. The subject of Jordan's death seemed to dissolve her professional manner.

"I'm sorry, Sergeant," she said evenly. "I'm sure you think that I am hopeless."

"No, Ms. Skeffington," he replied. "It happens. I do have to get some answers sooner or later, but I could come back."

She shook her head slightly. "I shall try," she insisted, waving him once again into Jordan's large handsome office.

Having seen Jordan's other offices, Montgomery wondered why this one differed so markedly. He could hardly believe the same man had used it. Compared to Jordan's claustrophobic study and his small, indifferently crowded rooms at J & T headquarters, the Talbot office was spacious, uncluttered and casual.

"This is quite an office," he remarked, admiringly. "It's not like the other one. At Jordan and Talbot."

Ms. Skeffington sat on the desk with an unconscious playfulness sharply contrasting with her red eyes and smeared mascara. She shrugged slightly and smiled. "I wouldn't know. I've never seen it."

Her response surprised Montgomery. She had worked closely with the man for some time. Could she really not have been to J & T even once? "How long did you say you worked here?"

"Four years," she answered proudly. "I've had plenty of offers for higher paying jobs, but I loved it here."

"What will you do now?"

The thirty-four year old Skeffington set her square jaw in determination. "I'll stay and carry on," she stated. "No matter what."

Montgomery understood that her comment led directly to Madelaine Jordan. Skeffington had not disguised her antipathy for "the monster". Since no one liked Madelaine, questions about her got Montgomery nowhere. He went directly to his real questions. "If you have worked with Mr. Jordan for so long, then maybe you can tell me what I need to know about his personal habits?"

"If I can't, no one can," she replied almost defensively, as though someone else would try.

"Alright, then," Monty began carefully. He could see that was emotionally unstable. "You can help me out, Ms. Skeffington. You do want to help?"

Her face stiffened and her shoulders settled, as she contained her emotions. When she nodded gravely, Montgomery decided that she would hold up for a couple of questions, no more.

"Mr. Jordan had taken some kind of medication, Ms. Skeffington, he explained again. Repetition helped calm many if the people he questioned. "You knew him well enough to know where he could keep something like that, didn't you?"

"Yes, sir," she said, her breath still coming in spurts. he had kept any here, I would know about it."

He felt the usual churning in his stomach that started when a whole line of inquiry evaporated, leaving no mark on his case. Still, he pressed on. "Would he ever want to hide this kind of thing from you, Ms. Skeffington? Some people don't want to worry those around them when they're having problems.

Shock surged through her face. "Thomas Jordan," she said evenly but sharply, "never kept anything from me. I was his confidante. He trusted me. And I told him everything."

Montgomery knew what the last sentence had to do with his question.

"What did he tell you?"

"Oh, everything," she blurted. "I know all about the problems we had here. More than anyone. And he told me all about his personal problems, too. Like about his family." She stopped, abruptly. "I can't repeat that kind of thing," she apologized.

The stale air of a dead-end street filled Montgomery's head. The young woman's giddy assurance told him that she did not know anything. One thing he learned about Thomas Jordan: He had kept most of himself inside. He would not have burdened an adoring Skeffington with his troubles. Montgomery understood that type of man and knew better than to waste his time. "Did you see any indication that he would commit suicide?" he asked roughly.

Indignant, she leaped from the desk. "Good God, No!" she cried. "Not Mr. Jordan! He lived for his work here. He had goals, Sergeant. And great men don't give up until they have finished what they set out to finish."

At lease, he thought, the interview was finished. He watched Skeffington start crying again. He would leave her be and get back to one of his normal cases. The Jordan case had a quality about it that Montgomery disliked. It felt unreal, to everyone involved. Whatever the reality of Jordan's death, Montgomery knew that Jean Skeffington would not like it. He was not sure he would either.

~ ~ ~

The pilot of the Talbot Instrument's Learjet moved the plane gently the Allegheny County Airport's taxiway. From the corner of her eye she could see the helicopter waiting outside the Jordan & Talbot hanger, its blades slowly rotating. The J & T crew had encountered her often enough to know that Madelaine Jordan did not intend to be kept waiting. She wanted to be in and out of the city of Pittsburgh as quickly as possible.

Once the plane had pulled to a stop near the hanger, Madelaine unstrapped herself and waited. In a moment the J &

T Chief Pilot was in the seat beside her. She nodded and left the cabin. Outside the air was, as usual during the summer, hot and humid. Though the weather was not substantially different from that in New York, she felt much more uncomfortable.

The helicopter was air-conditioned, which helped keep her temper cool. Its pilot greeted her without ceremony. "Miss Jordan," he said. "We have clearance for Chatham Center."

"Good."

As the helicopter whirred on its way over the backed-up traffic, Madelaine said nothing. She ignored the terrain, the skyline, the man next to her. All she could think about was the adversary she was going to see first, the one who gave her the most difficulty.

The time passed so quickly that she barely noticed the landing in the middle of the city. Automatically she stepped out of one seat and into another, in a Lincoln Continental Town Coupe, its motor running. She could feel her aggravation growing as the car, caught in traffic, edged closer to its destination.

He back locked in its sitting position, Madelaine stared straight ahead, glowering at the small office building that housed her nemesis, Stapler.

Her expression registered little of the intense annoyance she felt, but her left foot rapped out beats to each block. To her, little was worse than being trapped in the city of Pittsburgh, except being trapped there with the man she had to see.

She examined the dirty stone and brick that composed the faces of the old buildings on Grant Street. Only an occasional steel and glass structure jutted into the skyline, contrasting its dynamism with the sturdy stagnation of old eyesores like Stapler's building.

One of the sturdiest and one of the dirtiest, properly enough, she thought, belonged to Richmond S. Stapler, Esquire, courtesy of Jordan money and influence. The Haller Building had survived worse plagues than Stapler and it showed the scars of everyone of them. The imposing sandstone front had recently been sand-blasted at the first two levels. The other four floors, right up to Stapler's "penthouse" office, still wore the grit of decades of Pittsburgh's industrial greatness.

As the car pulled to a stop in front of the Haller Building, Madelaine prepared herself for the interview to follow. She fully expected it to be unpleasant. She and Stapler had been acquainted for almost five years and hostile for even longer. Madelaine had disliked him long before she had met him in person. Her father had described Stapler in terms obviously dredged from her father's misty vision of himself as a youth. She had wanted no part of any such mythology or its idols.

Her resistance had not prevented their meeting. He had arrived one night for a quiet little dinner with the three Jordans. Madelaine had assumed that Stapler, as an ambitious associate at Sinker & Lyne, had been willing to coddle the firm's largest client. His insistence upon taking her everywhere during the summer following her graduation from MIT, reinforced her opinion. She had informed him, without hesitation, that she despised him. He had smiled and asked, "So?"

From that cold beginning, their association had deteriorated until, in the last confrontation, he had physically demolished her with a wicked left cross. Since they had been boxing at the time, she did not so much object to the punch as to the deliberateness of the target. More than once, he had referred to her nose as a symbol of her personality. That he had intended to break it, she had no doubt, anymore than she now doubted that she would suffer abuse for having had it properly repaired.

Rubbing the newly formed bridge, she prepared to face the coming insults and strode out of the ancient, gated lift. Her low leather heels snapped out reports of her approach to Mrs. Carpenter's desk.

"Good morning, Miss Jordan," Mrs. Carpenter said amicably, rising.

The secretary's attitude, the friendly informality, annoyed Madelaine. She was not in the mood for it and the impatience seething beneath her expressionless "Hello, Mrs. Carpenter," was unabated by the mockingly appreciative smile the greeting elicited.

"If you will wait just a moment, Miss Jordan," Heloise said, her finger on the intercom button, "Rick will be right with you."

Madelaine could see that none of the lines on the phone were lit. The tactics of delay she understood too well. Her eye on the door, she said. "Thank you, Mrs. Carpenter," and without hesitation, she stepped over to the door and threw it open.

Stapler, standing in the corner of the room, stared at her. Attired in a solid brown, French-cut suit vest, he at least looked the part of a lawyer. His long, dark hair drawn back from his forehead told her that he had been running his hand through it as he did when puzzling over how to handle her.

Out of the corner of her eye, Madelaine detected a shrug from the secretary who had followed her bolt into the office. Stapler gave them both a half-smile, as he moved toward the safety of his desk. Many of the men she dealt with used their desks as a protective barrier against Madelaine.

Speaking before he achieved his position, Madelaine said in staccato, "I want a meeting of the full board of J & T within the week."

"And how are you, Madelaine?" he asked politely.

Her large, gray eyes glaring at him from under the high, naturally pencil-lined eyebrows, Madelaine snapped, "Wretched and you know it."

His smile seemed to be one of pleasure, for her benefit. "Good," he said, sitting. After a glance toward Heloise, he added, "I love that white suit you're wearing, Madelaine."

Madelaine ignored an urge to look down at her outfit. She had absentmindedly selected the white and gold suit, but saw nothing wrong with it. "Why?" she demanded.

Stapler pondered her inquiry for a moment and then intoned, "White is for innocents, virgins and brides, Maddy. Those who grieve wear black."

Sitting as she let a one syllable laugh, Madelaine rejoined, "And since I'm not in black, I'm not grieving."

"I didn't say that, Maddy," Rick protested.

Stiffening, Madelaine paused a moment to set her broad, bony shoulders. "I am not grieving, if you must know. I may miss him, but his death is not particularly unexpected."

Evenly, he replied, "I won't argue the point with you, Madelaine."

"Good."

Stapler settled back in his chair trying to relax. "Did you fly in yourself?"

"It is much more convenient." As Rick leaned back, Madelaine herself leaned forward. She corrected the tendency. "I have a favor to ask of you.

"There is no one I'd rather do a favor for."

"I would like you to exercise your power as trustee of those trustees you established for my father."

He tried to interrupt. "Madelaine. Let me explain."

In her best frozen manner, Madelaine continued. "I want to be the new chairman of Jordan & Talbot. The Board will not elect me unless the Trustee, you, are behind me. It should be done immediately. Before opposition can be organized." She knew already that several important people had approached Rick for help in blocking her accession.

"Your personal feelings toward me should not influence you in this matter."

His face had gone as white as Madelaine's always was. The muscles in his jaw worked to clamp his teeth together. "They won't, Maddy. I'll be honest with you..."

"How refreshing."

Stapler couldn't hold back a smile. "I suppose it is."

Madelaine decided to defuse his honesty. "I know that DeJong and Einberg have contacted you."

Without showing his surprise, he said "And that I am inclined to agree with them."

"That I didn't know for sure until now." Madelaine had guessed that he would side against her as he always had, but she was disappointed. She had hoped that her father's death would have made him feel sorry for her. "You are wrong in your assessment of me, Rick."

Tilting forward in his leather chair, Stapler stared straight into Madelaine's large gray eyes, "I hope so, Madelaine. In any case, any arrangement will be temporary, until things settle down."

She stood up and looked down at him. "I have plans, Rick. If you, and the others, try to delay them, I will have to find some way around you. It will make working together impossible."

"Madelaine," he countered firmly as he rose, "we have to cooperate on the estate." He started to move around the desk.

Her sharp words stopped him in his tracks. "Not necessarily."

Testily he asked, "What do you have in mind?"

"Contingencies," she said vaguely. "In case we don't get along."

"You've made your point." He was finally annoyed. Madelaine had laid it out before him. Fall in line or fall out. "The last thing I want to do is upset you. I know you are under a strain. We'll get along. Somehow."

"I'm sure we will." Her thin mouth curved into a shallow smile. "There is too much at stake for both of us."

Holding back, Stapler kept his voice emotionless. "If you have finished with me for the time being, Madelaine, please remember that I am always at your disposal. That door is open to you at any time. Don't hesitate to take advantage of it."

As she turned to go, Madelaine glared back at Rick. "Perhaps we can spar a bit later."

For the first time, he noticed how well her nose had been fixed. He hurried to catch her as she swept out of his office. In front of Heloise's desk, Rick caught Madelaine's arm. "I'm not as sorry about breaking your nose now that I see the results."

Suddenly angry, Madelaine pulled away from him. "Someday, I intend to return the favor." Without another word she pivoted and stalked out into the corridor.

Furious with her, Stapler took a step after her, only to be restrained by Heloise. "I can't even compliment the bitch." He stormed into his office and over to his window, waiting to see Madelaine come out of the building and climb into the silver Lincoln.

"You two will hurt each other someday." Heloise said.

"Someday soon," he said towards the glass. "We've got to work on this Goddamn estate together." Rick watched Madelaine as she strode out to the car. "By God, she is something."

"What was she so upset about?" Heloise asked quickly.

Rick left the window, to stalk about the room as he answered. "As you know, one of our clever devices was to put Mr. Jordan's stock in Jordan & Talbot Incorporated, by far his largest asset, into a foundation and a series of trusts.

"I should remember," Heloise said. "I had to type up several hundred amendments to them." Her fingers hurt just remembering.

"Don't worry," he laughed. "I'll get you a memory type-writer eventually."

"When did you become trustee? I thought Jim Carstairs had a backup trustee," she said, pretending not to hear his promise.

"Yes," he agreed, trying to disguise a grimace. "But our alternate trustee died even before Jim did. Jordan didn't want a bank to be trustee, so he made me the fall guy until we could come up with someone else he could trust to stand up to Maddy. Christ, it's unbelievable. I'm sure, Maddy thinks I maneuvered it. She must think I'm the slimiest creation since her mother." He laughed again at the thought. "Hell, I didn't even know about it until he showed me the executed amendment he wrote himself. In long hand!"

"Did you do it for tax reasons?" she asked to keep him talking. Rick would calm down if he talked to her. "The trusts, I mean."

"Tax?" he repeated. "Oh, yes. Always for taxes. Actually, he had a couple other reasons. He wanted to keep J & T out of Carolyn Jordan's unstable little hands, of course. And he was afraid to leave it outright to Madelaine. We just couldn't predict what she'd do with it. I think the poor guy was afraid that she'd tear J & T apart out of spite."

"Will she?" Heloise asked hopefully.

Rick looked at her and wondered what her tone implied. He measured his words. "I think, after today that she will let us know all too soon. And I'm afraid she's going to start with me."

Heloise smiled, displaying most of the small white teeth behind her generously drawn lips. "By the way," she said sweetly, "I have a letter of apology typed up. Do you want to sign it now?"

"Apology.'" he cried. "Never. I was right, wasn't I?"

Heloise put the paper on his desk. He stared at it for a minute, his palm on his forehead.

"You would think," he capitulated with a sigh, "that a man of my stature would at least hesitate to grovel before such a stony, sexless statue of a woman." A feeling of amusement overcame his anger. He would have to give P1adelaine what she wanted. She would be his stern, unloving goddess. "Okay. But bring me a cheap pen, will you?"

~ ~ ~

Skeffington was not at her desk when Carleton finally reached the office of the Administrator. That did not surprise Carleton. Skeffington had an exaggerated view of her own importance and tried to be everywhere at once, as if things could not run smoothly without her presence. As far as Carleton could tell, life proceeded rather better with Skeffington in the ladies' room.

Sitting nonchalantly on the administrative assistant's desk, Carleton surveyed the mountains of messages that Skeffington had taken or made for her own reference. Like other bureaucrats Carleton had run into, Skeffington created paperwork mostly for herself which she later would deem too insignificance even for her own reading. One note, however, was arresting.

"Dr. Raymond Carleton" read its heading.

Craning his neck, Carleton digested the note. Skeffington, it appeared, was leery about renewing his building pass. She thought he was a "trouble-making little creep". Not a very compelling reason, he told himself. If Skeffington could bar everyone she thought was a trouble-making creep, the Talbot would be empty most of the time.

The note concluded with "Talk to Mr. Melton about it.

Melton! Carleton already knew what that old prune thought of him.

He had voted with Jordan, Carstairs and the others against him. If Melton had his way, Carleton suspected that he would be out in the street in no time. But if Melton was the new Administrator, he had to face him.

The door to the Administrator's Office was closed. Carleton put his ear to the wood and heard voices, though not well enough to recognize them. Feeling defiant, he knocked and opened the door, without awaiting a reply.

Inside the office formerly occupied by Thomas Jordan, Carleton found Jean Skeffington and in a chair beside Jordan's desk, Howard Peabody Melton. At seventy-four Melton looked shriveled up like a month-old tomato. The old man looked Carleton straight in the eyes.

Carleton shifted his glance over to Skeffington, who stood with her hands tight to her sides, obviously outraged by his intrusion. Her face was nearly as red as Melton's if not so natural.

"The guard told me to come see you," Carleton said innocently.

"That was over two hours ago," she replied over clenched teeth.

"I know you're busy, so I waited."

Melton rose slowly from the chair and walked over to Carleton, politely offering his hand. "How are you getting along, Dr. Carleton? I understand your pass has expired."

Wary, Carleton moved sideways instinctively. "I suppose it has."

"Quite frankly, I'm not sure what to do about it. The pass was intended only as a transitional thing, to help you move and find other facilities."

"There aren't any other facilities, damn it! Where am I supposed to go? Nobody has any use for me, now!" His own anger caught Carleton off guard. He cooled it quickly. "I mean, I've started a project that I can't finish anywhere else. The Talbot is unique."

Putting his hand on Carleton's shoulder, Melton was sympathetic. "It is, Dr. Carleton, Very unique. I understand the problem, but I can't make exceptions for every former member of the staff. That would not do at all."

Baring his teeth, Carleton asked, "Is that it? You can't make an exception for me because all the other stooges you cut down don't deserve to be here? Well, you should make an exception. I am an exception. You'll find that out."

Carleton stormed out of the Administrator's Office, slamming the heavy door as hard as he could. It barely made a sound. He raised his hand to throw his briefcase at the name plate on the door when he saw that it said Thomas Jordan. That reminded him that he did not need to be angry. Not now, not anymore. He could deal with Melton–and others like him–effectively without violence or temper. All he needed was the force of his superior mind and the flick of a switch. That was all he would ever need again.

~ ~ ~

Upon her arrival at Jordan & Talbot's headquarters, Madelaine found Francis DeJong implacably awaiting her. A skilled negotiator, DeJong maintained his look of composure despite his apprehension in dealing with Thomas Jordan's forceful unpredictable daughter.

DeJong had known Madelaine since 1961 and he had learned enough to remain inscrutable. He smiled impassively before every statement after each question. He found it difficult, but it had to be done.

Cleveland, DeJong, Planter and Bolton had served Jordan & Talbot as underwriter and acquisition broker since 1961. Jack Cleveland and Tom Jordan had helped resurrect Carstairs Paint and Chemical in 1958. They dad worked so well together that Jordan had convinced Cleveland to form his own firm with J & T as a principal client. The relationship had endured, profitable for both parties.

It was DeJong, however, who Jack Cleveland had insisted would be more objective and informed than he. DeJong, he had said, "was born crusty," as a final endorsement. In the time since, DeJong had seen his influence at J & T grow and wane, but never cease. Tom Jordan had always respected

DeJong's opinions, if not necessarily agreeing with them. More importantly, in Jordan's view, DeJong had always given his opinions.

DeJong feared that with Jordan's death, his tenure on the board was in jeopardy. DeJong realized, as did many other board members, that the cold, young creature seated across the small conference table from him, wanted complete control of Jordan and Talbot, as she had at Talbot Instruments three years before. Madelaine shared authority, and apparently whatever else she had, with no one. That, at least had been the pattern she had followed at TI.

DeJong, while respecting Madelaine's obvious talents, had long felt that she had exceeded her abilities in turning a faltering TI around. She had little rapport with people. Her subordinates despised her personally despite their admiration. In waves of hirings and dismissals, acquisitions and divestitures, Madelaine had completely changed the character of Talbot Instruments. The short-term effect had obviously been beneficial, in the extreme. The future, however, seemed to DeJong to hold less promise. It was all Madelaine's, an uncompromising organization, driving too hard and almost always overextended. Phone calls from Directors ranging from a panicking Heinrich Wozheim to a disapproving Josh Einberg indicated to DeJong that the others accepted his analysis of their heiress apparent.

He observed her with conscious nonchalance, as she addressed him.

Her brow furrowed so slightly, the eyes narrowed so little that she seemed uninterested in what she had to say. A wicked scythe of a mouth flashed out its words.

"As Vice-Chairman and a member of the executive committee, Mr. DeJong," she said in a sharp even tone, "you should be interested enough in J&T to call a board meeting as soon as possible."

DeJong smiled at the reiteration of the theme. Only the committee or the President of J & T could issue that call.

Madelaine was neither. "In time, Madelaine," he replied gently, hoping it would be a long time. "Your haste is for nothing and it is most unseemly. Josh and I can handle things for now."

"Josh?" she asked as though she had forgotten he had ever existed. "Josh Einberg? Don't be silly. Poor Josh is totally preoccupied over at Tylton. As well he should be. You can't expect him to carry that load as well as that of running J & T."

Her overstated doubt seeped in under DeJong's calm facade. His words were measured, and clear. "He is not alone, Miss Jordan.

"I am not criticizing, Francis, only pointing out the problem." She explained. "Your first obligation, of course, is to Cleveland, DeJong. Shouldn't Jordan & Talbot have a full time Chairman? Now."

She had made her accusation sound as though he shirked his duty to both his firm and to J & T. "Perhaps," he agreed, suppressing his anger. "Whom do you suggest?"

Madelaine bore the insult without expression. The glint of silver in her eyes could hide any emotion. "I prefer myself, but I am prepared to entertain any reasonable alternative," she responded. "From within the organization, of course."

The unveiled slap to DeJong broke through his reserve. She had flatly ruled him, as an outside director, out of consideration. The affront proved too much. DeJong came very close to an outburst of complete rage.

The scarlet in his face, he was aware, gave him over, despite his struggle for silence.

Madelaine took her eyes from his face and stood, daring him to look up at her. Near victory, she began to prowl about along the bank of windows.

"Personally," she said, not pausing long, "I think that the Board itself is a bit weak. Only Josh Einberg and you have proven any real expertise in actually running anything nearly this big. I understand that even TI isn't Jordan & Talbot. I suppose either of you as chairman would satisfy me."

The merry-go-round had come full circle and DeJong began to feel nauseated. He tried to anticipate her next direction. Undoubtedly she would attack him through Cleveland-DeJong, depriving it of TI's immediate securities business.

"Of course," she went on, "Josh would have to give up Tylton. And your affiliation with our underwriting firm would have to end." She paused long enough in her thinking aloud to ask, "Could you give up your position at Cleveland-DeJong?" with emphasis on the DeJong.

"Give it up!" he cried. The firm meant everything to him, he realized. More than the Chair of J & T, much more. "No, that I could never do. Cleveland-DeJong is my life," he added with emphasis.

"No, no, of course not," she said. "I shouldn't have insulted you by asking." Leaning back against the window, Madelaine looked DeJong in the face, her lips almost curved into a smile. "I know you dislike me, Mr. DeJong. And I know that you are not alone in that, but that doesn't matter. I admire your dedication to your firm, honestly," she continued without any sincerity in her voice. "It must be a fine feeling."

Grudgingly, he admitted, "It is, Madelaine."

She smiled, baring her teeth. "You and Jack Cleveland have done a pretty good job. J & T is going to need more of you, if I have anything to say about it," she promised. "I want to restructure the business. We've got too many marginally profitable lines. We will have to dump some of them or recapitalize them. Basically, I think J & T needs more equity capital and less debt," she added evenly.

DeJong gazed at her with admiration. He began to see her scheme for dismantling J & T and recreating it in her own lean, hard image. It seemed paradoxical, perhaps, that she wanted to let the public in on the largely privately held enterprise, but he liked the idea. More than once, DeJong had suggested to Tom Jordan that going more public would be beneficial in the long run. Even though the market is in weak shape, he mused, they might be able to trade on J & T's record and Madelaine's reputation. Yes, indeed!

"In fact," she went on, offhandedly, "I sent Jack a request this morning to prepare an underwriting for a possible issue of TI common before people realize how slow this recovery will be."

"Really," he croaked, astonished at the speed with which she worked. "How much?" He knew it would be generous.

Madelaine looked at him as if she were deciding then and there. Before she spoke, however, she turned her gaze to the windows. "I was thinking in terms of roughly 50 percent control outstanding."

The shock brought DeJong to his feet. "That's $175 million dollars!" he shrieked. "In this market!"

"Jack and I figured more like 188 million," she said casually.

"Who approved this madness?" he demanded,

She looked at him in mock wonder. "TI's Board of Directors, of course. It was decided that we needed the money to finance our excursion into semi-conductors. Jack told me he thinks that you two can get it." Returning her eyes to his, she added forcefully, "Francis, we're hot. When my financial results are out, we'll be hotter. And I think, if you will pardon the expression, I think we ought to capitalize on it."

"When did all this planning take place?" he asked sharply. "Before or after your father's death?"

Her answer was tinged with the proper trace of regret. "We had an emergency meeting yesterday afternoon," she replied. "And no, I did not call it. The board panicked at the news."

"He would never have allowed it," DeJong stated sadly.

"No," she agreed coolly, "Thomas Jordan would never acquiesce to sharing anything with anyone else, Francis. But you and I know better."

DeJong knew he should be enraged at her presumption, but he could muster no more than incredulity. "I will have to consult with those in control of the corporation," he said slowly organizing his retreat.

"Tell Josh, certainly," she concurred. "And the finance committee, but let's try to keep it as quiet as possible. We don't want the information to get out. The securities laws complicate matters terribly when that happens," she added matter-of-factly.

DeJong's voice shook as he capitulated. "Of course." The reference to the Securities Acts reminded DeJong of the profits the firm had saved for select clients on inside information the previous winter, in violation of those laws. "Perhaps that is best."

When DeJong had closed the door, Madelaine stretched her long arms in front of her, and looked down at Grant Street with its tine, crawling cars and its hurrying little pedestrians. She felt she could seize them all and gather them to her. No, she thought. She could probably do it, but she did not have any particular use for them.

Her large gray eyes traveled down the crowded street towards the Monongahela River. She could see the Haller Building from there. Somewhere in that squat old building, Stapler was conniving to thwart her ambitions. She did not mind so much. Not now that she had pushed DeJong into her corner. There was Einberg, too, of course. She had plans for him, but Stapler with his control of so much of J & T stock, was the main problem. Hiding in his little office building, Stapler felt secure, she thought. He had replaced her father, in some ways, at least. He had betrayed her in merely meeting her the first time. He had always aligned himself against her with her father. Nothing had changed now that she was alone.

Like Stapler, his Haller Building had no distinctive feature. It was not particularly tall, dignified or important to the skyline. Nothing about it made it stand out, but the mere sight of its profile jutting out beyond the very similar building next to it made her feel ill. How did it attract tenants when the perfectly fine building next to it had "FOR RENT" signs all over it?

It bothered her that the question so nagged at her in a moment of considerable triumph. Just once, she determined, she would have a victory she could savor without feeling the craving for something else. She would have it and, glaring at the Haller Building, she knew against whom it had to come.

CHAPTER FOUR

Responding to the bell, George discovered Madelaine outside, in a state of fury. She barely gave him time to pull the door open before she brushed past him. The pink color in her cheeks told him she had been with Stapler again.

"Christ!" she snarled. "I've been here two days already and I don't have a goddamn key!"

She was headed toward the study before George could speak. "If you need one, Madelaine," he said cautiously, while following her.

"I don't want to be waited on like a little girl," she snapped. She tore the doors open to the small room and disappeared through the opening.

George hesitated before joining her. He knew that he had better let her cool down a little.

Her long, white hands feeling cold, Madelaine seized a bottle of brandy and poured herself four ounces. With both hands on the glass, she swallowed several long sips until the heat soothed her chest. Taking gulps of air, she steadied herself with the edge of the bookcase.

She stiffened as she heard George approaching her quietly. His hand reached toward her glass and deposited a set of keys on the ledge. She stared at the ring of metal for a long time, not daring to speak.

George let a moment pass and said, "I believe that all of the keys are there."

Madelaine swung her head first up, then down and finally to the side where George stood. She summoned her warmest smile for the aging butler. "George," she said. "You are incredible."

Dryly, he replied, "Thank you, Miss."

Releasing the glass, she clutched his shoulders and stared him right in the face. "How could you have gone through all those years with me and not hit me once?" She grimaced, drawing the thin, pink lips over her front teeth. "I apologize. It's not your fault that I have to work with Richmond S. Stapler, Esquire."

"I assumed that you had seen him today," George said.

She spun away from him in exaggerated anguish. "Oh, he called," she said. "Now I know why poor father had his heart attack."

The brandy ran down her throat, feeding her desire to throttle the impossible attorney. "George, you have known me for, well, for forever. Tell me, honestly," she asked evenly. "Do I remind you of a female impersonator?"

George pondered the question for a moment. "I haven't really known any," he replied.

She laughed out loud, as she rarely did. It felt good for a change. It was, of course, the brandy.

To George, Madelaine's laugh had a glorious sound. It was not the throaty, almost harsh sound everyone else heard. He heard only the thin giggle of a Girl under ten years old. It seemed like that long ago that he had last heard her really laugh.

His dour expression brought Madelaine to sobriety. She wrinkled her expensive new nose and said, "Let's see, what did we fight about today?" It didn't take too long to remember. "Ah, yes. That God-awful autopsy. How in hell did he manage that one!"

"He didn't tell you?" George asked surprised. It was, after all, in spite of Rick that the autopsy had been ordered.

She looked at him, her pewter colored eyes keeping the light for themselves. "He hung up on me before I had a chance to ask."

George decided to set the record straight, for the sake of both the combatants. He liked Stapler and wanted him to

Get along with Madelaine, especially now that her father was Gone. "A detective named Montgomery was here. It seems that there was some drug in Mr. Jordan's coffee."

"What do you mean, George?" she demanded.

"I don't know," George admitted with a light lift of the shoulders. "It was Dr. Morex who requested a formal autopsy."

Madelaine was not really listening. Montgomery's name hung in her mind. She thought it over several times. She would have to meet this Detective Montgomery. "What do you think?"

It was a sensitive subject for George, for he knew that he was the one who had the responsibility for the coffee. "I don't understand it," he declared. "I made the coffee myself as usual. Dennison Decaffeinated. I don't see how it could have gotten in there, unless he did so himself. But he didn't use sleeping aids."

The thought of it made Madelaine feel vaguely ill. "Suicide," she said. "I don't see it." A wave of nausea upset her balance. "Get that Montgomery for me," she ordered, steadying herself again, "and then I'll deal with Rick."

~ ~ ~

Heloise hated to switch Madelaine over to Rick at a time when he was half-drunk. He had not stopped since talking to her last. Conversations between the two had become so taxing that Rick could not relax again without several shots of Old Grand Dad.

Madelaine's tone had left Heloise no choice. If anything, the Jordan heiress was more agitated than Rick. Though Madelaine hid strain well, the lines deepening in her smooth, white skin indicated something to Heloise. Neither she nor Rick could afford a blow-up with Madelaine, Heloise quickly composed a note she hoped would help.

"Madelaine, please," she heard Rick say into the phone. "No, I can't think of any reason. Suicide is out of the question... As far as I am concerned it is. Unless you know... Okay, Okay. Montgomery said today or tomorrow? Good." Rick's face contorted into a grimacing smile when Heloise joined him behind the desk. "I'll be happy to have him call."

"She's killing me," he said, in an aside. "First thing, Maddy..."

"I'm sorry, Madelaine. I will let you know first thing. Yes. No, don't hang up," he said, reading the note from Heloise. "No, don't hang up. Madelaine!" Rick was exasperated. "For Christ's sake, Maddy, you are the executrix!" he shouted, He almost threw the phone on the desk, and clenched one fist threatening to kill the plastic receiver. "Hel, please, you talk to her."

When Heloise refused, he relented.

"I did petition this morning, Madelaine," he told her. "Thank you, I think I am half-competent, too," he said grinning at Heloise.

Heloise returned his smile with an impatient frown and a nod of her head toward the note.

"One more thing, Maddy," he went on. "I want you to go to dinner with me tonight. That's right. Dinner at the La-Mont. With me. No, of course not. I'll pay. You're right, Madelaine, it's not my idea of a good time either, but Hel... Yes, Hel suggested it. She says we can't fight in a restaurant. I'm not particular either, but she thinks you're too civilized."

He nodded and said to Heloise, "She said to say Thank You."

"She is welcome," Heloise responded.

"You're welcome, Madelaine," he told the phone. "Please, Maddy. How's eight? Yes, seven is better for me too. You'll meet me there?" he said. "Remember, this is for fun only. No business. That's my girl. Goodbye. Oh, and wear something sexy," he suggested. "Sure you do... No, for the waiter. We'll get better service." Rubbing his ear, Rick returned the phone to its cradle

"I hope you two won't tear the place apart," Heloise commented. Rick stood and stretched. "I don't think so. She was pleasant, relatively. She even apologized to me."

"How nice."

"For thinking me the most heinous, soulless monster on the face of the planet.'"

"After the way you treated her this afternoon, I agree," Heloise said. "You still didn't tell her anything about the autopsy yourself. That was the worst thing you've done to her yet."

"Are you through, Mrs. Carpenter?" he asked.

"No, as a matter of fact, I'm not," Heloise said, suddenly upset with him. She rarely lectured him and never got mad anymore. "You, Rick Stapler, know perfectly well how badly you treat her. She's bad; you are supposed to be better. You have never shown a moment's kindness to that poor girl and you know how much she must need some now. For God's sake, Ricky, you haven't come an inch since I first met you."

Staring at her, Rick said calmly, almost dreamily, "Heloise? Didn't you tell me in college what a wonderful woman you were?"

She was still mad at him, but she smiled, "I did, several times."

He heaved a sigh and smiled lightly. "Yes, I guess you did. You're too good a judge of character, which I suppose, accounts for your marrying J.J."

Something made Heloise turn to leave. She didn't know what it was, but she always followed her instincts. "Shall I get Monty on the phone?" she asked over her shoulder.

After a moment he answered lightly, "Yes, and cancel any dates I have for tonight and the next week. I'll need the energy."

He stared at the door she used to escape his gaze. Sometimes he simply did not understand her. Perhaps he never really did. In twelve years, he thought, he should have gotten some insight. It didn't matter. He had her around when he needed her. That was good enough for anybody.

~ ~ ~

Carleton felt good.

The mailgram lay beside him as he watched the two sets of green lines come together on the table top computer screen. The good news made it difficult to concentrate on keeping the intensity of his readings up, but the matching was so obvious that he finally tore the contact pickup from his forehead.

Earlier in the day he received the mailgram from old man Jordan's daughter, as executor of the estate. Madelaine Jordan informed him in concise telegram prose that he had been selected as a candidate to receive one of the special Talbot Research Hospital fellowships being established in Jordan's name. He had, as suggested called to set up an interview "as soon as possible," the following afternoon.

It was a nice irony that Thomas Jordan, who had in life so slighted him, should provide him with the opportunity to return to the Talbot with full funding. With more money he could greatly expand his horizons. He thought of the Mayor and laughed. If he wanted, he could probably do anything.

His good spirits, however, did not intrude upon his determination to first finish the project at hand. The insult of the month of April could not be retracted by a tardy restoration of status. Had he not confronted Jordan, the money would not be available even now. It was because of him, Carleton, that he was being rewarded with the new fellowship. That was as it should have been. He only wanted his due.

Quickly, Carleton ran a system's check, to assure himself that the device was in proper electrical order and was hooked up in the proper sequence. Punching program numbers into the desk top TI 125 computer, he verified each step. The amplifiers were recording, as was the transceiver.

Satisfied with the final check run, he turned off his equipment.

The hardware that he had designed, branching off from Madjerin's original brain wave detection devices, was working perfectly. The raw data on H.P. Melton had long been programmed onto its own cassette. The synchronization would be more than adequate.

He did not bother to cover the machinery, since he would have to install it in the van by evening and, more particularly, because he had an errand to run with the van. Most of it he wouldn't need soon anyway. That fellowship money would go along way.

His laboratory was lined with shelves, once used to store jars of preserves. Now he used them for technical manuals and books. Also he kept a small box of a white powdery artificial sweetener that he had taken from the basement of the Talbot. The sweetener had come in handy. Beside the sweetener sat a tiny bottle of another white powder, a sleep inducing material also pirated from the Talbot. With the two mixed together, the sleeping powder was not at all noticeable. Just like him, he thought. Not physically noticeable, but dangerous, powerful. That was the best way to be.

Measuring the proper amounts, Carleton spooned the powders into a small plastic sweetener dispenser. It was the kind of dispenser that was included free in the boxes of the Dennison Foods Sweetener, the kind Melton used. The cap snapped into place, sealing the powders inside. Only the plastic lever would release them, mingled together.

Turning out the light, Carleton swung the door closed and locked it. The two flights of stairs were treacherous because they were so dark and rotted, but he didn't mind anymore. He opened the door and stepped into the light.

"Raymond."

She had been lying in wait for him. Quickly, he thrust the plastic bottle into his pocket. "Yes, Mrs. Gergorian." He was growing more impatient with her all the time. He wished that he had a printout of her mental activity, if there were any.

"Are you going out? I need some things at the store."

"You always need something at the store," he snapped.

She ignored him. She did not hear anything unpleasant. "I'm out of paper towels, soap and Jell-O."

"That's impossible.'" he cried. "I just bought you Jell-O."

As if she hadn't heard him, she corrected herself. "No, that's not right. I have Jell-O. Cat food. It's cat food."

"You don't own a cat."

Nodding, she agreed. "Not anymore. I use it for the plants. You can get the cheapest kind."

"Cat food for the plants! Of course. How many?"

"Three." Mrs. Gergorian patted his arm and retired to her section of the decaying mansion, adding, "Not tuna, though.

Shoving his hands into his pockets, Carleton remembered that he had never run errands. The others could drive. The others were always off doing something, while he stayed home and read or studies. They had not amounted to much. Both his brothers were businessmen, inmates in that great American institution called The Corporation. Neither had to use his brain, fortunately. His sister didn't either: She was a mother.

He would be the only one to make his mark. He had already started.

Leaping into the Volkswagen van, Carleton congratulated himself on his intelligence. He hadn't far to go to be recognized for what he was, a true genius. Hell, he thought, he'd gladly pit his brain against anyone else's. He had five silent testaments to that.

Pumped full of self-confidence, Carleton put the bus in gear and headed for the market. From there he would drive to the University Club. He had a delivery to make there before dinner time.

~ ~ ~

Montgomery paced nervously down the hall from the coroner's office. He hated even talking to the people at the coroner's, let alone visiting their offices. When he saw Stapler wandering his way down the corridor, however, Montgomery felt a wave of relief.

"Hello, Stapler," he said. "I needed the company. Thanks for hustling down here."

Shaking the detective's hand, Rick replied, "I've got to explain this to a very tall, very temperamental girl. I want first hand information."

"I'm glad she called me, in a way," Monty went on. "The idiots finished yesterday and didn't tell me. Christ, you give them a rush job and they lose your phone number!"

"What did they find?" Rick asked impatiently.

Montgomery frowned. He was embarrassed more than anything else. "The moron I talked to wouldn't tell me. I don't get along with these guys. God damned bureaucracy."

Stapler nodded and the pair advanced to the entrance of the Office of the Allegheny County Coroner. Inside the, door, the main office looked like most other county offices. Paper inhabited every cubic inch not reserved for human beings, few that there were.

After brief bouts with three secretaries, Montgomery convinced a fourth to take him to see Dr. Timothy Brewster, the Senior Assistant, who was in charge of the Jordan autopsy. After the young lady located the room where Brewster was waiting for Montgomery, the detective vented his frustration.

"Why the hell couldn't you talk to me over the phone, Brewster!" he demanded without introduction.

Brewster, a retired pathologist, was new in the office, so he just smiled and said, "Montgomery, right?"

"Yeah," the cop growled.

"And you must be Mr. Stapler," Brewster said, amiably. "Sergeant Montgomery mentioned that you might come along.

While Rick and Brewster shook hands, Monty snapped, "What've you got, Doc?"

Having been warned about Montgomery in advance, Brewster had prepared himself for the detective's short manner. "Your Mr. Jordan must have been a light sleeper."

Receiving no response from either of his visitors, the assistant coroner continued, "He took a mighty heavy dose of," he paused, deciding to avoid the use of the generic name of the material, mostly because it had slipped his mind. "Let's leave it at sleeping powder," he said trying to sound condescending. "Common enough stuff. I don't think matters anyway. I'd estimate that he took enough to guarantee that he'd sleep through yesterday."

The report did not please Stapler very much. "Lethal?"

"Not this stuff," Brewster said. "It's fairly safe. In any case, the drug didn't kill him, in my opinion. All it did was allow him to sleep peacefully through an awesome heart attack."

Montgomery offered his own query, "What about the violence?" a nightmare, Sergeant. In fact, it's suggested that weak hearts often give out during a dream."

Rick shook his head. "But Jordan had a pretty strong heart."

Brewster did not help, he agreed. "I know."

"Shit," Montgomery interjected.

"Thank you, Dr. Brewster," Stapler said, preparing to leave. The doctor smiled and replied, "My pleasure, Mr. Stapler."

Once outside in the hall, Montgomery lit a cigarette and commented, "Funny thing is, I think he meant that."

Rubbing his forehead as if to smooth out his thoughts, Rick said, "How about a drink?"

"The magic word," Monty said grinning. "I'm off duty as of now. Where?"

Stapler responded quickly. "The University Club, alright?"

Annoyed, Montgomery nodded. "Can I get in?"

Pittsburgh's University Club, like most University Clubs, was nicely done in a baroque fashion. Stapler had joined because "it made me feel stuffy, had playable squash courts, good food and tall drinks."

He had suggested it to Montgomery for another reason. At that hour he was sure to run into H. P. Melton. Melton, his only remaining supporter on the Talbot Research Hospital Board of Trustees, could give him a sense of the mood of the rump board regarding his tenure as counsel.

~ ~ ~

Discussing bureaucratic psychology, Stapler and Montgomery took seats at the bar. Montgomery's stubborn opinion of coroners became quite colorful after two quick bourbons. Stapler offered to exchange one Registrar of Wills for any three coroners.

"Soft life, Stapler," Monty said suddenly, "Xerox a form, change the name and a couple of figures and you guys collect thousands."

"Huh?" Stapler pretended not to know what he meant.

"You God damned lawyers."

"Us?" Innocence widened Stapler's eyes.

"Probate lawyers like you, Stapler," Monty explained. "You guys are really smart."

"Yeah," Stapler agreed. "I'm so smart that I'm about to go out of business."

"Good," Monty congratulated him. "Get back into criminal work. Then we can make you sweat a bit."

"Christ. You bastard. You personally drove me to civil practice with your fabrication on that Johnson case." Stapler shook his glass at the detective, with mock indignation.

"'He dropped the heroin, your honor.' Such innocence doesn't look good on a cop."

Montgomery downed some peanuts. "Oh, come on, Stapler, you won your God damned appeal. He's running loose still. Besides, that son-of-a-bitch was guilty as hell."

"Sure he was," Rick admitted. "So were you. Illegal search?"

"But I'm a cop," the cop said. "And anyway, Counselor, I only said that I picked the dope up off the ground. I didn't say he actually dropped it," he pointed out with a lilt in his gruff voice. "Shit. He killed for it."

"I didn't want to be a public defender anyway," Stapler said. "No money in it."

"Speaking of money," Montgomery interjected, "How much was Jordan worth?"

"More than you'll ever see under any table, Monty." "A coy lawyer is not appreciated in my department." "Directly and indirectly?" He asked. Monty nodded. "About 50 or 60, I'd guess. Most of it is in Jordan and Talbot, some in real estate and miscellaneous securities, of course."

"And you handle it?"

"Since spring, I have, yeah. We were going to appoint a new trustee as soon as we could find one we liked." Stapler looked down into the empty glass. "Only we didn't. Jordan became convinced that everybody he knew was dying off. Hell, everybody was. He thought it was a plot or some such."

"Maybe it was." Montgomery added cryptically.

Stapler rubbed his forehead. Often since May he wondered why so many men should die so unnaturally close together. Five members of the Talbot board had succumbed since then. "Five heart attacks."

"Maybe, but I don't like it," Montgomery said, pulling a recently typed report from his jacket. "I've been over this damn thing a thousand times," he said, "and I can't find an explanation for it. No fatal dosages of drugs or anything.

Those other guys from the Talbot just died in their sleep, too. Sweet dreams and Sayonara."

A frown of confusion bent Stapler's mouth. "Well, it was a pretty hectic spring, Monty," he suggested. "The recession was at its worst. I know that a couple of the trustees were on the edge of bankruptcy So was the Talbot. We had to cut way back on the grants at the hospital. These men were all pretty tough, but in the course of two weeks, they had to decide what careers to scrap."

"They don't really give a shit about anybody, do they?" Montgomery asked.

Stapler glared at him over his glass. "God, you're a jerk, Monty. That's just ridiculous. Jordan gave a lot of time to the Talbot because he was interested in the research going on there. Most of the others were, too. All the people denied grant renewals had been sponsored by members of the board, promised continuing funds."

A new voice joined the conversation. "Richmond, my boy, you are a splendid advocate."

H.P. Melton thrust his white-haired, red-faced head between them, Chuckling to himself, Melton joined Stapler and his guest at the bar. His creased face was long and very thin, but never gaunt. Melton played golf every day out in the blazing sun, forever unable to get a tan. Instead, he turned bright red. Melton at regularly crushed Stapler on the squash court.

Stapler introduced Montgomery to the smiling older man.

"Sit down, young fella," Melton said. "Save your energy for tomorrow."

"And what's so good about tomorrow?" Stapler asked.

"Tomorrow," Melton intoned wisely, "tomorrow you will have to clean up after a murder."

Montgomery did not smile. "Anyone I know?"

"Yes, indeed, Sergeant Montgomery," he continued. "He may even be sitting with us now."

Stapler nodded grimly. "You've been talking to Madelaine."

"You are perceptive, Ricky," Melton replied brightly.

"I thought you hated her," Monty said. "Which I can understand. She really let me have it about that autopsy, today. Besides, I hear she's homely.'

Melton's eyes danced as he looked at Rick. "I find Madelaine to be very attractive in her own way. Striking, even."

Stapler said nothing on the subject, studying Melton silently. The retired airline executive had some news for Stapler, and Rick knew it. Undoubtedly, Madelaine had hinted something to her old family friend concerning her plans for him. A man of strict ethics, Melton might not tell Rick outright if Madelaine had spoken confidentially.

"She did tell me," Melton was saying when Rick finally listened, "she needed a new attorney and asked me for a recommendation."

"You mean a personal lawyer," Monty asked, growing increasingly curious about Stapler's relationship with the Jordan heiress.

"Oh, yes, personal," Melton said deliberately. "For a real estate deal."

Stapler smiled. "I hope you put in a good word for me, Redhead."

Melton rose effortlessly as he spoke. As a matter of fact, though it was inappropriate, I did."

"And?" Stapler did not betray his anxiety.

"She accused me of senility!" he explained as he walked away. "Good evening to you both."

~ ~ ~

Madelaine entered LaMont the way she entered any building.

Ignoring a gentleman's gesture, she threw the door open in a single, sweeping motion. Her long legs made their entrance well before the rest of her. Purpose and direction shone so clearly in her face that the Maitre d' retreated several steps as she strode by.

She paused at the front of the cocktail lounge, so that only Stapler could detect the hesitation. Emotionless, she surveyed the scene, spotting her target before he could raise his glass in salute. Madelaine fixed her mouth in a tight, grim smile, and approached Stapler, sitting on a stool at the bar, as was his custom. Madelaine's drink was awaiting her.

Rising, Rick grinned at her. "Madelaine, I love that way you walk. Do you realize that every man, woman and child in this room watched your entrance?"

She did not expend her attention on the others staring at them. "Good evening, counselor," she said picking up the drink. "I don't like sitting at bars. Could I prevail upon you to move to a table?"

"As God is my witness, Maddy," Stapler began, "I will bow to your every whim tonight." He picked up his scotch and led the way to a window table. "Besides, Heloise insisted that a table would be more romantic," he said without a glance as she moved past him.

Madelaine sat down without admiring the view. She had always disliked Stapler's sense of humor. She felt he used it to mock her every move. More than that, however, Madelaine envied Stapler his ability to belittle her, no matter how viciously, with that ingratiating smile "Heloise is usually right," Madelaine said finally.

"Usually," Stapler replied, pausing to glance out the huge window at the towering fountain. "She also thinks that I am a cad for the way I treat you. Do you agree?"

Madelaine knew that Stapler expected a retort, but she had none. "Of course not," she said.

"Uh huh," he agreed. "I am a cad anyway. Aren't I?"

"Are you disappointed that I did not insult you on cue?" she asked evenly.

Rick smiled and patted her hand. Her candor always annoyed him. "You never disappoint me, Maddy," he said icily.

"I've come to expect so little. With me, you hoard your imagination."

Madelaine slumped in her chair, not much, just enough for Rick to perceive it. She normally had a back straight as a Prussian in traction. Stapler felt a flush of guilt. "I'm sorry, Madelaine. I am trying to be good tonight."

Stiffening her back, the lady replied, "I don't care to match wit with you."

"Wit, no. Wits," he chuckled, "in that you over-match me."
"You flatter me, Counselor," she stated.

"They never told me in law school that 'Counselor' could be such a dirty word," he said lightly.

"Sorry."

"Tut, tut. Drink your drink."

They lapsed into a silence, concentrating their respective glasses. Madelaine sought vainly to divine Rick's motive for a so-called friendly dinner. Was it his interest in the estate work? She knew he would do anything to keep it. Further, she understood his fear of losing his connections. Or did he have bad news for her?

Stapler, for his part, considered how best to approach his companion. He had the coroner's report to relay to her. He had to discuss details of the trust administration, at some point, since they had had so little success at his office. He was far behind schedule,

Such an approach, however, would probably cost him Madelaine's cooperative, if suspicious, mood. Heloise had suggested that a casual evening together, without any purpose, would establish a rapport between the two that could be beneficial, even enjoyable.

Stapler shook his head just thinking about the idea. He had met Madelaine several years ago. At Mr. Jordan's subtle prodding, the two had shared some evenings together. "You two are perfect for each other," Jordan had confidently insisted.

Unfortunately, Madelaine despised Rick for being her father's nominee and told him so. Rick, assuming that she had to be kidding, made matters worse by reminding her that he squired her about only to pacify her father. They developed a mutual disregard for one another that, Rick felt, was the only rapport likely between them. They sat in strained silence at LaMont, ignoring even the view. Some rapport! Rick thought.

At his signal, the Maitre d' approached to inform them that the table was ready. Madelaine's glance revealed that she knew the table had been waiting for some time.

Having seated the couple at the best table in the restaurant, the Maitre d' suggested several specialties and departed with a renewed order of cocktails

"Madelaine," Stapler began carefully. "I want to explain what the evening is all about."

"That isn't necessary, Counselor.

"If you call me that one more time, I'll give up the practice of law tomorrow," he groaned.

"I am only trying to keep our relationship on the professional level," she explained. "We don't get along very well on the personal level."

Stapler put his chin in his hand and stared at her for a long time. "Madelaine," he sighed. "That is the point. We have to get along. This business is very important. And besides," he continued, now surveying the view, "I think you and I should be friends."

"I don't see why," she replied matter-of-factly.

"Well," he said, conjuring no reason. "Heloise said so, and I do everything she tells me to do."

Her laugh was harsh and cold. "Is that the only reason? I should have suspected as much."

Stapler reacted quickly. He began to laugh along with her. "If I had had Heloise when I first knew you, you and I'd probably have three kids by now."

Unsettled by Stapler's usurpation of her insult, and her laughter, Madelaine stopped. "I doubt it. I understood you then, Rick and I understand you now," she stated. "I like to choose my own company."

Gazing deeply into her wide gray eyes, Stapler put on a warm smile. "Your father had the gall to impose upon me his petulant, impossibly intelligent child, nudging me in the side and winking the whole damn time. And, if you imagine that you did all the suffering, your insensitivity is beyond my expectations, Maddy, it really is," he said gently. "Christ, I have on occasion hated your guts. You have directed me about and abused me terribly," he said, looking hurt. "And you're right, I have taken it for as long as I have because of your father. Now unfortunately, he is dead. I don't have to take it on his account anymore."

The kindly smile on Stapler's face seemed totally incongruous to Madelaine. His tone was so pleasant that his speech did not seem the diatribe it was. She was not, however, persuaded. "Good!" she snapped.

"Yes, that is good," he agreed. "That was all very distasteful to a guy who claims to be independent. It is over. So let's forget we've ever met. I will even resign as trustee if you like." Stapler even impressed himself with his reasonableness. He hoped that he had not overplayed it.

Across the table, Madelaine said nothing, her eyes revealed nothing. His capitulation came so suddenly, so absolutely, that Madelaine could not even process it. A full second passed before she began to consider the alternatives.

Stapler did not, however, give her much chance to digest his act. "I can live without my only major account. Not well, but I'll get by," he said with mock stoicism. "It is not worth it to me to fight with you every time I see you. Forget it. Seriously. All of it. Do what you like with the business, the estate, everything. I know you can handle it perfectly well alone." He paused dramatically, at least it seemed dramatic to him. "Now that that is all forgotten and you have what you want, we can eat our dinner without devouring one another."

After he finished speaking, Madelaine automatically waited a moment, expecting him to begin again. She actually hoped that he would for she wanted time to collect her thoughts. The silence disturbed her more than his sudden resignation. "What are you saying? Is that it?" Had she wasted $600,000 on a rundown office building for nothing?

"Of course not," Stapler replied. "Everything has a catch." When Madelaine visibly relaxed, Stapler scratched his forehead. "I insist that, since we can't be enemies anymore, we be friends."

The timing was perfect. The waiter arrived as per cue with the drinks, asking for their order. Stapler ordered for them both: Chateaubriand for two. Madelaine, who never allowed anyone that presumption, said not a word. Heloise had been right, after all. Stapler had little idea of what he had done, but Madelaine was disarmed. He felt that somehow, behind that white, angular face, Madelaine was talking to herself. Not only would she hesitate to demand his resignation, she might not accept it. She would depend on him, if not trust him, and maybe learn to like him.

But then, he thought complacently, he was not greedy.

~ ~ ~

Melton's footsteps landed heavily on the thickly carpeted stairs to his room. Long before he had reached his townhouse, a peculiar drowsiness had overtaken him. Nothing annoyed him more than feeling tired.

At his age, he took it as a sign that he was old. You age faster when you walk slower, he thought.

It was only a little after nine o'clock and yet he knew that he would fall asleep any second, perhaps before undressing. Melton prided himself on his physical condition and did not tolerate fatigue. Unlike his old friends, at lease the few left, he had remained athletic and trim. He assumed that the others suffered their heart attacks because they had neglected maintaining their vigor and tone.

The realization that so many of his associates were either dead or dying haunted him. In the past, he had avoided the very thought of death, but since Tom Jordan's death, he thought of little else. Tom's death brought the others suddenly together. A man like Tom Jordan did not just die for no reason. Melton knew that something, somehow was wrong.

His feet seemed to drag even more as he opened his bedroom door. In the dark, his sleepy eyes surveyed the small, cozy chamber. Formerly a den, it now served Melton as his sleeping quarters, because in the bedroom, too big for his taste, he felt secluded, like a dried insect rapping against its shell. The decorations took up more space than they should have. He had crammed the room so full of pictures, chairs and nick-knacks that one could hardly move. Even he, in the obscurity of the night and his fatigue, ran into several "objects of clutter," as Tom Jordan used to say,

Unable to switch on the light, Melton managed to find his bed clothes and exchanged his tailored suit for plaid flannels from K Mart. The Wall Street Journal lay on the bed stand, as it did every night, but he ignored it for the sheets. His head rested on the pillow for only seconds before sleep overtook him.

In those last few seconds, Melton wondered why he should feel so tired. At the University Club, after his little chat with Stapler and the policeman, Montgomery, he had eaten dinner as usual. No heavy starches, of course, not much wine. A standard dinner, he thought, designed to keep his weight down and his energy up. He had after all consumed four cups of coffee.

He liked to linger over coffee after dinner. It gave him a chance to see his friends and chat with the staff. The marvelous new sweetener that Jordan had designed himself and forced on Melton, allowed him plenty of coffee without the useless calories of sugar. He had a terrible sweet tooth but had eschewed sugar for years as part of his diet. Now, however, he could drink whatever coffee he wanted and not gain an ounce.

Notwithstanding all of the caffeine, Melton was asleep. Sleep had not been peaceful for the aging redhead for several years. Morex suggested that age and the fearful pace of Melton's life had conspired to make sleep more difficult. The doctor had finally prescribed sleeping pills to aid Melton on difficult nights.

Melton hated drugs, another quirk he picked up from Tom Jordan, but he did find that Morex's prescription often came in handy. He had gotten to the point at which he required one pill every day. His mind remained active, however, and vivid, often frightening, dreams possessed him all night.

It took several hours before Melton's normal sleep pattern asserted itself and he began to dream.

~ ~ ~

It proved to be a nice dream, mostly about his younger days and his many accomplishments. Suddenly, however, he found himself an old man, sitting at a table with his aged friends. All of the guys from the Talbot were there. Jordan, as usual sat at the head of the table, set high atop the US Steel building.

Eighty stories up, through fog and soot, Melton sat drinking coffee, too much coffee, with his companions. It was becoming a familiar dream, if not the same scene, the same idea. He grimaced when the first man went to the edge and leaped off the building. All heard the splat against Grant street a second later.

They all hurried over to the side to pay their respects to the blot on the asphalt below. Sorrow was expressed by all with a shake of their heads as they returned to the table. No sooner had the group resumed its place, however, than a second member arose, Jim Carstairs it was, bowed slightly and strolled off the building. Again they responded by gathering at the railing and waving. He had landed in the Plaza below. One at a time they went, every man sitting with him. Some went more dramatically than the first two, most defying the force that led them to the brink, but all ended upon or near the pavement in front of the skyscraper.

Finally, only Jordan and Melton remained. They looked at each other, Melton with fear in his eyes, Jordan remaining strong. Melton terror deep in his bones. Jordan smiled that sad smile of his and talked about their days together. Melton tried hard to listen, but his own thoughts pounded too hard against the inside of his head.

Finally, Jordan rose with a heavy sigh and a glance about in case anyone else had shown up to see him off. He shrugged at his old comrade, fixed his shoulders and walked out of sight. Melton covered his ears and screamed, but he still heard the sound, the sickening, crushing noise that Jordan made against the steps leading to the fountain below.

He could not move, refusing to look at the sight that had once been his best friend.

H. P. Melton knew he was next. In his sleep, he understood. His arms and legs had stiffened and his head physically shook from side to His teeth clenched hard grinding defiance out against the gods or whoever wanted him. He would not give in so easily. He could not, for he had a terrible fear of death, a dread of leaving his life, his wretched, uncompleted life, behind for all to see. He desperately wanted to hide it all.

The dream, so vivid for so long appeared to fade for a moment, but something was wrong. Melton could feel it, a strange pain in his head along with the confusion, the fear. Slowly, somehow, he was no longer alone on the roof. A shadow grew, deepened, congealed into a man standing in the increasing winds. The man, if he was a man, did not belong there, and they both knew it.

Seconds passed with the two figures in the dream simply staring at each other. Melton experienced more horror than ever, feeling that he had yielded his soul already, part of it at least, to the ominous figure that appeared of its own will, on his building.

When the shadow began to move, Melton backed away. Soon his dream motions translated into physical movement. Melton tore at the covers, flailing about as he fled the stalking fury that promised to take his revenge. Though Melton rand and ran, he knew that he could not escape from the top of the building. He tried the elevator and the stairs, only as a matter of form. Like death, his adversary maintained a steady, sure pace, easily closing the gap between them.

Trapped against the railing at the edge, Melton responded like the cornered animal he was. He kicked, he bit, he swung his arms violently, destroying the tidiness of his bed. The struggle continued for a full minute, but Melton knew that defeat was inevitable. He could feel the force of death seeping into his mind, strangling his will. He begged to wake up. The familiar face laughed without a smile.

~ ~ ~

Carleton tried to maneuver the VW back into its familiar slot behind Mrs. Gergorian's house. His eyes were not working very well and he over shot his mark, flattening a couple of the neatly trimmed shrubs. What the hell, he thought, they were practically his bushes anyway. He had to trim the damn things. Until the money came in.

The night swirled before him. His mind shoved the bizarre discordant images aside, but it took great concentration to do it. He had to get some sleep. Jordan was coming to see him that afternoon. No, he was dead. The daughter, she was the one. Soon she would give him the wherewithal to escape Mrs. Gergorian, her lawn, her bushes, her cat food.

Stumbling out of the bus, Carleton felt his way to the back of the VW to check the lock on the rear doors. He didn't want anyone to see. The doors opened with a twist of the handle, revealing the TI 125 computer, the lamp and the transceiver inside. In a daze, Carleton admired his handiwork. It was a brilliant device, in all modesty: the Carleton Brain Wave Synchronizer and Sender. He liked the sound of the name, a very official sounding label for a sophisticated piece of electronics made from scratch. It, like Carleton, had unlimited possibilities. For the moment, of course, it was only his little dream machine.

The door latched and locked, Carleton inched his way through the darkness toward the house. He wanted to sleep. His machine demanded an awful lot of him and he had to be prepared to make the proper impression on Madelaine Jordan in less than twelve house. For that he needed sleep.

He could not chance sleep without the tape recorder, he remembered. The tape recorder let him sleep. He could no longer do it alone. Halfway to the house, he noticed that he did not have the recorder with him. It was still in the van. Damn it! he thought. He was becoming forgetful. Just when he had to be at his best. Was the strain getting to him? No, it was not a strain. He was just tired. That was all. Tired.

CHAPTER FIVE

Madjerin sat in her tiny office in the Talbot Research Hospital, her mouth contorted by the desk top. Ink black hair covered reams of charts and printouts. Custodian Hank Washington let her sleep, even though his generosity forced him to crawl under the desk to secure an overflowing wastebasket.

Hank and the sleeping doctor were old friends by this time. They shared the same nocturnal hours and the same lonely building. The Talbot bustled so during the day, that both preferred to perform their tasks after Midnight. Hank would wake the exhausted Madjerin to free her of discarded papers and they would talk. Occasionally, Madjerin accompanied "Dr. Washington", as she called him, on his long rounds.

That latter practice ended in the spring as the grant trimming for her section approached. Madjerin, fearing that her Talbot funds would be cut off, worked constantly to perfect her cerebral mapping procedure. Her presentation had impressed the board, but not enough to convince five of the members to continue funding, leaving her dependent on Criminal Science Foundation money.

Many of her colleagues proved less impressive. Madjerin, at least, retained her office and access to the computer facilities. Others were forced to leave by the budget crisis, several giving up research altogether. Even her assistant had had to leave. With so little for herself, Madjerin could not retain Ray Carleton, no matter how useful he was, costing her an innovative mind and doubled her workload. Every morning now she collapsed on the desk.

Before leaving Madjerin asleep, Hank Washington noticed a scribbled memo taped to the door. "Hank", it ran, "please wake me this morning. I have a presentation to make before noon. The Jordan estate has some grants to make and I have to get one. CSF runs out in October."

The request notwithstanding, Hank hesitated. He knew that his tired, little friend would fail to impress the Jordan people without the required preparation, but without sleep, Madjerin's clarity of expression English disappeared. Still, if the Criminal Science money ceased in October, Madjerin would desperately need any available funds. Hank shook the narrow, hunched shoulders.

Madjerin did not react. Hank shook his head. He hated to take extreme measures to disturb so deep and needed a slumber.

"Wake up, Madj," he said firmly, poking her side.

Normally, a solid thrust at her side brought Madjerin around with a jump. That morning, however, she responded slowly, with great difficulty. After she had finally raised her head, her body swayed.

Washington seized her shoulders and shook her vigorously. "Come on, Hindu," he said with authority. "You say you got work to do? Do it!"

"Hennnry," she sang softly, dreamily. "I'm aslee-eep." He laughed. Ordinarily when he woke her, Madjerin would insist that she was awake. "And you are not all you should be, if you want the Jordan money."

"Jordan? Here?" She asked, her eyes still closed. "Money." Hank was gone when she half opened her eyes. She was sure that everything was a dream. Hank's voice, the open door, the Jordan money. She closed her eyes and recited, "The brain, Ms. Jordan, is like a transmitter," she giggled. "I have developed the receiver."

"Coffee!" Hank boomed, as he strode in the door with a tray supporting two cups and a pot.

Madjerin swung around in the chair, no longer giggling. "Come with me to the meeting today, Hank," she pleaded in sing-song. Washington ignored her request as he poured the coffee. Too strong, he thought. No matter how much cream and sugar he put in it, the damn stuff would still be too dark and bitter for Madjerin.

"Oh, Henry," she complained thickly. "This is black." "You need it that way, Madj," he explained.

"I like it light," she said petulantly. After lowering the cup she grimaced. "And now I remember why."

"Finish it. The bitterness helps wake you up."

She gagged on the next gulp. "You're trying to poison me, Hank."

"If it will wake you up," he agreed, his uneven white teeth showing under a bristly mustache. He took a seat on her desk despite the printouts and drank his coffee. "When's the big meeting and with who?"

Madjerin threw her head back in despair, catching her hair and jamming it behind her large dark ears. "Madelaine Jordan. She's inheriting millions from her father and has some to give to me." She sighed as she examined a brain-wave chart. "But only if she likes me. And from what I hear, she doesn't like anybody."

"Ever meet her?"

"Nope, but she's bringing a man I showed to before." Madjerin racked her brain for the name. "He's the lawyer."

"Stapler?" Hank asked. After she nodded he said, "Oh, yeah, he handled an injury case here once. Too much wax, they said." Hank looked at his floors and smiled. "Better too much than not enough, I say."

Madjerin rose from her chair and sat on the computer representation of the cerebral functions of one H.P. Melton, next to Hank. "What happened?"

"Stapler rented a Rolls Royce and called on the idiot woman who claimed to have slipped on my floor," he said, reveling in the memory. "She took one look at that car and decided you don't fight a fat cat lawyer."

"Smart, then?"

"More clever than anything else," Hank said. "Don't worry about him."

Madjerin was worried. Her whole career hung in the balance. She needed time–and money–to overcome the obstacles to her research The practical uses of Brain-wave mapping were many, she was certain, but so, too, were the difficulties in making the procedure remotely practical Since losing Carleton, she had made too little progress to suit the CSF, or herself, for that matter.

"The key to an improved mapping procedure is a highly amplified reception of the impulses," she said, thinking out loud. "Hank, I just can't figure out what to do."

Hearing her speak so desperately, Washington felt a frustration he rarely experienced. Being only a janitor had not bothered Hank in all the years he had swept and cleaned miscellaneous buildings. Even though still fairly young–he was only 41–Hank had no ambition to "improve" his station. Pay was good and the work carried its own satisfaction. He had rubbed shoulders with executives, lawyers, engineers, doctors, even bookies. He never felt envious of them, nor coveted their suburban homes and migraines. He had what he needed and most of what he wanted. He didn't aim to be more than he was.

When Madjerin found herself stymied, however, it was Hank who would feel frustrated. She became confused, discouraged or unhappy, but he paced floors, slammed doors and felt useless. The problems that stumped Madjerin eluded him altogether. They were in a different language, of a different world. Then, and only then, he despised himself for rejecting the education he could have gotten, the training he refused when he stormed out of a small New England college. As a freshman, he quit just because his adviser suggested that, despite his F, he had done "well for a negro boy with a Southern education". At these times he regretted his hasty, emotional reaction, but it was too late to correct. That is why he frowned at her when she asked him again.

"Will you come with me?"

Madjerin did not know Hank's background very well. She envied him his normal job and certain outlook. Often she hated what she was doing. She had slaved for years to earn an opportunity to come to the United States on a technical scholarship to escape India. After it all, however, she was almost as miserable. More comfortable, of course, than in her home outside Bangalore, but still unhappy. Only Hank's pleasant interruptions had gotten her through the grueling spring. She had to have his reassurance to survive the morning's trial.

"Alright," he said finally.

~ ~ ~

Stapler stared out the window, surveying the morning's hazy horizon. He wasn't sure that the air was the villain. More likely it was the morning; his eyes failed to function since he had gotten to the office. Not accustomed to rising at 5:00, he had downed three cups of coffee without really waking up. Madelaine insisted on meeting with applicants for gifts under her father's still unprobated will, beginning at 9:00.

The early start had been her one demand on him the night before. In exchange, she promised she would consider keeping him employed "for the time being". Wine mellowed Madelaine Jordan and she had had enough during dinner to admit that she might need help in taking on the responsibilities her father had left her.

Madelaine had said many things, some about her plans for J & T, a couple about her problems at Talbot Instruments, even one or two things about her life with her parents. But their discussion of the autopsy on her father had thrust her into silence for the evening.

"It's not important," she had said, in answer to his question about her mood. "I just have so much work to do."

She had looked at him in a funny way when they had parted. The expression on her face was the usual impassiveness, but her floating, mercurial eyes had said so much so fast that he had grasped very little. So much was concentrated in those two, singular outlets of hers that her gaze frightened him.

He didn't look forward to her early visit, for that and other reasons. Madelaine had, if anything, become more difficult than ever, since arriving in town. Everything he said, most of the things he did seemed to upset her. In spite of their reconciliation the night before, Stapler feared that the pattern would continue that morning. He had to get ready.

A good deal of work, therefore, had to be done before he could think of taking Madelaine to the Talbot. Rick had gathered the files of applications and dismissals for the hospital's staff positions. Fortunately, Heloise always kept the files beautifully organized. Even more fortunately, Heloise had come in early herself to do most of the work. Together, they succeeded in having a decent briefing prepared for Madelaine's arrival at 8:00, which a billboard clock informed Stapler was only two minutes away.

Her car had not yet come to grace the front of the short, stocky office building that ignored the glass towers down Grant. It was an old-fashioned stone edifice, elegantly attired in the soot that characterized the more established members of the neighborhood. Stapler had purchased the anachronism with a modest inheritance and a substantial mortgage. The rentals paid for the interest and taxes and most of the maintenance, while the depreciation sheltered some of his income. More importantly, Rick got a beautiful old penthouse suite as his office for free.

The worn penthouse image suited the one Stapler sought to project for himself. Estate lawyers, he was once told, should appear prosperous. Solidity and stability, as well as competence, were suggested by this office. Even he was convinced.

Heloise, too, aided that image. When a client entered the suite, Heloise greeted him, or her, with an air of confident grace that those with money admired in one so young. She had always had looks, but her difficult years of marriage had imparted to her face that wisdom-through-pain look that reassured the most insecure.

Because of his office, his building and his Heloise, he had arranged to meet Madelaine at his office. He wanted the psychological support. Few people intimidated Stapler, but Madelaine Jordan always did. She was physically so large and mentally so strong that in both ways she was at least his equal.

In business, she was a conspicuous success. More than one national magazine devoted its cover to the triumphs of the "Angular Amazon" as Time had called her. Women's magazines adored her, constantly seeking her endorsement.

Madelaine, however, endorsed nothing. She permitted only the shortest interviews. Any further information would have to be gleaned from the P.R. department at Talbot Instruments. Some writers claimed that she could not handle the social aspects of life and could not talk with people about anything but business. Others postulated that she had a torrid sex life that she had to conceal. One rag claimed she was bisexual but not man enough to admit it.

Stapler had such a publication on his desk when she arrived. Madelaine strode into the room, briefcase in hand. With a sweep of her long fingers she pushed the cover portrait of the "Woman Wunderkind" to one side. In a motion almost too quick to reveal any grace of movement, she brought the valise to rest where the magazines had been.

"Good morning, Rick," she stated, allowing no room for dissent.

He turned to look at her, the throaty declaration drifting through his head. "Good morning, Maddy," he replied, staring at her stainless eyes. Often flecks of green or blue would appear in the iris, as though floating dreamily through a forbidding cloud. Not today. The uniformity of the shimmering silver made the view look unreal, as Stapler watched, like that down the plated barrel of an expensive pistol.

Madelaine looked down to open the case. She did not seem disturbed by his attention. Nor did she appear pleased. Not quite ignoring his mindless scrutiny, she said, "I hope you have something to tell me about these people. I couldn't find much useful in my father's files at the house." She pulled some papers from her case and handed them over toward Stapler, without bothering to look up at him. "This top one is a list he made up of people from the staff. I assume he meant to rehire them if the hospital raised additional money this Fall. You probably have copies already."

His hand went for the sheath of papers as he watched the transaction. Her hand was long and the slender fingers assumed a graceful attitude that gave them an even longer appearance. Her nails were clipped to the top of the fingers, eschewing the lengthy extensions may women crave. The nails had never felt polish nor seen a manicurist. By example, she had ended the fad of manicure among her top executives at TI

Though she hated jewelry, Madelaine wore a single silver band on her right ring finger. Stapler had asked her about it once, because it looked so tiny on her hand, like a miniature silver wedding band. She had snarled that it was only a ring. She wore it because she liked it. Whoever had given it to her had long been forgotten, she had said. It didn't matter to her whose gift it was; she liked it and she had it. She never took it off.

"Do you want to read the list over, Mr. Stapler," she snapped. "Or have you already memorized it?"

The sharp tone catapulted Stapler out of his daze. "I have," he said, "Hel and I have drawn up a summary of the work of each applicant, or supplicant," he added with a smile.

"We don't give succor, Rick," she said humorlessly, "only money." He buzzed and spoke into the intercom. "Hel, bring in those summaries that you have so kindly prepared for Madelaine."

She stared at him. "I'd thought that she could read your mind," she said without emphasis. "I'm surprised that thing even works."

Heloise entered, walking carefully, but deliberately, up to Madelaine. "Here you are, Miss Jordan," she said with measured good cheer. Madelaine started. Her eyes swung to Heloise without blinking. They darted from her face down to her waist and back again. For some reason she always expected her to be pregnant. Heloise remained smiling, with what appeared to be tolerance.

Madelaine did not speak for several seconds. Finally she said, "Thank you, Mrs. Carpenter." She obviously wanted to say something else but did not. Heloise annoyed Madelaine. A woman of good sense, if not necessarily intelligence, Heloise remained devoted to an employer uniquely disagreeable. Madelaine, having brooded about it the night before, was certain that they had some deeper, more intimate connection, which she also failed to understand.

Without a touch of irony, Heloise said, "It is always a pleasure to work for you, Miss Jordan."

Stapler rolled his eyes and scratched his lip. Heloise took the signal and departed. "This information should help you limit the number of people you'll want to meet. Your father had his favorites among this list.

"And a couple he did not like," she suggested. She ran her finger down the page. Twenty-five names, four with stars, five with crosses. "Father starred people he assumed were unworthy of his attention," she explained. "'Prima Donnas he called them. He despised them because they reminded him of mother."

Stapler smiled placidly recalling Jordan's description of Madelaine. "She plays the prima donna, gives a fine performance and then won't accept the roses." Did she even want them? "The crosses, of course, represent those he favored. You're not bound by his inclinations, you realize? Or won't be, once the estate is set up."

"I know that, Rick," she said. "I never have been." She smiled a tight sarcastic smile for his benefit. On those thin pale lips, the smiles ran from sarcastic to vicious. "We will start with these nine designated by my father."

"The summaries begin with those nine, Madelaine," he pointed out, congratulating himself on anticipating her. Madelaine had both despised and respected her father. His favorites, she would–and did–feel, would have merit. Those he had disliked would have characteristics she sought, as well as talent enough to make an impression. The un-marked applicants would interest neither of them.

"We will begin with this much admired Corbett, the psy-chologist" she began. "What's this? Madjerin?" She asked approval for pronunciation only. "She's fourth on this list."

"She is working on a project to chart the impulses gener-ated by the brain'," he read.

"I can read, Stapler," she said. "What do you know about her?"

Stapler sat back in his chair. Madjerin. The Indian girl. Dark skin, black hair and eyes, slender ankles, tiny wrists. "She has a small grant from the National Crime people.

They think that Brain Wave mapping will lead to a new means of identification and lie detection."

"Christ," she commented.

"Madjerin is a cute, half-starved petite Indian who fled to the U. S. to live. And I mean live, period. She is kind of pathetic as I recall her. Her assistant had to go when the funds went down the drain this spring. And she's gone nowhere since."

"Sounds wasteful," she decided.

Stapler spoke quickly and earnestly. "Give her a chance, Maddy. Seriously, she works hard as hell. She has a limited visa and without money she'll have to return to India next year."

"I had to return to Pittsburgh," Madelaine said unsympathetically. She frowned. "Alright. If she's cute enough for you, I'll give her a chance. Who's after her? He's on the hate list."

"Carleton," Stapler read. "He was her assistant. Clever son-of-a-bitch and knew it. I think he's a little nuts. He insists he is Nobel Prize material."

Carleton left a sour impression on everyone. Present when Madjerin demonstrated to the members of the board of trustees how her mapping apparatus worked, Carleton did most of the talking, and some of the mechanical work. His intrusion ruined Madjerin's chance to keep her funds. Jordan, who liked the frail little Indian girl later promised to Stapler that he would not allow Carleton to stay. "Intelligence," Jordan had said "is no substitute for perspective."

"Is he?" she asked.

"Maybe. He's smart enough." Stapler stated. "And he is very ambitious. After his ouster, if I can call it that, he started to work on his own. My guess is that he is already ahead of Madjerin."

Madelaine nodded. She put an asterisk by Carleton's name and an X by Madjerin, a very dark X.

~ ~ ~

Montgomery had been a cop too long to like it. He prided himself on his instinct, as most good detectives do. Police procedures and coroner reports had their place, but hunches meant a knot in the stomach, a germ of an idea jumping up and down near the back of the head. He had been around too long to accept six deaths of close associates in less than two months as entirely natural. Something about the Jordan case, as he called it, followed him around all day and hid under his pillow at night. That explained why he was driving out to the Melton place at 8:30 in the morning. That and the call that had awakened him at 6:00 anyway.

At 5:18, H.P. "Red" Melton's early morning squash partner, Jack Freed, had called as usual. As usual, he had gotten no response. Melton, an early riser, liked to jog before a match. Freed had gathered his gear and strolled over to Melton's remodeled townhouse to snitch an English Muffin while Red prepped for the game.

The housekeeper had confirmed Freed's conviction that Melton's breakfast was to include Thomas' English Muffins, and little else. Ordinarily, she had said, Melton's jump rope was enough to rouse her, but she had not awakened until her alarm went off that morning at 5:30. Finding neither a note nor an indication that Melton had arisen, the two of them had chuckled, anticipating Melton's embarrassment which, they had expected, would turn him several deeper shades of crimson. Two solid raps on the ancient sportsman's door had brought no response. Neither had a sound upbraiding for laziness. That made them worry.

By the time Dr. Anthony Morex had arrived, the door lay against the wall of the corridor, its hinge pins on the floor. Ordinarily a very quiet sleeper, Melton had strewn the wreckage of his bedding about the room. His clock, its alarm turned down, had deserted its place on the bed stand for the shadows under the bed.

Morex, accustomed to the symptoms by that time, had wasted no time phoning the coroner's office and Montgomery's people at Homicide. The aging physician, drained by the experience, had remained, seated in the hall, until Montgomery had finished looking around. "Doc," Monty asked, grimly, "this is the same?"

Without raising his head, Morex replied, "It cannot be."

"Another heart attack?" Asking the question made Monty's empty stomach burn.

With great effort the Doctor looked at Montgomery. The remnants of tears made his eyes glisten even in the dim hallway. "It is impossible. Impossible," he cried, rising painfully from the narrow wooden chair, as though he had to. "I examined his eyes first, of course." He shook his head. "He's worse than the others. My God, I cannot understand what's happening to them?" He shuddered, not wanting to know, and retreated down the corridor.

Montgomery had seen enough to leave the Doctor to himself for the time being. As personal physician and friend to Jordan and Melton and their four associates, Morex deteriorated a little bit with each man's death.

The first four deaths had gone down routinely enough, no fuss, but since Thomas Jordan's death, Montgomery's curiosity, stirred by his talks with Morex, had led him to investigate the deaths of the four members of the Talbot Board of Trustees preceding the two more recent ones. Each was the same: An early morning heart attack, striking them in their sleep. Each accompanied by evidences of violent discomfort, struggle with... with what? Themselves?

He began the process of ordering the bodies exhumed even before leaving for Melton's Monty mustered his most professional attitude and approached the covered stretcher. The rough blanket felt harsher against his experienced hand than expected. Melton's mouth was twisted in an aborted scream, but, with eyes closed, the corpse had the look of serenity that came with death. Seizing the loose, sunburned eyelids, Montgomery prepared himself to face what had so shaken Morex.

As though someone had rammed his foot through the back of Melton's head, the eyes stood on the brims of their sockets; dark red spots marred the clear white Montgomery remembered. One eye turned grotesquely toward the other, the detective saw the eye torn away from its bounds on the left side. Coupled with the severe contortion of the mouth, the eyes screamed wild terror deep into Monty's throbbing head.

He staggered out of the room of the once lively little man he had met only twelve hours previously. In the living room, Morex had brandy waiting. Montgomery drank hungrily enough to crack the lip of the fine crystal. Some blood mingled with the hot alcohol as it swirled down his throat.

"Forty years I have been a doctor," Morex said gazing into his glass. "Not all of them in this soft service to wealthy men. Forty years and I have never, never seen a man like that."

The brandy doing its job, Montgomery managed to reply, "I've been around myself, Doctor. This is different." Montgomery had almost always been surrounded by death, of one kind or another. He was seeped in violent death in his job. He had seen everything and yet, and yet he had never blanched at a corpse before. "No. This is different."

"He was a strong man," Morex said absently. "Strong heart. Low pulse and blood pressure." He poured them both more brandy. "Last night," he continued, "it must have gone on forever!"

"But why, Doc?" Monty asked anxiously. "What could cause that to happen?"

Morex looked at him with glazed eyes. "Nothing, Sergeant. Nothing that I know of."

"For Christ's sake, he was asleep!"

A practical man, Morex disliked philosophical speculation, but he had no other recourse. "Some men, Sergeant, like Red Melton they don't want to die. He wouldn't admit it, but Red hated reunions and did not look forward to one with his maker," Morex explained slowly. "His life was not flawless. He desperately wanted time to do penance. I think that he felt it coming... sometimes, we see it approaching in our minds, in our dreams, perhaps. He knew he was dying and he fought it with all of his considerable strength."

"Why in God's name didn't he wake up?" Montgomery demanded. "I always do when the going gets tough." His eyes lit up. Drugs, Doc! What about it? Was Melton drugged?"

Morex' face clouded over. He remembered Jordan's death. "Red always took sleeping pills. By my prescription. He was an active driven man. Without pills he'd keep thinking too long into the morning "Last night is all I care about."

"We'll have to check," Morex said, leading the way to Melton's medicine chest.

Unlike most men his age, Red Melton used few drugs. The sleeping pills stood alone on the second shelf. The bottle was nearly full. Morex checked the date.

"No unusually large doses from this bottle," he said. "Filled a week ago and only about half a dozen are missing by my estimate."

A frown creased Monty's face. "How strong are they?"

"Not strong enough to keep a man asleep through that kind of attack," Morex replied thoughtfully. "That took time."

"Yeah?" Monty sighed. "Well, something kept him under. Maybe the coroner can find out."

By the time the coroner arrived, Montgomery had left for Jordan's He had left his subordinates instructions to go over Melton's place as if it hid a winning lottery ticket. Something had to come up somewhere. Maybe at Jordan's.

Thomas Jordan was the key. Jordan ran the Board of the Talbot. Jordan alone did not use any kind of sleeping aid. Except on the night of his death. On that night he had enough in him to keep his asleep through a train wreck.

Someone had spiked that coffee, Monty was sure. That someone would help Montgomery explain, at least to himself, how a heart attack could be the most terrible way to die. Nature alone was not so cruel.

He had a feeling. That feeling was his lead. Without it, he had nothing but six men, all members of the same board of trustees, all rich as hell and all dead of the same thing. It was too much an MO to be coincidence. Montgomery's ulcer told him to keep looking.

~ ~ ~

Madjerin did not see Madelaine and Stapler when they entered the conference room just yards down the hall from her office. She and Hank had been reviewing her presentation for the third time at the moment they passed her door. Hank, facing the open door, caught a glimpse of Stapler and his striding female companion, but decided not to alert the pacing speaker. The mere sight of the tall, stern woman would panic Madjerin.

The coffee had done its trick and Madjerin was at her intense best. Her slight British accent gave the technical nonsense she so earnestly spewed the sound of erudition. At least to Hank, it did.

Not a word made sense to the custodian, but in her demeanor he observed growing confidence. The mumbo jumbo about brain nerve-energy impulses sounded increasingly convincing to his unenlightened ears. Any failure she might experience at the meeting would stem only from the weakness of her project. That, Hank figured, was all anybody really wanted.

Had Madjerin received the thought riding Hank Washington's brain waves, she would have dissented from his conclusion. In fact. her worst fear was that her work, on its merits, would justify only her defeat. With so little progress on the practical model, the potential of the whole project was in question. Over the past few months, Madjerin had ceased to care about the success of the project except in terms of retaining her funding to keep her in the United States.

She did not, however, consider such matters as she went over her speech. All of her concentration went into perfecting her delivery. The mapping of brain wave functions seemed to her a sufficiently well accepted idea, allowing her to focus her dissertation on the possibilities of refining the procedure to practical application. Currently, sophisticated machinery and programming were required to pick up the impulses generated by the chemo-electrical activity of the human brain. The resulting mapping proved equally intricate, capable of confusing all but a couple of experts in the field.

With Carleton's aid, Madjerin had succeeded in distilling the maps into several distinct basic functions, four in fact, common in all of the tested subjects, yet individual to each. Other impulses changed constantly, impossible to pinpoint or identify, but the four remained incredibly constant, varying only occasionally in intensity of output. Madjerin didn't know to what the functions related in the brain, whether to conscious thought, or background electrical activity of the cerebrum. To her it didn't matter. What counted was the fact that the graphs produced by those four functions were unique, unchanging patterns generated by an individual's brain. "The key to personality," Carleton had mused upon the breakthrough.

While vital to the project, this breakthrough was the last one Madjerin could claim. Repeated testing, after Carleton's discharge, had helped her perfect the procedure for isolation of the four functions, but she had failed utterly to simplify the method of pickup. If that question arose in her meeting with the Jordan heiress, Madjerin would have to concede defeat and pack her few suitcases.

Finished a third time, Madjerin looked up to find that Hank had fallen asleep. His chair tilted back against the desk and his chin on his chest, the janitor dreamed peacefully under her amused gaze. To others, Henry Washington would have appeared an immensely comic figure in his suspended position. To Madjerin, he was a picture of reassurance, for she knew that Hank would never fall asleep unless confident that she was ready to proceed alone.

CHAPTER SIX

Stapler paused outside the meeting room to catch his breath. Inside, Madelaine was grilling the first of the candidates for the grants bequeathed by her father's will to the Talbot. He felt he had to somehow steady himself before going in.

The phone call he had just finished came from Heloise. From the moment she had said hello, he had known something was wrong. Heloise had spent a few minutes on miscellaneous matters, such as Carleton's insistence that his interview take place at his lab, Montgomery's failing to call, calls of panic from Skeffington, Einberg and Mrs. Jordan's lawyer. All important, but no reason to suppress trill in one's voice. Finally, she had cleared her throat and said, "I also got a call from Phil Hammermann."

Phil ran a nice active accounting business on the third floor of the Haller building. He was dull, but he paid his rent promptly every month. "What's he want now?"

Her breathing had almost roared through the receiver. "Nothing," she had said, "He's moving out."

The news had left him speechless and angry. Hammermann & Still had rented half of the third floor from day one. Their rent was ridiculously low and their offices very nice. Worse, they were the third and biggest tenant to leave in the last two days.

"Where are they going, the bastards?" he had demanded, knowing the answer.

"Across the street," she had said.

"Find out who owns that God damn building!" he ordered and hung up. Whoever it was, seemed intent on stealing his tenants. And at rents that had to be ruinously meager.

Shaking, Rick resorted to a small flask he was carrying in his coat pocket, in order to steady his nerves. He had brought the whiskey along, fearing that Madelaine would have him a wreck before he could get to a bar. Now it was this.

Still, the liquor worked its wonder and he felt ready to resume his seat next to Madelaine at the conference table.

The pair inside the room was talking over the experimental work that the researcher had been doing at the Talbot before losing his position. Dr. Corbett concentrated on the mechanics of learning and particularly on the workings of memory, which Madelaine had already tested to the limit.

"What is your model of the human brain, Dr. Corbett?" Madelaine asked once Rick was seated.

Alfonse Tobias Corbett stroked his beard while pondering Madelaine's question. An experimental psychologist, Corbett usually avoided such questions with a shrug of his round, seemingly tired shoulders. He knew, however, that Madelaine Jordan would not appreciate it, if he did not respond satisfactorily.

"My model of the human brain?" he asked, drawing out the words to allow him time to conjure an answer. "Well, of course, I don't really deal in anything so theoretical," he continued. "We cognitive psychologists are more concerned with the relationship of sensory input, memory and the learning process. I specialize in long term memory, as I explained before."

Madelaine gazed out the window. "My 'short term memory' is excellent, Dr. Corbett. Please answer the question."

"I merely wanted to point out that I do not have a detailed model of the working of the mind," the harried psychologist explained.

"Which, I increasingly understand, Doctor," Madelaine commented. "But you must have some ideas on the matter. Otherwise your research would lack depth." She smiled gratuitously.

Corbett had succeeded in delaying the answer long enough to recall an approach confusing enough to get by. "The human brain is a collection of nerve complexes. Not unlike a computer, it operates as a series of tiny, electrical circuits powered by the chemical processes of the nerves. A sensory input enters the brain as a series of chemically produced electrical impulses. These impulses are channeled into short term memory circuits where the pattern of the impulse is retained for a short period before, in most cases, it is transferred into a permanent circuit in the long-term memory region of the brain." It sounded like Psych I to him.

Madelaine frowned approval. "Sounds elementary enough."

Corbett looked to Stapler, seated off to Madelaine's side. The attorney managed a grin, but offered nothing more. Stapler knew his role, and, at that point was happy with it.

Madelaine was in charge and doing quite well in finding out what was what. Rick had his own problems and had even ceased to pay close attention to Corbett, watching instead the movement of Madelaine's nose.

The new construction, he decided, was more appealing than nature's edifice, certainly more consistent with the sharp lines of the rest of her face. Most fascinating to Stapler was the fact that the tip of the nose never moved when she spoke, not even on the M's. More than ever, he was convinced that she was not human.

"I suggest," Corbett was saying, "that you can get a better theoretical model from Dr. Madjerin. She seems to be oriented to the electrical nature of the brain." He hesitated a minute before adding, "And, of course, there is "Nobel" Carleton if you can find him."

Madelaine's ears moved though her face expressed no particular interest. "Would you be so kind as to offer an opinion regarding Mr. Carleton's merits, Doctor?"

"I'd prefer not to," he replied.

"I'm sure," Madelaine countered without inflection.

The message did not escape Corbett. He sought complimentary phrases to satisfy what he took to be her preference. "Very bright, I suppose, is first," he said, despising himself. "His grasp of the subject is sure. He seems to see the bulb when others see only light. I think much of the progress of Madjerin's work derived from his insights."

Corbett was making himself sick and decided to relieve himself at least a little. "He is, however, decidedly weak in the hard core work needed in these areas. He feels that he is above the mundane, the detail. He and Madjerin made an excellent combination: She did all the work; he provided some key insights. He openly derided her on the brain mapping project, insisting he had more interesting plans for their procedures."

"This Madjerin," Madelaine said, rubbing the tip of her nose, sounds a bit weak."

Like most of the staff at the Talbot, Corbett felt sorry for little Madjerin and became defensive when she was attacked by an outsider. Perhaps, he felt that way because he, too, ridiculed her at times, is smothered in detail, that's all!" he declared. "She works so damn intensely that sometimes she loses perspective. That is why Carleton helped her so much," he added with a sneer, "because he never did anything to speak of."

In silence, Madelaine's gray eyes settled on the increasingly red face of the anxious psychologist. She watched for a time as beads of moisture congregated on his forehead to mock the calm imparted to his face by a bushy, rusty beard. The scrutiny, so emotionless itself, produced an agitation in the stooped scientist, to the point that his damp ruddy hands shook.

"Dr. Corbett," Madelaine said at last, "You have been most cooperative. Thank you. When we have reached a decision, Mr. Stapler will be in touch with you."

Dr. Alfonse Tobias Corbett rose with difficulty and left the room. By the time the next hopeful was sitting in his vacated chair, Dr Corbett had already finished his second double bourbon.

~ ~ ~

Anyone desiring to tramp about in Kelly's gardens did not merit his cooperation. Sean Kelly had tended the Jordan grounds for twenty-five years, gaining the admiration of sensitive folk, who understand fine grounds-keeping. Policemen in recent weeks had become his least favorite species of garden pest. Not surprisingly, he refused to accompany Montgomery on his fifth tour of the curtilage.

George Bestral substituted himself for the testy "yarder" He did so with pleasure. Even more than the detective, George felt that something untoward had been involved in his employer's death. The sleeping powder in Jordan's coffee, coffee so carefully prepared by George, had given the butler a week of sleepless nights.

They stood under Jordan's bedroom window. Montgomery looked this way and that praying, almost, for some sign. The brick was unmarred, the fine wooden casements undisturbed. The window was very high off the ground, due to an elegantly soaring ground story. While the study window, on the bottom floor, reached near the upper one, no means of scaling it appeared to Monty's schooled, frustrated eyes.

As George watched, Montgomery waded into the lush shrubbery separating him from the base of the house. He scoured the scene, alert for so much as a broken twig. The soil, soft and rich, retained no evidence of imprints. Kelly, scrupulous in his care of even the hidden beds extending several feet between the hedge and the window, would have seen to that.

The window and the surrounding wood were untouched. Inside, the study lay richly shadowed and somberly silent. Jordan had received his first cup of coffee for the evening while at his desk, preparing some paper or other. His memory haunted that room still. And Montgomery felt it. Monty paralleled Jordan's path from the study to the hall. The soft humus gave beneath his feet as he ran his hand along the old brick.

The hall window, smaller than that of the study, revealed the same hauntingly quiet scene. The view appeared unreal through the glass, streaked with age and blurred by a smudged hand print.

Monty, continuing to follow the imagined path of the victim, suddenly returned to reality by the hedge, breaking sharply toward the house. The greens scratched at his eyes and he stumbled backward, arms flailing. Only the casement of the small hall window saved him falling on his back as his hand instinctively sought support.

Then he saw the hand print, there on the window, beside that by the heel of his palm. It was smeared, and, therefore, not identifiable, but it was unmistakable. He spun to call George and found Kelly glaring at him instead.

"You God damned son-of-a-bitch!" the gardener cried. "You'll ruin twenty-five years of hard, finger-gnawing work, you bloody bastard!"

George ran over to calm the feisty Irishman.

Monty grinned sheepishly, too satisfied with his discovery to be angry. He began to retrace his steps to get out of the bushes.

Kelly roared. "What are you doing now?"

"I'm trying to come out," Monty explained.

"Why the hell don't you come out where you went the hell in!"

Before Monty could utter a word in his defense, Kelly set about assessing the damage. He knelt down in front of Montgomery and carefully examined the torn bushes.

George spoke up. "But, Kelly, Sergeant Montgomery did not go through there."

Kelly ignored George completely. "I will have to pray to the Savior that these crippled branches may heal."

His mind racing, Montgomery asked, "Mr. Kelly, when did you last tend these hedges?"

"Every week," Kelly snapped. "And every three weeks they are trimmed. Tomorrow. That's why the damage'll be so obvious."

"What about the windows?" Montgomery queried. "When are they done?"

"Ask the butler!" he answered curtly. "I am not a window washer!" Kelly got up from the ground and stomped gently off.

"Well?" Montgomery directed his question to the butler.

George did not hesitate. "One week, the front and right side are cleaned, this last week in fact. The next week the back and left."

"All of 'em?"

"Of course. Mr. Jordan insisted on it," George explained.

Monty's face and heart fell.

George detected the marked change in expression. "Is something wrong?"

Monty waded out of the bushes again. "Yeah," he said unhappily, "My clue got washed out."

~ ~ ~

Stapler was having a swig from his portable bar when the bleary eyed Henry Washington shuffled by. Madelaine had ordered a short break in her meeting with Madjerin, while the dark little researcher prepared a demonstration of her apparatus.

Rick was peeved at the heiress Jordan for her brusque manner with the researchers. Toward Madjerin, she had acted literally ice cold Madelaine had a way of being haughty that surpassed anyone that Stapler had ever seen. That rigid back, the cold gray eyes set deeply in her angular face made her forbidding on the friendliest occasions. Did she like anybody? Yes, he remembered, she did like George, the Jordan valet. That he'd try to figure out later.

Hank saw the figure leaning against the blank white wall and rubbed his eyes. He had just awakened to find Madjerin gone and the light in her office off. Rising, he had detected her voice down the hallway as she left the conference room for her computer lab. The interview should not be over, he thought.

"Washington!" Rick cried. "You slippery devil, you." Rick waved his flask and ordered Hank to find a glass for himself. Hank went automatically into the conference room, where he kept a set of glasses in the cabinet by the window.

Madelaine looked up when he entered. She was, as usual, poring over some papers, her brow furrowed, her teeth clenched. "You'll have to wait," she snapped. I'm not finished with the Indian girl yet."

His eyes still a bit unclear, Hank gawked at the intense face and the large, bony hand dismissing him. He broke into his toothy smile when he realized that this creature was the awful Miss Jordan that Madjerin so feared. "Hello, Ms. Jordan," he said slowly. "I'm just passing through to get a glass from the cupboard over there."

Her reddened cheeks worked in and out as Madelaine glowered at Henry Washington as he strolled over to the cabinet. She devoured his every move as he casually removed two glasses.

"This, my dearest Madelaine," Rick's voice rang in her ears, "is Henry Washington. He keeps the floors bright and shiny around here."

Washington chuckled. "Sometimes, Mr. Stapler, I keep 'em too bright and shiny."

"Hank," Rick continued, "this is Madelaine Jordan. She is rich and famous, but you, somehow, will probably like her."

Madelaine seemed to ignore Rick as she rose and offered her hand to Hank. They exchanged strong grips. "You are the custodian here, Mr. Washington?" she asked mechanically.

"Well, I'm the janitor, if that is the same thing," he replied "I always figured that I didn't have the education to be anything harder to pronounce than a Janitor."

Stapler entered his two cents. "Madelaine, you should call Hank 'Hank'." he said. "Especially since he made you blush."

Suddenly, she swung her head around to Rick. Son of a gun, he thought, she did it again. Madelaine started to snap at Stapler, but when she saw that he had noted her embarrassment, she stopped.

"Sure," Hank insisted, filling the moment of silence.

Noticing the two glasses in Hank's hand for the first time, Rick asked, "Can't you get enough in one glass, you old booze-hound?"

Hank filled the pair of glasses up in a kind of salute. "One is for Miss Jordan here, Mr. Stapler."

"Excellent idea, Hank," Rick agreed. "Poor Maddy has been dry all morning, haven't you Maddy?"

Madelaine felt agreeable. Worse, she did not suppress the feeling. Something about Washington's casual, smiling attention intrigued her, even soothed her. "Yes," she said softly. "I would like a drink, Hank. Thank you."

Stapler recoiled. Something was amiss with his Madelaine. He had never heard her sound gracious. Henry had an effect on his stiff, gruff Madelaine that Rick had not seen before. Maybe George could make her speak so quietly, but not in front of him. It was maddening. Besides, it was his damn whiskey!

The three of them toasted the Talbot and drank slowly without a word. Madelaine used the minute or so to restore her. Something about Hank seemed so distantly familiar, as if obscured by the haze of time. Like a dream she had once had long ago before she learned not to remember them. The clanging of the phone startled Madelaine out of her reflection.

Stapler picked up the receiver and nodded to Madelaine. "We'll be down there in a second, Madj."

Madelaine began to collect her papers. The cool sheets felt reassuring and familiar in her hands. The linen lining of the valise restored her to her senses. "We'll leave from there," she said. "This demonstration had better be worth my time," she added skeptically.

Without looking her way, Stapler said, "Don't you want to come along, Hank? After all, Madj is your protégé, as I recall."

Hank's eyes lit up. "Could I, Miss Jordan? I'll stay out of the way."

To her, he sounded so refreshing, like a child, the way he spoke. Except, of course, Madelaine disliked children. "Certainly, Hank," she said with effort. "If Dr. Madjerin is a friend of yours."

Hank came close to jumping off the ground. "Thanks," he beamed. "Maybe I'll finally get what the hell she's always talking about."

"I am hoping for the same thing," Madelaine said.

The two of them left Stapler in the room arranging his attaché case. He knew the way to the Goddamned lab and would take his time, which included another shot from the flask. Something was wrong with Madelaine and he did not understand it. Furthermore, he could not assess what effect this nonsense would have on Madjerin's chances, or his, of gaining Madelaine's approval. Somehow, he felt it couldn't help.

~ ~ ~

The cassette tape expended itself, stopping the machine. Carleton leaned forward to press the "arreter" button on the recorder. He was not really fully awake yet, but he felt the little speech he had just reviewed pulsing in his head. Sleep-learning was not of particular interest to Carleton. He used, as now, only in a pinch, because of its simple efficiency. Limited in time because he had been so busy the previous night, Carleton resorted to the hypnotic techniques he had perfected as an off-shoot of his research.

He was certain that Madelaine Jordan would be impressed with his presentation. He had read up on her at some length. She was generally credited with an excellent mind and a thorough understanding of electronics. Hadn't she already picked him as one of the candidates of the fellowships? If she were as intelligent as the magazines said she could not but see his merit.

Carleton couldn't be too overwhelming though. That might alienate her. Intelligent people don't like to be made to feel stupid. One of his weaknesses was that he often made others envious of him. Besides, of course, he could not reveal that he had adapted the brain wave mapping techniques to other uses. That would not do at all. He would stick to the basics, his innovations on Madjerin's project.

He was tired of it, of holding back, of being passed over. Most of his life he had spent unnoticed. It was, perhaps, natural for someone as small as he was physically, in a society that placed an idiotic emphasis on size. Even standing up he would not be counted in a land of high school football heroes. He found very early on that his head would never be very far off the ground, but that his mind could be. That was what he concentrated on.

Now his work was paying off. He had overcome his potentially ruinous setback at the Talbot. Madelaine Jordan, homely and smart, different–she would pick him out of the crowd.

Flukes and favors were of no interest to him. No guesses or gifts for Raymond Carleton. He would now take what he deserved. One thing he deserved was to be back at the Talbot, back in a real lab. He looked about him in anger. Since he had been expunged from the rolls of the funded in April, Carleton had taken his work underground. Literally. Now he would be resurrected.

Resuming his seat, Carleton took the tape machine, flipped the cassette over and pushed the play button. If the contents of the cartridge had eluded him for a moment, his own voice soon reminded him. "Good evening, Carleton," he heard himself say. "We botched it last time, but we're more prepared this evening. Everything you need to know is on the rest of this tape. "Now" the voice continued, changing its rhythm, "You are going to sleep, Carleton. Sleep, perchance to dream. Sleep."

Carleton cut off the machine. He had done that already. Thomas Jordan's final education, he thought, smiling: That particular lesson had been taught. The time had arrived to go over the mechanism in preparation for the receipt of his reward: Tenure at the Talbot.

CHAPTER SEVEN

George entered the study with a tray of coffee and expensively small sandwiches. He placed the tray on the side table adjoining the desk. Serving the coffee, he suddenly stopped. "I don't know how you take it," he said. "I didn't have to ask Mr. Jordan."

Montgomery laughed. "Okay. We'll suspend our reenactment for a minute," he said. "But only for that."

"I said nothing while I poured the coffee," George recalled. "Mr. Jordan was seated, of course, as you are. He was looking over a list of some sort."

"Do you have it?" Monty asked.

"Madelaine took it with her this morning," was the response. "It was a list of some people cut from the staff at the Talbot Research Hospital."

Nodding his head, the detective motioned George to continue.

"We exchanged few words, Sergeant," he went on." I could see that Mr. Jordan was preoccupied."

"By the list."

George smiled sadly. "Oh no, sir," he explained. "Not at that point. Not the list. It was several days after his sixty-fifth birthday, you see."

"Getting old bothered him?"

"It bothers everyone, Sergeant Montgomery. Especially men like Mr. Jordan."

"Enough to get sleeping pills?"

Emphatically, George responded, "Absolutely not! He was not completely satisfied with his accomplishment. He wanted more time not less."

Montgomery sipped some coffee and attacked one of the tiny sandwiches with a polite ferocity. In a way, he could understand what Jordan may have felt on his last day. Sixty-five years was a long time to live. His own forty-three years seemed short by comparison, yet, occasionally, Montgomery felt the time flying past him, ripping holes in his dreams, mocking his achievements.

He was an excellent cop, the best of the county's homicide detectives, as he had been in Philadelphia for a time. He was good enough to be offered a promotion to Chief of the Bureau and good enough to turn it down. By any standard, his career had been a successful one, and he had never feared looking back. Now, he was beginning to wonder if it would be enough when he turned fifty, let alone sixty-five.

"In any case," George continued, "what bothered Mr. Jordan was that he had no one near him, I suppose. Specifically, Madelaine had no time for him except for business

Monty sneered. "I got the impression that she doesn't waste her time on anything else."

Indulgently, George said, "She can. She and I do, sometimes."

Recognizing the silly look in George's eyes, Monty apologized. "Sorry. I didn't mean anything by it. I don't really know her." Monty recognized that look from a snapshot of himself with his own kids taken years ago in Philadelphia.

"No one does, Sergeant," George said with a smile that wasn't a smile. "For all of that girl's brilliance and success, with all the fame and attention, no one knows her, Sergeant Montgomery. I think that haunted Mr. Jordan, that he knew her so little," he speculated. "Madelaine did not send a card."

"Until the day after," Montgomery said grimly.

"Yes."

Screw it, Montgomery thought, what makes a girl a bitch! "Let's go on, George. What happened after the coffee?"

"I had brought a piece of birthday cake along with the coffee," George related. "I spent several minutes convincing him to eat it. He accused me of trying to make him feel his age, but finally took it. He loved birthday cake," George added with a touch of nostalgia. "I'll never forget his fortieth. Madelaine–she was four then–Madelaine insisted on baking the cake. It was her first cake as far as anyone knew. It was a spectacular four layer edifice. That is the only word for it. She had apparently been practicing for weeks, stealing flour and sugar and the other makings without any notice from the kitchen."

"Crafty little witch, even then."

"Adorable, Sergeant," George corrected him. "At that age she was adorable. She was terrible with her mother, mind, but, when Mr. Jordan came home, she was truly a wonderful child."

"Swell." Montgomery was disgruntled. He was getting absolutely nowhere. "How was the cake anyway?"

George shrugged. "I haven't the faintest idea. No one else ate it."

"I suppose not," Monty said, feeling foolish. Servants surely didn't eat their master's cake. "What next?"

"Mr. Jordan told me to leave some coffee, because he wanted another cup for bed," George said. "After that he dismissed me."

"You left the tray?"

"No, I just left the pot and his cup."

"Cream and sugar?"

"They were in the pot," George remembered "You must be pretty good, George," Monty said.

George laughed. "Usually. He uses that awful coffee creamer and an artificial sweetener. He owned the company that made them," George said. "Why, even the cake was made with it."

"Can't stand the stuff myself," Monty began. Suddenly his face lit up. "How about you?"

George was appalled. "Never."

"Anyone else here use it?"

"Of course not."

"Visitors that day?"

"Several came, but none had coffee." George was puzzled. "What are you suggesting?"

"My men did not check anything but sugar and the creamer out on the counter," Monty said. "Is any of that stuff still around?"

Together the two men headed to the kitchen. George opened a cabinet, reached back into the shadows and produced a small open box. Montgomery seized it and held it up to his nose. With one sniff, he looked up at George. Then he walked to the telephone.

~ ~ ~

The table, like most hospital tables, felt hard despite the thin cushioning between the surface and Madelaine's back. She could hear Madjerin's machines humming gently in the background. Combined with the drink she had consumed earlier, the whirring sound had lulled her into a state of relaxation. When Madjerin placed the contacts against her forehead, however, Madelaine jumped.

"It is only the sensors, Miss Jordan," Madjerin said calmly. She was used to the procedure and the subject's reactions.

"Sorry," Madelaine apologized. "Are these the problem?"

Madjerin sighed as she fixed the final contacts against the back of her benefactor's scalp. "Yes. It takes too long and is so cumbersome. As you can see."

"Any ideas as to how to avoid this?"

The question arose so abruptly that Madjerin did not respond at once. She racked her memory for Carleton's proposal, the one she had only begun to review before he left. "Only one that appears feasible," Madjerin finally replied. "The brain, as I have said, is a generator of electrical impulses, of brain waves. It does, therefore, radiate or transmit these waves just as a radio sends out its signals."

"You would need some sort of receiver, then?" Madelaine looked up at the spotless, sterile white ceiling.

Stapler's voice cut into her musings. "Glorified ESP."

Extrasensory perception, or at least one theory of it, co-incided with the brain wave transmission approach Madjerin considered correct, but she knew it was a phrase used to discredit the work of serious scientists probing the workings of the human mind. "Certainly not, Mr. Stapler," she said. "ESP assumes that one person can receive an-other's brain waves. Nothing could be more absurd. The patterns of different people–the graphs we reviewed up-stairs–are markedly distinct. To receive a signal, one brain must be on the same fundamental frequency, as it were, as the transmitter. I have yet to find any two people whose patterns harmonized sufficiently to even suggest the possi-bility."

Madelaine was impressed, but she wondered if Madjerin had really studied the problem. "How many of the hun-dreds of functions of the brain... I mean the electrical graphs we've seen. How many of those functions would have to coincide?"

"Oh boy!" Rick was astonished at Madelaine's grasp of the strange subject. He didn't even understand what she was talking about. He and Hank exchanged glances and helpless shrugs.

Madjerin did understand, but she did not have an answer. "Perhaps the Four Basic ones, but I don't think it matters. In any case, it is impossible. The power of the out-put is too low to be received except by the sensors of this machine, which greatly amplify the impulses." She hurried to start the procedure hoping to forestall further questions. "Are you ready?"

"Yes."

As her fingers played with the variety of switches, Madjerin watched the oscilloscope, comparing it with the computer scan printout. The two men moved closer instinctively. The level of output disturbed Madjerin. It registered almost 10 percent below normal and, if anything, Miss Jordan would read higher than normal by her estimate.

Turning to check the electrode contacts, Madjerin discovered her subject looking straight at her. Incredibly, at least one of the electrodes had fallen off.

Madelaine detected the look of amazement on Madjerin's face. "What's wrong?" she demanded, assuming the doctor had detected a serious problem.

The response proved surprisingly harsh. "Lie down, Miss Jordan!"

Orders usually repelled Madelaine, but she did as she was told. She knew that something was wrong. Even though she did not credit Madjerin's research with very much, Madelaine recognized that, such as it was, this was Madjerin's bailiwick. A woman who insisted on obedience in her own realm, Madelaine submitted to others competent in theirs. The small, dark hands, damp with perspiration, secured the suction electrodes to Madelaine's forehead. Two of the four had come loose, but all were now in place. The Indian hesitated to turn around.

A whistle by Stapler forced her, however, to look. The peak readings were off the scale.

Stapler shook his head and whispered in admiration. "Are those your standard settings, Madj?" he asked.

"Believe it or not, yes," she replied.

The oscilloscope reflected Madelaine's frantic concern. "What's wrong?" she croaked, for the first time, considering that the problem could rest with her and not the machine.

Before answering, Madjerin reduced amplification by about thirty percent. The reading dropped abruptly to standard levels. "Wrong? Nothing, Miss Jordan."

"You were off the bloody screen, Maddy!" Stapler laughed.

They all laughed as Madelaine sighed and her readings dropped slightly more, reflecting decreased brain activity.

"Try to relax completely, Miss Jordan," Madjerin suggested. "We've certainly seen your active state."

Relaxation was foreign to Madelaine Jordan. She tried. The graphs declined in amplitude a bit more and the disturbances diminished. "Alright," Madjerin said. "That wasn't much, but it demonstrated–you'll see in a minute," she barked at Madelaine, to keep her still. "It demonstrated how the readout tends to those four basic functions, I've found. Here, look. No, not yet, Miss Jordan."

She flipped another of her many switches. On a second oscilloscope four distinct, separately colored functions appeared among the jagged lines on the face. The equipment needed to produce the effect had been terribly expensive, but worth every penny. The sight always struck those who viewed it. Confident, Madjerin allowed Madelaine to look.

"If I could only put you to sleep," Madjerin said, "Then the four stages would stand almost alone. Until you dreamed, of course. Dreams mess up everything. The four functions seem to be a stable background, while all that interference is semi-conscious and conscious brain activity. The latter ones vary, but the basic ones, see, they are almost constant."

The wired subject of the experiment sat up, removing the suction pick-ups, "Alright, Dr. Madjerin. We've seen enough for now," Madelaine said. "We have some others to see this afternoon. Including your former associate, Raymond Carleton." Rising, she shook hands with the anxious, little woman garbed in laboratory white. "I must admit I am intrigued by this work of yours, but I can't let you know how you stand until later."

Madjerin felt good. Even though she had to compete with the others, she was certain that she had had an impact. "Thank you, Miss Jordan."

The tall, pale heiress smiled almost benignly. "Thank you, Doctor. For a minute, you had me worried. I thought I looked like a dwarf on that green screen of yours."

A nervous laugh shook the tiny frame. "It was the highest reading I've ever seen, Miss Jordan."

"I'll sleep better for that," Madelaine said. "Goodbye, Doctor."

"Goodbye, Miss Jordan," Madjerin responded, her confidence growing. "Goodbye, Mr. Stapler."

"So long, Madj," Rick said. "She'll be hell to live with now."

Hank Washington accompanied the two to the elevator. After his good-byes, Hank returned to Madjerin who hugged him with a violence seemingly beyond her small arms.

Rick and Madelaine walked briskly to the car without exchanging a glance or a word. As she opened the door, Madelaine said, "I'll bet that multi-colored-function oscilloscope cost $15,000 if it cost anything."

Rick laughed. "Probably." he agreed. "It's from Talbot Instruments."

~ ~ ~

Carolyn Jordan had a way about her. George could recognize her even from the distance. Seeing a ground attendant carrying some passenger's bags, George simply looked at the woman beside him to find his charge. Mrs. Jordan always took some sort of mysterious baggage with her on the plane, but somehow, never carried it off.

Shortly after Montgomery had departed to check up on the findings at Melton's, George received a directive from his former mistress's maid to fetch the lady at the gate of Flight 880, TWA, at 3:52. George knew well enough to be there, waiting.

She saw the valet from the ramp and nudged the attendant, as if they were old friends. The abashed young man only nodded. When the three met, the attendant entrusted the carry-ons to George's custody and fled without a tip.

"You don't know, Georgie, my old friend, how difficult it is to get decent service these days," she said without a greeting.

He smiled and said, "How difficult were you?"

"I have missed your sense of humor, George," she admitted ruefully. "How have things been?"

"As might be expected," he said cautiously. "The police have been visiting often since Mr. Jordan died."

Carolyn Jordan shook her head, without disturbing her still brown hair. "I don't quite understand what the police have to do with she said quizzically. "I don't like it much."

"Sergeant Montgomery, whom you will meet before long," George explained, "suspects foul play. So do I."

The full, bright red lips parted in wonder. "Foul play? I thought it was a heart attack."

"So it was, but Mr. Jordan had been drugged." George added, motioning a porter. "He never took sleeping pills."

She furrowed her forehead and bit a fingernail. "That is true. Not even when I left him." Silently, she recalled all of the difficult scenes she and her husband had had prior to the separation The subject repelled her. Her thoughts went elsewhere. "How's my vixen?"

They had reached the baggage area, where the bags had already begun arriving. George ignored her question and sought her bag. It slid down the chute and onto the turntable. With feigned interest.

George watched as the porter seized it and returned to Mrs. Jordan. She had watched George the whole time as though he would answer her by his silence.

"She hasn't said anything about me?" she asked when he remained inscrutable. "Besides making damn sure I don't get anything to speak of from the estate."

The relationship between Madelaine and her mother was arena that George sought to avoid. The pair had never gotten along at all. Plates, paperweights and epithets they had exchanged but little else. They had contended wickedly for Mr. Jordan's affection when Madelaine was young. Increasingly, however, they had tended toward the opposite extreme, each outdoing the other in their disaffection with the confused head of the household.

Upon the separation, matters had worsened. None of the three had really spoken to others for sometime. Only when Madelaine took over Talbot Instruments did she pay any attention to her father.

"Madelaine is very busy," George said looking straight out the window for the car. "She has really only had one chance to note that she despises you."

The woman sighed forlornly. "I see," she said quietly. George looked at her in surprise. She had had nothing but vile words for her daughter in the past. The pair had expressed dislike for each other in more ways than George could remember.

It seemed, that Mrs. Jordan was upset about Madelaine's opinion of her. "The car," he said.

Without another word, they walked out of the airport and into the limousine. Mrs. Jordan did not offer a word until half of the route to the house had been negotiated. When she did speak, she stopped before completing the thought and dropped back into silence. While George did not enjoy the silent tension, he could not think of anything sensible to say in the situation.

The only consolation in her arrival, he thought, lay in the timing. Madelaine, out on her grant interviews, would not arrive until after her mother had occupied the house. George was not sure that he had done the right thing in inviting Mrs. Jordan to stay at the house, but her attitude in the car led him to believe that, perhaps, he had guessed right.

~ ~ ~

The basement storage room at the Talbot Research Hospital proved every bit as cramped as Jean Skeffington had warned. While a large enough room, it contained cartons of all descriptions, a few heavy, sophisticated machines and even Hospital records. The aisles for access had been intended for one with less bulk than Montgomery. The acting head of the Hospital led him toward the rear of the storage room. "It's back here somewhere, Sergeant," Skeffington said, uncertainly. "I've never looked for it before."

Montgomery peered around the boxes piled around him. "Who got you the box you used to make the cake?"

Her round shoulders shrugged. "An orderly, I guess."

"Everyone has access to this room?" Montgomery asked, aggravated. Skeffington looked embarrassed. "Technically, no," she explained. "But, I let the key out to just about anyone. And there are three others."

"Whose?"

"Well, Mr. Jordan, of course. Let's see." Her mind took its time to remember. "Hank Washington. He's the night custodian. And the Chief Janitor, Ted Fillings."

"Are they as loose about their keys as you are?" he demanded. She had that look of annoyance on her face that people get when they were criticized rightly. "Yes. Mr. Jordan wanted everyone to have easy access. For the Sweet Tooth."

Grunting at his bad luck, Montgomery searched for the cartons of Sweet Tooth. It wasn't too difficult, once he put his mind to it. The cartons were neatly piled up in a corner of the room. The top one was open and half-empty.

He took out one of the boxes, opened it and smelled for the odor. "This one is Okay," he said, mostly for his own benefit.

"What did you expect?" Skeffington demanded.

"Nothing, I guess," Monty admitted, going through several other boxes. "And that's what I got."

They walked back through the stacks of supplies to the door. There, they met the stern, questioning eyes of Henry Washington. Washington blocked the door suspiciously until he recognized the red hair of Jean Skeffington.

"I'm sorry, Ms. Skeffington," Washington said. "I couldn't see it was you."

Skeffington smiled. "Aren't you asleep yet, Hank?"

"It's hard to tell, Ms. Skeffington," he replied. "I'm pretty close."

"This is Detective Sergeant Montgomery, Hank," she said. "Sergeant, this is Hank Washington, the night custodian."

Montgomery examined the black man's face for a hint of fear or anxiety. All he saw was a man near his own age with a big smile. "How do you do, Washington? Mind if I ask you a question or two?"

Hank's eyes narrowed as he wondered what would be asked. "Sure, Sergeant, but I doubt I know anything you'd want to know."

"Maybe," Montgomery allowed. He doubted it as well, "Have you let out your key to this room indiscriminately?"

"No."

"No?" Montgomery asked.

Skeffington flushed. "But Hank," she said hurriedly, "Mr. Jordan wanted everyone to have access."

Washington nodded. "I know that, but I work at night. I don't want just anybody getting in here."

"Who have you given it to," Montgomery asked, "say in the last few weeks?"

"Nobody."

"Are you sure?"

"Why should I?" he asked. "I come in here at about 9:00. Everyone's gone by that time."

Montgomery's interest began to decline again. Skeffington gave her key to everyone, Washington to no one. It seemed typical of the Jordan case. He was, as usual, wasting his time. "What about that Fillings character?"

"Ted Fillings leaves the door unlocked," Washington said.

"Shit," Montgomery hissed. "What a way to run a Hospital?" He stomped into the hallway. "Thanks anyway."

Washington and Skeffington watched the detective storm down the corridor.

Hank ran his fingers through his short graying hair. "What was that all about?"

With a disgusted air, Jean Skeffington replied, "He wanted to know who had a chance to get to the Sweet Tooth, for some reason he kept to himself."

"Oh," Hank said, not bothering to understand. "Well, I'm going home, Ms. Skeffington."

"Good. I'll see you tomorrow, Hank." Jean Skeffington turned and headed to the elevator. She thought about Montgomery's questions and what they could mean. The detective's refusal to even hint at the basis for his questions about the Sweet Tooth annoyed her. So she had baked Tom Jordan's birthday cake with it. It was perfectly harmless She did a lot of things like that for him. And why bother to check the contents. She had seen that it had just been opened before being left on her desk. Besides, Tom had assured it could never go bad.

~ ~ ~

Stapler thought it a bad sign that Madelaine accepted Carleton's proposal for a meeting at his East End apartment. He had insisted, however, that he had equipment there that merited display. Madelaine did not bat an eyelash at the request, even though she had demanded of the others that they appear at Talbot for appointments as she arranged them. Stapler knew better than to ask her the question bothering him. Why was Carleton so special?

During their drive from the Talbot in Oakland's campus section to the Point Breeze address given them by Carleton, Madelaine discussed her first impressions of the various researchers interviewed that morning. Only two had apparently gained her attention to any degree. The psychologist Corbett, with his strange fascination for computers, word categories and memory, had largely secured his grant by boldly, impulsively, analyzing Carleton. Madjerin overcame Madelaine's preconceived dislike for her and her exotic subject by exhibiting a command of the mapping's procedural details. Madelaine approved of those who insisted upon ruling their domains no matter the consequences, unless it was her field as well.

Carleton was the only one that Madelaine had favored from the outset. Stapler's dislike for him, coupled with her father's disfavor had led her to believe that he would be something special. As far as she was concerned, neither Stapler, nor her father, judged character and ability as well as she. While both men appreciated talent, they avoided those not fitting their prejudices. Madelaine actually preferred those people that differed from herself or her expectations.

Though she hated to admit it, Madelaine was like her father in many ways. Intelligence, independence and strength characterized her father's personality and Madelaine had the same virtues, even more thoroughly developed in her opinion. Father and daughter differed in several respects, however, particularly in their respective approaches to people. Mr. Jordan liked people usually for themselves. Madelaine found herself mostly repelled by people, drawn only by their abilities, ideas and idiosyncrasies.

The best example, she thought, was Rick Stapler. Her father had taken to the young lawyer immediately. He had insisted to Madelaine a dozen times that Stapler had the warmth and decency that comes with dishonesty and guile, whatever that meant. Madelaine admired the attorney for his ability to confuse an issue when necessary, while clarifying it for himself. She also liked him because she so disliked him. That anomaly did not in the least baffle her, as it would Stapler had she admitted it to him.

Remarkably enough, both passengers in the Jordan Lincoln maintained their independent thoughts while conversing on the subject of Carleton's research. Fortunately, their combined knowledge of that work was so minimal that they did not miss any information by not listening. The "future Nobel Prize winner" had a surprise in store for them, in his landlady's fruit cellar.

The note he had left on the door suggested that they enter and descend two flights to his "Laboratory". Madelaine stepped back to examine the house and shook her head. A large, three-storied structure of indeterminate age, it looked like a plausible place for a laboratory to Boris Karloff. Stapler was thinking of Vincent Price, by the time they reached the lab door.

A single knock brought Carleton to the door and an exchange of greetings. The trio proceeded into the dimly lit, bricked chamber. The ingenuity of the lab's accouterments brought words of congratulations the visitors. Railroad ties, beer kegs, old, rewired televisions and radios seemed the main components of the equipment. A canvas sheet covered what was obviously the key to the operation. The insignia on the white cloth revealed the owner to be either sailor or thief.

"I used to," Carleton responded to an unasked question. "I quit when my brothers took my boat. Besides, I don't have the money to sail anymore. I've kept myself in this fruit cellar ever since your daddy canned me."

The malice in Carleton's voice reminded Stapler of the repellent aspects of the researcher's personality. Acid dripped from every word, venom spilled from each phrase. Carleton did not seem to like anyone, or appreciate anything. No compliment sufficed. Gratitude was as foreign to Carleton as affection was to Madelaine.

Madelaine examined the room quietly before saying, "We might be able to reverse that action."

Taking her words as his cue, Stapler began his spiel. "As you may already know, Mr. Jordan has left a sizable estate, much of which he directed be donated to the Talbot, to fund individual projects," he explained, confident that Carleton had already figured out how much was available. "Miss Jordan, as executrix of the estate, is to make the determinations as to whom the funds will be granted."

"You happen to be one of the candidates," Madelaine stated.

"The standards for the grant," Stapler went on, for Madelaine's benefit mostly, "are the potential of the work involved, the potential of the candidate and the usefulness of the outcome."

Tired of hearing the speech, Madelaine said, "Which I alone shall evaluate. What do you have, Dr. Carleton?"

The expression of Carleton changed from one of amusement to one of scorn. "What I have, Miss Jordan," he said, "is a right to that money. More than you'll understand."

"Right," she replied thoughtfully. "is a word overused in this country, Doctor. If you have a project of merit, however, I might confer that right upon you."

The two faced off for what felt to Stapler like an hour and a half. Madelaine's giant, battleship-gray eyes were half closed with disinterest as she locked the shorter man's anger in his throat. She was not really uninterested, but she looked as though she could live forever without Carleton or his computer research.

Carleton decided not to waste his valuable time on a homely behemoth, one who reminded him too much of his brothers. He'd let his work get the grant for him. "I have," he began before correcting himself. "I had been working with Dr. Madjerin on her National Crime project before the spring boot located my behind."

Stapler, happy that someone had finally spoken, commented, "We have just left her, Dr. Carleton. You don't have to review your work with her. She did indicate that you had a slightly different direction in mind though."

Carleton acted surprised that Madjerin had given him credit for anything. He did not assume that she could understand his methods. Grinders, he found, had insuperable difficulty in grasping broad concepts. He did not think that Madjerin lacked intelligence, just genius. "That was very nice of her," he said finally. "She didn't view my concepts as meriting money, but mention is some consolation."

"What is under the sail, Dr. Carleton?" Madelaine asked coldly. "I assume that you have your terminal there.

Impressed with her observation, Carleton launched into his sleep-learned dissertation. "I have accomplished what Madjerin wants. The electro-chemistry of the brain is my subject, Miss Jordan. Wave mapping is only one of the possibilities involved in that field. But it is an important one from a practical standpoint." The "canned" material rolled off his tongue easily and convincingly.

"You are right, Miss Jordan. The sail here, protects my computer terminal from the cold and the moisture. I have constructed other devices to provide the proper climate, but canvas is a great material to fall back on." He whipped the sail off of the device. It was not actually just a terminal. It proved to be a minicomputer, itself linked to the central computer at the Talbot.

Madelaine nodded. "A 125," she said. The machine came from a recent entrant into the small computer market, Talbot Instruments, Inc. "At a 25 percent discount, that runs $18,000."

"I'm leasing it from a new company here," he explained, with sly cheer. "I got them the Talbot Research discount, so they gave me one year free."

The sham discount did not bother her at all. "Very good," she said.

Disappointed by her lack of response, Carleton got back on the programmed track. "As I said, I have solved Madjerin's difficulties while working in my own direction. Some kinks remain to be hammered out, but I think she can do that." He felt generous. "Her problem is that she can't receive the signals put out by the brain. We had started to work on my idea late this last winter, but didn't get very far. The fact is that the brain does indeed transmit energy waves, however weakly. The beauty of my receiver approach is this: Conscious and semi-conscious brain waves are the most quickly dissipated. They are directed by the body to one use or another. Most of their energy is wasted on internal consumption."

Carleton turned to his TI 125 and started it up. "With me so far?"

Madelaine nodded. Stapler shook his head, but said, "Don't worry about me. She's the one you're after."

That was Carleton's intention. "Good. I'm going to use you as my subject anyway."

Stapler shrugged. "It is my turn. Madelaine got her chance earlier."

"With Madjerin?" he asked rhetorically. "Did she get that new oscilloscope yet?"

Madelaine responded. "It looks very impressive."

"It is," Carleton retorted. "The set up and programming are very intricate. She does that sort of thing better than anyone I know. She'd make a marvelous assistant for someone."

After checking to see if the arms of the mechanism had reached their operating levels, Carleton continued. "Assuming that the two upper levels of brain energy are internally dissipated, then what do we have left? We have the basic subconscious functions that we isolated last December. You see Madjerin's system of contact electrodes is not only impractical, it is inefficient. A computer must expend an enormous amount of time sorting out the various functions. If we can seek to pick up only an extra-body transmission, we will receive only the four personality functions, as I call them. The others do not transmit to speak of. Which explains why those who have tried to construct machines to read minds across a room have all failed. You can't read thoughts very well. But you can easily receive the subconscious electric activity of the brain."

"Which is?" Madelaine broke in.

A grimace betrayed Carleton's frustration. "I haven't had the money or the time to figure that out," he said. "Anyhow, that puts the cart before the horse. Theory is worthless, if it doesn't help something work," he declared. "I know enough if I know it is there."

"Good," Stapler said. "I have a feeling that if you tried to explain that one, I'd have to leave the room."

"I'll have the answer before I'm through, I would think," he suggested. "If I have the money to continue."

Madelaine rubbed the bridge of her new nose. Sometimes it hurt for no reason. "We shall see."

The white clad shoulders rose and fell in a shrug. "Okay. In any case, I have received the signals, even with this makeshift equipment. The 125 doesn't have to do much. Mostly, I use it to organize the reception into the readout. The real key is this little, homemade amplifier, under the computer. The receiver picks up all sorts of energy transmissions, including radio. Part of it was a radio once. Part a TV set. The input, however, is boosted by this device and the computer screens out all background reception. I run the system before testing," he said turning on the receiver. The TV set in the other corner of the room lit up with a scramble of wave activity. "The computer processes the reception and screens all of it out." He switched on the computer interposing himself between the receiver and Stapler as he typed commands.

The TV screen went blank except for a bright white line across the middle. Carleton and Madelaine stood side by side at the control panel. She examined the terminal, the amplifier and the receiver. Aside from the substantial re-wiring, it all looked pretty conventional.

"You see," Carleton said, "everything has been screened. The background will no longer be passed on by the receiver and the amplifier can work only on what I want it to."

"Rick," she stated.

"Exactly," he concurred, smiling at the confused attorney. "Come on over here, Counselor," he commanded.

Stapler exhausted his reservations with a sigh and ap-proached the machine. Carleton stepped aside, his hand on a dial on the amp. Rick stopped beside Madelaine, who watched the screed. "Nothing," she said.

"No," Carleton agreed. "Not yet. I don't waste energy when I can help it," he explained. "Okay now. Ready?"

Both of the others nodded. As Carleton twisted the knob on the machine, the TV screed began to show signs of life. The jumbled deflections from the middle line began to ap-pear as little bumps then grew slowly into mountains against the charcoal sky of the electron tube. "Like it?" he asked.

"So far," Madelaine replied. "Kick in the second program."

Admiration and distrust filled Carleton's head. This tall, broad-shouldered, transvestite knew what the hell was go-ing on, he thought. She's dangerous. "Coming up," he said.

By typing on the TI 125 keyboard, Carleton brought his other computer process into play. The TV screed scrambled briefly add when the image reappeared, four distinct, over-lapping graphs appeared Carleton allowed the spectators to savor his genius while he rummaged among his papers. Shit, he thought, I couldn't have lost it. The file of graphs that he had photocopied several days before did dot con-tain what he wanted. He was desperate.

Madelaine's crisp voice brought him a mixture of relief and apprehension. "I believe that you are looking for this," she said, handing him a Xerox copy of a braid wave graph that he add Madjerin had taken eight months previously.

"Yes," he said staggered. She had already made the comparison that was his coup de grace.

"You've got a pretty good match, Dr. Carleton," she said clinically. "I'd say you've caught our Mr. Stapler very well."

CHAPTER EIGHT

Melton's townhouse yielded, unfortunately, only disappointment. By the time the Sergeant had returned to check his investigation's progress, no key to the sweetener aspect of the case had appeared. The housekeeper insisted that Melton used no sugar or sweetener in his coffee at all. None turned up around the house.

"I'm sorry, Sergeant," she said. "But he gave sugar up several years ago. I've been making this coffee for him since 1965, so I know. And he knew I disapproved of sweeteners."

Monty nodded wearily. If one more theory were knocked to hell in this case, he would have to tear his hair out. "Would there be any way he could have had some somewhere else?"

She pondered this situation carefully. "Well, he eats his dinners at the Club," she said. "It saves me the work and him the loneliness."

"Is that what he said?" Montgomery inquired doubtfully.

"That is my opinion," she replied. "H.P. needed company constantly. He didn't play sports like a maniac for the exercise. He wanted an excuse to have someone around."

Personalities did not seem to influence this case and Monty had no patience left. "What about last night?" he asked brusquely. "Did he follow his routine? Dinner at the Club?"

"Yes," she responded meekly.

"Then what?"

"He came home," she began. She paused as though something struck her. "Well, to be honest, he did go to sleep earlier than usual He usually goes to bed at about 9:45 and reads the Wall Street Journal for a bit. Last night he came home and went right to bed."

Excitement built in Montgomery's voice. "When?"

Disturbed by his intensity, she hesitated before answering "Before nine, actually. That is very early."

"He didn't say anything?"

"No."

Montgomery turned to a young subordinate and barked, "Call the University Club and tell them not to disturb any of their supplies of sugar and sweeteners. I don't want them serving it to anybody. Tell them we'll be right over." Once the young man had departed for the phone, Monty turned to the stocky, paling housekeeper. "Thank you. We could be making some progress."

As he abandoned Melton's, Montgomery tried to fathom what was going on. Someone seemed to be going to a great deal of trouble to help the entire Board of Trustees of the Talbot sleep at night. Assuming that each of the board members had been slipped a similar mickey before they died, he had only to discover a person with common access to the men.

Someone able to contaminate their food or coffee with a slightly bitter, slightly acrid substance that allowed them to sleep–permanently.

Whoever it was, he concluded, also had access to the University Club. No problem there. He himself had been there the previous evening, apparently just before the number had been done on Melton. Stapler came to mind immediately. He had access to each man as the attorney for the Talbot; he also had access to the University Club the night Melton had gotten his dose.

He didn't like it. Stapler was too smart to be obvious. He also had plenty of competition. The living members of the board, for example. Sure, competition between giant retired egos. Hard feelings on a board exercising such power as the Talbot's had that spring, torpedoing the careers of so many of the staff.

That was a thought, Monty mused. The staff had suffered badly in the spring as the recession forced out second-rate researchers, and probably first-raters, too, ones with enemies on the board. Montgomery understood organizational politics as well as anybody. After all, he had struggled against a couple himself. Professional jealousy, power, money all rivaled love as murder motives. In fact, love had lost much of its popularity as a motive for homicide. That was a shame, he thought, as he pulled into the University Club lot.

The parking attendant took custody of Montgomery's car with a we've-been-expecting-you nod. The manager of the Club, Horace Turner, greeted him at the door with expressions of a similar sentiment, tinged, Monty thought, with minor resentment. People don't like cops messing with their club's privacy, Montgomery figured. He knew he wouldn't like it.

Turner led the detective to the dining room where Melton had eaten. Monty knew he was too late to gain anything but a feeling for the place where Melton had been doped. The staff had cleaned up after night before and was in the process of preparing for the coming evening.

"What do you know of H.P. Melton's eating habits?" he asked.

Less annoyed that he would ordinarily have been, the manager replied, "Quite little, I'm afraid, but some of the serving people should know something. Mr. Melton dined in this room every evening at 6:30."

"Find someone who knew him well," Montgomery ordered.

Once Turner had left him, Monty collapsed into a chair. Did anyone know a man well enough to know why he died?

Melon had died of a heart attack, "natural causes", the certificate would read. Yet, to Montgomery, there had to be something unnatural about the causes, because the death was too violent, too ugly to be natural. He had seen hundreds of murders more peaceful than Melton and Jordan's "natural" deaths.

Something about the Jordan case plagued Montgomery. It eroded the stoic satisfaction in his job that made it worth all the trouble and pain it had brought him over the years. He knew that he wouldn't let it go until he had some kind of answer.

Two people stood beside the manager when Monty responded to the nudge on the shoulder. Both had intimate knowledge of Melton's habits, as members of the evening shift. One, the tall, chubby woman had waited on him the previous night. Montgomery started with her.

"Did he sweeten his coffee?" he asked abruptly.

"Yes," she said, after a moment's reflection. "He had stopped for several years, he once told me. I've only been here a couple years," she explained. "But he said he took it up again last winter."

"He blamed Mr. Jordan," the other, a reedy black man, interjected.

"Jordan?" Montgomery asked quickly. "Why?"

He had an unusual accent, Jamaican perhaps, when he spoke. "Mr. Jordan developed as new sugar," he explained. "Mr. Jordan wanted all of his friends to try it. Mr. Melton said his sweet tooth was reborn."

Montgomery began to feel a warm glow. "Did he use it last night?"

"I suppose so," the lady answered. "But he didn't ask for anything."

"Of course not," the male replied. "He kept a little bottle of it in his locker upstairs."

"You know where?"

"Yes, Sir."

"Get it." This news seemed like a real break. Montgomery began to feel good for a change, and pressed on. "Now, Miss Simons," he asked, reading her name tag discreetly, "did anyone stop at his table last night."

She thought a minute. "Several people. He always called them over. He knew everyone."

"Regulars?"

"Yes. I recognized them all."

He sighed. He had hoped for a stranger. "Okay, Miss Simons. I'm going to have to have a list of everyone who came within a reasonable distance."

She took her turn to sigh. "Yes, sir. I'll try to remember."

"Thank you." Montgomery turned to Turner. "I hate to say it... Mr. Turner, isn't it?"

After Turner's nod, Monty went on. "As I said, I hate to impose on you folks here. You have done a hell of a lot for me already. But I want to find out if anybody, anybody, was up in the locker area last night. Everybody. We'll have to check them all out."

Scratching his cheek, the manager emptied his lungs. "Mr. Montgomery, there is very little access problem up there. Anyone can come and go, once they're in the Club. I'll see if I can find anyone who might help you, but don't expect too much."

Montgomery smiled. "I don't," he said. "In this case, I'm not expecting much at all."

~ ~ ~

The telephone continued ringing, while Heloise rapped out a tune on the cradle. The unanswered phone annoyed Heloise, particularly because she wanted the chore done before 4:30, when Stapler was due back. Heloise directed her impatience at the electric company.

"Duquesne Light," a voice finally said.

The secretary sighed and her voice reflected signs of her exasperation, "I have been calling for Miss Madelaine Jordan," she explained in an abnormally hard tone. "She is handling the estate of her father? Account number 473-22205."

"473 dash 22205?" the voice asked.

"That's right."

"Thank you," the phone replied.

Waiting for the right manager, Heloise tried to relax back into her comfortable chair. Stapler had gotten her the nicest executive swivel chair she'd ever seen. Every time she sat in it, she thought of the silly grin he had when he first showed it to her–even before she had accepted the job. With her husband badly injured, and perhaps because of it, she had been reluctant to accede to an old friend's offer of what seemed a cushy job.

Rick, of course, pleaded that he needed her. "I'm not a philanthropist," he cried, after hearing her objection. "I don't need a secretary or even a right arm." Just opening his own office, Rick insisted "I need... well, you." She typed adequately, learned fair shorthand eventually, and had a beautiful voice and presence.

Joe Carpenter had not objected strenuously, as she had expected, when she told him that she was going to work with a college sweetheart. Having known Rick longer than she, Joe waved her worries aside. If Rick's needs and theirs coincided, why not take advantage of the happy fortune, Joe had said.

The arrangement had worked out nicely and with Joe slowly recovering, she was happy. She had the two men she loved most in the world around her all of the time. To both, she had proved her worth and dedication. Neither, she knew, had any intention of living without her. She was an excellent secretary, or more, to Rick and a pretty fair wife, if she did say so, to Joe.

"Is this Mr. Stapler's secretary?" a voice asked.

Heloise answered quickly. "Yes."

"Good. I'm Tim Hirsch," he said. "I'm the account manager for Mr. Jordan's. I've been expecting your call."

She laughed, feeling better at the deep sound of his voice.

"You should have been. This mistake is enormous," she said. "Why didn't you catch it before the bill went out?"

Hirsch paused for a moment, as a rustling of papers delayed his response. "I'm sorry, Miss Carpenter. That is not a mistake," he told her apologetically. "As a matter of fact, I did catch it before it went out. That's why it's a couple of days late."

"You must be mistaken," she retorted. "Why, the amount due is higher than this office building pays."

She could almost feel him nodding. "I know, Miss Carpenter!" He sounded as exasperated as she was. "But, believe me, I checked three times. The computer did not make any mistakes."

"Mr. Hirsch, the Jordan household is gas heated, with a gas stove," she insisted. "How do you justify this bill? He doesn't even own a TV set!"

Hirsch's voice quavered. "I don't pretend to understand."

"Well, you should," she snapped. "Can you check again?"

"Yes." He was reduced to monosyllables.

"Then do," she demanded. Suddenly she felt guilty. The fault laid with the computer, probably from Madelaine's TI, not poor Mr. Hirsch. The fit of pique from Heloise was not intended for him. "Listen, Mr. Hirsch," she said conciliatory. "I'll call the house and find out if anything unusual happened during the billing period. You review your records and call me back tomorrow. How does that sound?"

"Okay, Miss Carpenter," Hirsch replied, audibly relieved. "I may even be able to pinpoint the peaks for you."

"That's not really necessary," she said. "I'll speak to you tomorrow. Goodbye."

After Mr. Hirsch bid her adieu, Heloise looked again at the bill. When it first arrived in the office, she didn't notice any problem. She even began to write a check for it, before realizing that the cost was about ten times what it should have been. The Kilowatt-hour reading was impossibly high. Unusually anxious about it, she had gotten immediately on it, but the solution would have to await her talk with Mr. Hirsch the next day. The delay seemed fitting.

Handling the estate had become more frustrating than expected. The autopsy had exacerbated tensions between Madelaine and Rick to the point that he could hardly work. Sergeant Montgomery never left her alone. Mrs. Jordan, as feared, had arrived that very afternoon, preparing, also as feared, to wage a bitter will contest. The bizarre bills Johnny Jordan dispatched from Vienna and Paris had not been anticipated, and contributed to the general disarray of Heloise's office.

Madelaine insisted upon an immediate restructuring of J & T and she had to have the damn grants decided yesterday, before even having any authority. At times Heloise so despised the high powered Madelaine Jordan, despite real admiration for her success, that she frightened herself more than Madelaine did. Madelaine treated everyone so coldly, that Heloise had decided that something was wrong with her. At least, she thought, she understood why Madelaine treated Rick so badly, but why she shunned everyone else whenever possible, Heloise couldn't guess.

Without a doubt, Heloise had concluded, Madelaine had a thing, something, for her Rick. There was too much emotion in that relationship for any other explanation. Hate usually derived from love, Heloise believed. Madelaine and Rick were both reluctant to admit any feelings for people. Rick she understood from their relationship in college. She was still certain that he had loved her, and had hidden his feelings, especially from himself. Heloise sensed something similar in Madelaine Jordan.

Madelaine now had all the attention in the world. She had seized headlines. Literally, she had made herself news by driving herself to a success that everyone, including Madelaine, could readily recognize and accept. When she received the admiration of all, paradoxically, she rejected it, repelled, or maybe disappointed. Nothing she did, no one she met satisfied Madelaine Jordan's elusive desires. Rick even approached wakening signs of life from the six feet of reservoir.

Heloise understood, or thought she understood, all of this about Madelaine Jordan. She did not understand why. Heloise, furthermore, did not care to find out. Not really.

~ ~ ~

"Shit!" Madelaine hissed.

Stapler started, for it was the first time he had heard Madelaine use that word. "What's wrong?"

Without answering, she pulled the car to a stop in the University Club lot. Rick assumed that she was just tired. He felt exhausted from the grueling day of interviews, coupled with the pressure generated by tenants fleeing his office building. For eight hours he had had to actively cater to Madelaine, realizing if the trend at the Haller Building kept up, he would need the income working for her provided. He might even have to ask her for a loan. He was in deep trouble, if she learned of his activities on behalf of DeJong and Einberg at J & T.

Madelaine stared straight ahead at the three police cars. Her mouth set in a frown and her eyes fixed, she said, "Is that Montgomery's car?"

Rick's eyes swung toward the parking lot. His stomach sank. "Shit!" It was Montgomery's car alright, flanked by two other cars from the county.

He cursed himself silently for suggesting the drink at the Club. Pushing your luck, he thought, never pays off. Now he would have to face Montgomery, with his paranoid insistence that Thomas Jordan's death was unusual. While he had come to like the difficult detective, Rick felt unsettled by Montgomery's unbridled drive for an explanation.

Complicating matters, he knew, was the presence of Madelaine. Though she had only talked with Monty on the phone, she despised him. The way she stared at the detective's car indicated that a confrontation with Monty was in the making.

As she drew herself from the Lincoln, Madelaine felt a wave of fatigue sweep over her. The day had been long, as had the night before. Madelaine could never sleep anymore. Coupled with the tension involved in dealing with Rick, worsening as his security collapsed, the lack of sleep drained Madelaine of her strength. The swirling feeling in her head bothered her so that she had to steady herself on the rear fender before heading toward the entrance.

The last thing Madelaine wanted after so miserable a day was to face Sergeant Montgomery. His telephone manner had been brusque and unrestrained. He had had the audacity to butcher her father, question her about her father's death and refuse to accept the fact that she had been in New York at the time. Montgomery's dedication to his little world was laudable enough, but she would rather stay in her own.

Stapler came up beside her as she walked to the door. Madelaine had almost forgotten him. "What do you think he wants?" she asked, looking straight ahead.

Holding the door for her, he replied, "I don't know, Maddy. But I don't think we'll like it. Not if I know Monty."

The absence of the doorman, the parking valet and Turner indicated that something was amiss. Yet, once inside, neither of them detected any real disturbance of Club routine. Members wandered through the lobby as usual. The help had no anxiety in their expressions.

A booming voice broke the image of calm. "There must be somebody, damn it!" Montgomery insisted at the top of the stairs. "Find somebody who was up there!"

"Guess who?" Rick said lightly.

When Madelaine did not respond, Rick looked over at her.

She remained perfectly still, glaring up the stairs toward Montgomery's voice. She was an extraordinary sight. Her legs were planted just far enough apart to give the impression of immovability. The rigidity of her back was stonelike. Similarly, the chiseled, sharp-lined features of her took an unreal cast, as though carved for exhibit.

As usual, only her eyes betrayed signs of animation. Cocked slightly upward, they caught the lights of the chandeliers, glimmering silver rings. Tiny, rainbow flecks of blue and green and even orange, reflected from prism crystals, capered about in the shining bands.

Slowly her eyes moved back and forth, lowering their gaze to ground level. Now they looked more like smoldering solder than anything else.

"Good afternoon to you both," Montgomery said, cheerfully. The voice startled Rick. Montgomery seized his hand before he had a chance to offer it.

"And this, I take it, is Miss Jordan," Monty said, grinning. He chucked Madelaine under the chin playfully.

The touch made Madelaine jump back, her eyes widened with hatred. No one, no one, had dared to do that to her since her mother when–whenever it had been! The blood of fury began to color the white skin of her face.

"Who'll buy me a drink?" Montgomery asked, feeling successful. "I deserve one."

"You'd better," Rick declared, laughing. Turning to Madelaine, Rick swallowed his invitation.

Only once had he seen Madelaine so terribly flushed: Thirty seconds later, she had blankly unleashed a punch that shattered his jaw, in spite of an eight and a half ounce boxing glove.

Distantly Madelaine felt Rick's firm grip on her shoulder. As his fingers dug into her taut shoulder, she became aware that her senses were fading. She realized that her buried temper had risen to choke off her oxygen and knot her muscles.

Battling for breath, she unlocked her jaw and opened her white-knuckled fists. Pain from her teeth, her hands and her neck gushed through her. She felt Stapler's hand slide down her back and nudge her forward at the waist. Her head was swimming but she could walk. Each step would bring her consciousness back.

By the time the trio reached a table in the bar, Madelaine knew that she would not black out. The glaze over her eyes had largely evaporated and she could hear the detective speaking.

"Finally, we got a break today," Montgomery enthused.

Stapler, his hand squeezing Madelaine's knee, replied loudly into her ear, "It's not possible to get a break investigating a heart attack, Monty. Is it Madelaine?"

Shaking her head, she said, "I'm sorry. I must be more tired than I thought. What did you say?"

Rick released her leg and said, "Never mind. Montgomery here has some news for us."

"Order the drinks first," Madelaine requested. "Please."

After the waiter had come and gone, Stapler whispered in Madelaine's ear. "Are you Okay, Maddy?"

She nodded.

Montgomery stretched his arms. "About the case," he said meaningfully. "We have our lead."

Rolling his eyes, Stapler said, "Your sense of the dramatic is getting to you, Copper."

"You're right," Monty admitted, grinning still. With an assertion of self-control, he forced a serious expression back onto his face. It was, after all, serious business. "Someone has been doping the artificial junk your father liked to put in everyone's coffee, Miss Jordan."

Rick grimaced. "That stuff is poison without any help."

"It'll do," Monty agreed. "But not for what someone had in mind."

"Oh?" Madelaine managed to ask.

"Yeah," the detective answered. "And last night, Melton got the same thing."

The name "Melton" fell like a hammer. Montgomery found his two listeners staring at him as if he were mad. He had forgotten that they could not have heard. The news was still under wraps. "I'm sorry," he said, too late. "I've been seeped in this all day and I forgot who knows what."

Neither Rick nor Madelaine responded. Stapler could only wrack his mind for images of Melton and Jordan as he had last seen them: Melton cheerful, ebullient and alive; Jordan twisted, pasty and dead. The images would not fit together.

Madelaine's head filled with scenes from the past, scenes of the Redhead and her father, inseparable, together. The pictures spun around and got farther away. She was drifting. And with no one to catch her, Madelaine drifted too far and slumped to the table.

~ ~ ~

For an hour after he had been left alone, Carleton sat in front of the TI 125 and brooded. The Jordan woman had been sharper than he had expected. She had taken to his ideas, but had she understood them too well? Perhaps he had not presented a convincing enough look at his achievements. He had not wanted her to grasp the full import of what he had accomplished, of course, but he began to fear that he had cut it too fine. Jordan and Stapler had come to see him after Madjerin. Had Madjerin's earlier audience made his work seem anti-climatic, derivative, and even redundant?

It was happening again, he thought, pounding his fist on the table.

No matter how good he was, no matter how much better, they didn't notice! It had always been, "Oh, that's nice, Ramie," and a pat on the head.

The TI 125 began to shake as his fist thudded harder and harder on the desk-top. Pain shot up to his elbow before he could stop. Disturbed by the intensity of his fury, Carleton stood up abruptly, spilling brain-wave graphs out of his lap. The 125 now sat serenely on the table. He stared at it, for a long time. Then he felt better.

He had the power, after all. He had the ability to impress himself on all of them, to remove impediments that stood between him and what he wanted, what he deserved. If it was a contest they wanted, between him and Madjerin, then a contest they would have. It wouldn't last long. It would be over by morning.

~ ~ ~

Madjerin and Hank did not speculate on the percentages in her favor. Both knew that Madelaine Jordan had been impressed and that was enough. The grant would come. Until then, a small dinner at a familiar local restaurant sufficed for their modest celebration

"She is so tall," Madjerin said in wonder, again. In India, few men were so tall as Madelaine. None of those whom Madjerin knew had the towering presence that made her benefactress seem even larger than others.

"For a woman, I'll say she is," Hank admitted. He had seen lots of guys bigger than Miss Jordan, but she was impressive alright. "She's kinda homely though."

Madjerin agreed. "I could barely see her face when she stood up."

The wine had the pleasant effect of making an early dinner more like a happy hour. Once Madelaine and Stapler had left, they danced about a bit, tried to sleep and met for their private party. Though neither succeeded in getting any sleep, they did not exhibit any symptoms of fatigue. At least, none that could not have been attributed to the wine.

Madjerin described in detail the part of the meeting that Hank had slept through. After a rocky start and some encouragement from Mr. Stapler, Madjerin had gained in confidence and clarity. The dissertation itself had helped Madjerin refine some of her own ideas and that had also aided her presentation. Madelaine Jordan had appeared completely at ease with Madjerin's model of the brain and all aspects of the computer operation. The idea of the existence of basic personality ID wave functions had drawn skepticism at first. Madjerin's various hopes as to how to improve the practicality of her procedures had brought the most objections, and also the most constructive discussion of the meeting.

An expert in the technology of instrumentation, Madelaine Jordan had suggested a range of solutions to minor problems that, in the aggregate, could improve the procedure enormously. A complete revision of the scan mechanisms would reduce the time needed to make a useful mapping. More efficient methods of recording and programming could be implemented with new Talbot Instrument devices, including an electronic graph reader. Time, energy and size could all be minimized. Only the major problem of impulse reception remained to be solved. On that she would pursue Carleton's path.

Hank listened without a word as his enthusiastic, little companion chattered away like her computer terminal. He didn't understand three words of what she was saying, but he knew that she felt successful and happy. He also grasped that Madelaine Jordan, Stapler's "Iron Maiden", had been interested enough to offer useful suggestions. Always a good sign, he thought.

When she got her grant, far larger than anything she had previously hoped for, Madjerin said that she was going to get a new apartment and a car and buy Hank a new suit.

The one he wore had only barely survived a decade of prior use.

And, she insisted, she would develop the mapping machine to the point that it could be installed in every hospital, to record every patient's and every baby's ID waves and in every police station, to check them, just as the National Crime Foundation had hoped. Maybe she would even get Carleton back to help her develop more beneficial ways of using the procedures: Detection of psychological disorders; evaluation of sleeping cycles and the mechanism of dreams; even the modification of aberrant personality.

Hank Washington marveled at the complexity of her dreams. The grandiose designs she dreamed of held little appeal for Hank. He assumed that they were good for her, but he couldn't see devoting himself to helping cops catch thieves or shrinks evaluate dreams. Clean floors attracted him more than the achievement of an inexpensive, simple mind reading device. He had no interest in what others were thinking or why they thought as they did. He was just happy that Madjerin would be able to stay at the Talbot for as long as she wanted.

Only recently, that minute perhaps, had the self-sufficient, contented Henry Washington come to recognize how much he needed the diminutive research scientist across the table. It was a new feeling for him and, though it scared him a bit, he kind of liked it.

~ ~ ~

George was returning the phone to the cradle when Carolyn Jordan entered the study. She gazed about the room as though remembering each corner and every volume in the bookcase. She moved to the desk and ran her hand over the smoothly polished surface. Tom Jordan had never accepted glass or Formica desk tops. One of his few demands was that the old mahogany desk given him by his Uncle Harley

Talbot, be polished every day. She was glad that George continued to have it done.

"Who was that?" she asked, assuming it was her daughter.

George hesitated to disappoint her. "Heloise Carpenter," he said. "She has a problem of some sort with the electric bill."

"Isn't she Stapler's secretary?" Carolyn asked, conjuring the face of the almost perfect young lady Stapler had somehow seduced into working for him.

"Yes," he replied

The face and the name came together. "Yes, I remember her. The only nice thing about that office of Stapler's." She had visited Stapler's suite only once, to sign the separation agreement he had drawn up, but the scene was clearly imprinted in her memory. "Whatever has she to do with the electric bill? I thought you handled it."

He had, of course, before Mr. Jordan died, but Madelaine had turned such details over to Heloise, in order, she had said, to keep some sort of official record. George shook his head. "Not anymore. And I am rather glad of it now. The latest one is apparently beyond contemplation."

"Oh?" She restrained that uncomfortable curiosity one retains about the running of an organization one once commanded.

"She wanted to know if I could think of any unusual events in the last month," George said with a trace of a smile.

Mrs. Jordan felt ashamed of herself for laughing in Tom's study, but she couldn't help it. "Did you think of any, George?"

For a moment he contemplated, for effect. Thoughtfully, he said, "Not that would use much electricity."

They both laughed. One of the few things in the house Carolyn Jordan had enjoyed over the last score of years, George's sense of humor rarely failed to amuse her. Remarkably, she mused, George had maintained an affection, or a regard, at least, for all the members of a divided household. More than once, Carolyn had cried on his shoulder, either to gain his support or simply to lean on it, she could not remember which, perhaps both. God knows she had needed both.

"How have you been, George? It's been a long time since I've seen you," she said, sitting on the shining desk.

The butler smiled. Her habit of perching on that sacred desk had been carefully developed first to tease and, ultimately, to annoy, her husband. "As well as can be expected for a lonely, old man, Mrs. Jordan," he said. "I miss Mr. Jordan, of course, but having Madelaine here helps keep me on my toes. All I need is someone to serve."

"To make your life complete, then, I have returned for you to serve," she said humbly. "With both Madelaine and me in the house, you'll need all ten toes."

"Assuming that Madelaine will not force you to sleep in the garage," George suggested, alluding to a familiar tactic of Mrs. Jordan in dealing with a strong-willed, teen-aged Madelaine.

After the smile faded from her face, Mrs. Jordan asked quietly, "How was he before he died, George?" The question did not come out as clearly as she wanted. It sounded too sentimental to suit her. She tried again. "I hope he was happy. Not too lonely, I mean. He was always, a little, but I was afraid he might be terribly so, with everyone gone."

"Mr. Jordan had little alternative," George observed. "His daughter had few words for him and all of those related to business. You were gone, of course. John wouldn't lift a pen. And his friends and associates were dying around him." George paused, to maintain his composure. He had watched as the man deteriorated over the years and the memory disturbed him.

For Mrs. Jordan, tears had always been her most effective and most used, tool. Sometimes, however, they were real.

She bowed her head so that George would not notice, or at least not feel compelled to say anything sympathetic.

George went on, if only to spare them both silence. "Springtime didn't help. Usually, he felt renewed in springtime. This year, he had to cut back on expenses at the Talbot. That broke his heart. The young researchers without the money to continue their work, he once said, reminded him of himself in his twenties when he didn't have the money for medical school. Still, he had to sacrifice them to keep the place open."

Without looking up or steadying her voice, Carolyn demanded, "Where was Madelaine through all this?"

"New York," he said with a sigh. "In New York, saving Talbot Instruments from receivership. That provided him some solace. If that child had been lost that would have made him very unhappy."

A wicked laugh forced itself out of Carolyn's throat. Talbot Instruments had been her husband's devil, his obsession. Created by Harley Talbot, Carolyn suspected, for the sole purpose of shackling Tom to him, TI had consumed Tom's life and, consequently, dominated her own.

The development work of Talbot Instruments had necessarily kept Tom Jordan out of the war, but in return, it had exacted a terrible price. "It bled us all for years," she hissed. "It took me too long to understand. Why didn't Tom do something?"

George looked at her sympathetically. "It is not important now," he said. "Mr. Jordan would never tell me why he did what he did. His motivation, I suppose, is one mystery he felt better left to him."

"God, we used to fight over that," she recalled. "That and Madelaine."

"He enjoyed seeing her picture in so many magazines," George said, changing the subject.

Rubbing her finger over one cheek, she said, "How could a homely girl like Madelaine ever become a cover girl?"

"Force of personality," George suggested.

Carolyn laughed. "When did she get that nose fixed?"

"She had to. It was broken," George explained.

"Boxing no doubt," Carolyn guessed. "What a nut she is. She is impossible with the press, from what I've read. You understand her better than I ever could, George. What's wrong with her?"

George pondered the question, the same one that Thomas Jordan and he had reviewed so frequently in the past. "I don't know. What ever Madelaine gets simply isn't good enough for her. Even the things she wants most and tries hardest for. Nothing satisfies her."

"She's always been like that," Carolyn said.

"I suppose."

Carolyn Jordan thought back, as she rarely did. Perhaps she was wrong. There had been a time when Madelaine, little Madelaine, had been different. "George, do you remember when she was little? Very young. About three or so?"

George nodded. It seemed that he was remembering a different person. "Madelaine was very good with her father."

"Yes, with Tom. Not with me," she said sadly. "Never with me." She shrugged and started to leave the room. At the door she stopped and stood staring back at the butler. "We're all lonely, eventually. Aren't we, George?"

He smiled as kindly as he could. "Only on the inside, Mrs. Jordan," he replied.

Wearing a frail smile, she nodded and went out to the stairs. George watched her as she trudged up the long curving staircase. She had come back, he reasoned, not to fight for more money. She had plenty of that. She had also had the kind of glamorous, carefree life she had always dreamed of. Yet she had come back, back to a house in which she had suffered, back to a daughter who hated her, back to the past that aged her.

They all expected that she would come back to fight Madelaine for control of what was left of Thomas Jordan. And surely she had. But George now wondered if that meant the house, the money, the corporation. Maybe there was something else left she wanted even more than those things: Thomas Jordan's love. Carolyn Jordan may have begun learning where she would have to go to find it.

CHAPTER NINE

The air was swirling about her head, long, wavy locks flying in her eyes. Madelaine found herself smaller, a child perhaps. Yes, a child. The world spun round and round the swing, but she did not get dizzy.

Clearer. The house stopped moving. The doors were open wide. She rolled out of a tire that hung from clouds. She continued rolling, down a hill that was flat, toward the house. The house, all stone and soot and majesty.

Inside, her mother screamed, Close the doors! Close them all. The flies, keep out the flies! All around her Madelaine felt them: Large gray-flannel flies, as big as brief-cases, and made of paper. She didn't see them. She never saw them. But she heard their leather-heeled footsteps, she smelled their burning cigars.

In and out, they went, invisible and whispering behind his doors. Only her mother shouted, one step ahead, slimming door after door as Madelaine reached for the knobs. That didn't stop the buzzing flies, of course, never the flies. But Madelaine, so small, so weak, could not open the towering oaken doors.

When her tears would not dissolve the door, Madelaine hammered with her fists, breaking the strong wood. She was larger now and the house responded, opening one door here, then another. Her mother ran from one to the other, slamming each as it opened.

The doors! The doors! her mother shrieked louder than ever. Stay out! Stay out of my house!

Suddenly, the flies were not there anymore. And the house was empty. Still, Madelaine could not keep them open, the doors. She was growing taller, taller. She was bigger than the house. Almost. She decided to tear the house down with her huge, ugly hands. The house would not stand. She would build another one, her own, invisible. One she could carry closer to her. She screamed and screamed without saying anything, her back turned to the old, crumbling house.

Like breathing, the screaming puffed her up, a balloon. She looked 360 degrees and stopped yelling. There was no way to stop. Her string that had been tied to the house hung thin and frail in the growing gale. Below her the house was gone. She was high in the clouds, climbing all the time, expanding painfully with the altitude. She would burst. Who would see? No one to see her explode.

At last. At last, hands were on her, stopping her. She did feel them compressing her, squeezing the gases out of her. Real. Too real. The hands were real. Rick? He was fuzzy, but he was there.

Hi, Ricky, she thought

She heard something. A voice, his voice?

Or her voice?

Hello, Maddy, said the smile. Yes, Rick's voice. She felt her head falling slowly to the pillow, throbbing as it went. Her room. She was awake. Her room at home, the deserted old mansion her father had left her to.

George was there, pumping up her pillow, as he always did whenever she was sick. And who was that face? The police were there! Monty, Montgomery. He had a funny, scared look. And Rick, Stapler.

Rick's eyes were open so wide. He usually looked so stern or sly, trying to fool her. Not this time, as he bent low to move her hair, her sad, short hair, from her eyes. He looked across her face from just above her lips, over her funny nose.

She felt a hand, as she looked at the ceiling with its carved antique beams. It no longer floated away from her. Clear, precise, Madelaine, obvious with details and knot holes. The hand brushed her cheek again, from the west side of her head.

Turning to look, her head hurt, her eyes saw a dense London pea-souper. Pittsburgh. She was back in Pittsburgh. Through the haze was a subtly drying face with a short woman below it. Kind, sad eyes gazed into Madelaine's, familiar but not very. Not like that. The mouth that did not speak, smiled timidly, like her mother did sometimes. Of course.

Hello, Mother, Madelaine said so slowly that it felt like molasses in her ears. She didn't like molasses If possible the expression that hurt the eyes, deepened and far away.

The mouth lied with its gay smile. Hello, you silly–you silly prima donna, it said.

Madelaine felt her temples pulsate, as she recalled that her father had called her that, with his silly wink. She spoke only to banish the pain. He's dead, isn't he, Mom?

As usual, her mother cried. Madelaine did not like that. Don't cry. Please, she pleaded. It's not fair.

~ ~ ~

Her other ear heard Rick say, We were worried about you, Maddy. You've been out for a couple of hours.

She turned, pounding eyes searching for him. Rick? No, instead she saw the cop. Montgomery seemed ridiculously relieved. She laughed at his expression. Hello, Sarge, she said. Were you worried too?

That sheepish grin running quickly across the thick, dry lips surprised her with its answer. She wondered why he cared, he was in homicide. It wasn't his fault, either. He had made her mad, but that was her fault.

The forty years of cop seemed too embarrassed to speak, turning instead to Rick Stapler. Richmond S.

After gaining the suddenly grim Richmond S's nod, Montgomery did talk. Of course, Miss Jordan. I felt responsible.

Even with her head rocking back and forth Madelaine knew people, but the lie didn't bother her.

Melton, the scrawny Redhead, was dead. Like a bolt of heavy fabric, her head unfurled the memory of the Club, the news. Like her father, her friend. Red was dead like her father.

I'm all right now, she said grimacing. She struggled against her weighty, broad shoulders and raised herself off of the quilt. Hard against her hair, she felt the headboard bounce. I interrupted you before Sergeant. If you'll give me a minute or two, I will join you all downstairs for a brandy and the rest of your aborted report. If you have time.

The detective gave a bravely deceptive smile. Of course, he said.

They trouped out, glancing her way as if to check on her condition. She nodded reassuringly to get them out. They had to go.

She hated being weak, defenseless. She was strong and wanted them to know. She had always been stronger and taller and smarter.

Bracing herself for the now familiar pain, she rose from the rumpled bed. A thorough dousing with cold water of her face and wrists chased the unconsciousness. She brushed the wet short hair away from her face, behind her ears. It obstructed her view of things. Substituting a white and gold pants suit for her stuffy, damp business outfit, she examined herself in the mirror.

The lines of her clothes accented the length of her figure, its only striking feature. She appeared taller and more important. A close look at the eyes revealed none of the redness she had expected, only pewter irises in the dim glow of dusk.

She paused before the glass, briefly, to inspect her nose the handiwork of three surgeons and $7500. Her fear of a collapse of the artificial structure once again proved misplaced. The defiant product of science thrust forward, so acute and so regular that it still amused her.

The misshapen lump that had formerly dominated her face, would still have distorted her life had force not intervened to rearrange it for her. Stapler, he of the vicious left cross, had caught her camel of a nose full that day. Even now she laughed, as she had through the pain and blood, thinking of they way her old nose had looked, trying to make a sudden left turn off of her face.

Now, it jutted out, ambivalent toward the long upper that had once maneuvered it up and down as she spoke. It stood alone before her, thin and proud, or maybe a little vain. It made her look even bigger than before, too big for ordinary woman.

Drawing herself to full height, Madelaine made the mirror admit that she was not remotely ordinary. She rested her set of white fingers on the narrow waist, both accentuated by the juxtaposition. That she was not beautiful did not make the least difference anymore. Not to her or to the maggots that feasted on the carrion that her father had left behind. Limb by limb she would restore life to the beast Stone by stone with her graceful, adept hands, she would rebuild the House of Jordan & Talbot,

Madelaine and the mirror nodded approval. She turned on the low heel of her shoe and headed downstairs to the attention of the others.

~ ~ ~

They had used to accuse Carleton of ignoring details which was only true of insignificant details. The important aspects of his projects he knew he had mastered. At first, of course, many things had gone wrong, but they had made him start from scratch, without the equipment he had used at the Talbot. Any system required debugging. His early mistakes had shown the way to refinements. They had cost him time and money, but that was at the beginning. Now, only a month later, he could show that he had the system down to such a point that he could be ready to act with only a few hours preparation.

He hadn't intended for it to be so soon, but the Madelaine Jordan interview had inspired him to be done with Madjerin. That was all right, considering that she would not tax his mind much. The machine, too, was pretty much ready to go. Only the final testing was left.

Sitting beside the TI 125 in the fruit cellar, Carleton affixed the single suction-contact to his forehead. Madjerin's contact method had advantages of simplicity for testing purposes. One contact would tell him whether his machine was working properly.

He typed several commands into the keyboard. He then placed a cassette with his name on it into the auxiliary unit, a TI Telcom 25, and typed more commands. After a second, the rewired TV set in the other corner of the room lit up.

Having checked the patterns for similarity, Carleton patted the machine on the top and varied the output setting. The screen brightened and then dimmed in response. Grinning, Carleton removed the contact and began his review of the non-technical aspects involved in preparation.

He had already called Madjerin, ostensibly to ask how the interview with Madelaine Jordan had gone. Then he had arranged to meet her and her janitor friend, Hank Washington, at the grubby restaurant that unnatural duo liked so much. That should do it.

With a single motion, Carleton seized his coat and switched off the light. Once the lock had thudded closed, he ran up the stairs. He wanted to catch Madjerin before 9:00 o'clock. That was the best time.

Everything had worked out so well that he hated to be near the end of his project. Still, he reminded himself, it did not have to stop with Madjerin. Certainly, there were many great things to do eventually, but his machine would assure that no one would deny him his right to success again. And, too, he admitted to himself, it was an indulgence of his ego. It deserved it, he decided.

As a matter of habit, he checked the coat pocket and cursed.

All the technical matters he had mastered, he still could not remember the funny, little ingredient that made it all work. He turned and descended to the lab. Even in the dark, he knew where to find it. He always kept his special, plastic bottles of "Sweet Tooth" on the top shelf of the preserve closet.

~ ~ ~

"You will pardon me, Sergeant Montgomery," Madelaine said, "if I sound skeptical. It seems to me that you are searching for something that clearly does not exist."

Montgomery's coarse features shone with confidence. He hardly expected any intelligent person to believe him right off. "Miss Jordan," he said with a patience derived from truth. "I have already found what I've been looking for. There is a link between all of these men who have died recently."

Offering his own two bits of wisdom, Stapler snorted. "Are you kidding? Monty, if all you're looking for is a link, you might qualify as the missing one."

Not even a rag sopped in gasoline could have wiped the glow from Monty's face. "The missing link is exactly what I've been after," he explained. "But you are closer to it than me."

Thunderstruck, Stapler snapped, "What the hell is that supposed to mean?"

Dramatically looking over each one in the room, as though he were a camera filming a murder mystery, Montgomery said "Of all the people in this room, Rick, old buddy, you are the one closest to this little discovery of mine. The character of each death, I have found, has been ridiculously similar. Each man sat on the Board of Trustees of the Talbot Research Hospital. Each man was wealthy and important. Each man died of a heart attack. Each was asleep at the time."

Madelaine's patience did not extend to melodrama. "Sergeant, she said from behind her father's desk, "Are you auditioning for something, or will you tell us what you have found?"

"I apologize, Miss Jordan," Monty said with a guilty shrug. "You're right. I am playing this up. I don't get the chances you do to prance about on center stage."

Madelaine sliced her face with a smile. "I'm not surprised. Your style is a little too ponderous to allow for prancing."

Since everyone was taking a turn, George spoke up. "We would all very much like to hear what is so significant, Sergeant. I am in accord with your theories and am especially interested."

Monty shot him a look of appreciation. "Thanks, George," he said. "Okay. One more thing seemed to be missing. Not motive or persons. We need them, too, mind you, but not at this stage. What we needed was something to indicate that Nature's was not the only hand involved in these deaths. Today, I think, I have uncovered the element that we needed to establish that."

The listeners sat nearer the edges of their seats and Monty reveled in the drama of his little speech. They would all, in a moment, think he was crazy. "Mr. Jordan was my entrée into this case and I felt he was also my key. I was right, but not entirely in the way I expected. Of all the men who died, Mr. Jordan was the one who moved Dr. Morex to suggest a full-dress autopsy. What he found brought out something that had been bothering him, subconsciously, I guess."

"The sleeping powder," George suggested.

"The sleeping powder," Monty agreed.

Madelaine frowned. "I still don't understand. Even though Father didn't use it ordinarily, it still didn't cause his death. It was a heart attack, plain and simple."

"Don't throw me off, Miss Jordan," Monty said. "You are absolutely right. But something was wrong. When Melton died, he too had been doped. Now, that was not so unusual for him, except that he was unintentionally doped. And he was doped at the University Club, not long after I left my pal Stapler there alone to fortify himself for a dinner with you."

"Why do I feel," Stapler said shaking his head, "that my name comes up in all the wrong places in this story?"

"I use you only as a reference point," Montgomery replied. "In any case, someone doped Melton's coffee just as they had your father's, Jordan. And they did it with this." With a flourish, Monty brought forth Melton's little dispenser of Dennison Foods Sweet Tooth.

Mrs. Jordan came out of her shell in the corner. "Sweet Tooth?"

Everyone exchanged glances that seemed to recommend a padded wagon for the detective. Of them, only George understood the significance of Montgomery's discovery. Madelaine examined the cop for signs of fatigue. Stapler looked for evidence of a leak in his friend's cranium. Mrs. Jordan did not look at all.

Montgomery savored the effect of his surprise. "Yep!" he agreed triumphantly. "Every single man who had died used this junk on the day of his death. At least so far, my information points that way. And in this little plastic bottle, there is enough dope to guarantee sweet dreams to an elephant for a week."

His revelation forced Madelaine to believe him, but it still puzzled her. Her mouth barely moved when-she asked, "So what?"

Montgomery had prepared for that question, but he had not prepared a very good answer. "That, Miss Jordan, completely eludes me."

"You think that they were all doped?" Rick asked.

"Yes," Monty said with a shrug. "I've got exhumation orders being processed to find out. Only Jordan and Melton were autopsied." Only the shudder of Mrs. Jordan reminded Montgomery of where he was. "I'm sorry, Mrs. Jordan. Miss Jordan. I didn't mean to be so damn rude."

Madelaine blinked once. "You needn't worry about us," she said. "Neither of us was that close to him."

Her mother's gasp contradicted Madelaine's bloodless statement. Carolyn Jordan turned away from the self-assured figure commanding the room. She had never really understood or liked Madelaine, but she despised her now.

The others simply wondered at Madelaine who did not acknowledge the attention. "If you think you are onto something, Sergeant, I think you are just simply wrong. People die, sometimes in clusters. Perhaps, usually in clusters. Until you can come up with some nexus between the so-called doping and the heart attacks, you will have to accept my complete inattention. I have too much work to do to tolerate grandstanding on the part of an aging Ellery Queen." With those words and a tired motion, Madelaine rose and left the study for her room.

Deflated by her even-toned scorn, Montgomery slumped into a chair. He had expected her to reject his theory at first, but he had hoped that she would listen to more of what he had to say. It struck him, however, as he slouched there, that she was right: He had no more to say. Madelaine Jordan, he thought, had effectively cut to the heart of the matter. He had no reason to suspect any connection at all except that he had to. It couldn't be the way it seemed.

The remaining three people in the room felt very uncomfortable. Madelaine had cast a pall over an otherwise grim day. Each in his or her turn, mulled over her rare ability to cause gray to become black.

Her mother had the privilege of breaking the silence. "She is a monster!"

Even George did not object.

Rick laughed. "Don't brag about your own offspring," he said. "It is very bad form."

"Doesn't she care about anything?" her mother asked desperately.

Stapler felt just morose enough to take it out on the woman he viewed as Mr. Jordan's premiere tormentor. "Madelaine merely spoke the truth, as usual," he said with venom. "Neither you nor she gave a shit in the sewer about him. She can admit it. Why can't you?"

Carolyn Jordan surprised herself with her reflection. She should have been enraged or crying by the time she spoke, but she was only very sad. "You don't understand everything, Mr. Stapler. I wish you did. Both of us would feel much better for it." She smiled feebly and departed for a quiet walk in the garden. She wanted to be alone, to get used to it.

~ ~ ~

Hank was already asleep beside her. Poor Hank. He had been up longer than she had. Two days without sleep had made them both giddy long before they had gotten to the wine. Coupled with the heady promise of the day, Madjerin and Hank had spurned all control. It had been the best day of her life.

That warm feeling ran up and down her body again as she looked at Hank sleeping so peacefully. Whatever their relationship had been, there was no question of what it would be in the future. Hank wanted her to marry him and she could not wait.

Despite the incredible excitement of the day, the length of it began to tell on the frail constitution of the overworked Madjerin. Only the coffee, which Carleton had insisted she have before driving home, kept her eyes half open. She wanted to stay awake forever and savor the dreams of the future with eyes wide and alert. Carleton, uncharacteristically, had painted a dazzling picture of her potential success when he dropped by the restaurant to congratulate her. Her head still swam.

He told her that Stapler had as much as told him that she would definitely get a grant. She giggled, half awake, half asleep. She had assured her former assistant that he would get a grant of his own, to follow the path of his choosing. They would then race to a Nobel Prize. Over coffee, the pair's mutual admiration vented itself to an extent that caused Hank to laugh at them so hard that he spilled his brandy.

After all of the drinking at dinner, Madjerin had refused to allow Hank to take the wheel of his oft-reconstructed Dodge. Instead, she had negotiated the route to her apartment herself and then had insisted that Hank stay with her, rather than trying to drive on alone.

The result of her concern had been the most wonderful moment of her life. Just before she fell asleep, Madjerin wondered if she would be lucky enough to dream about it. She was nearly convinced that it had been a dream in the first place.

Once she was asleep, however, she did dream about it. And, subsequently, the whole beautiful day re-ran itself for her several times. In her dreams, she assured herself one thing: That tomorrow would bring more of the same.

CHAPTER TEN

It was well after ten o'clock when Heloise shut off the lights of the penthouse office in the Haller Building. Rick's phone call fifteen minutes before had informed her that he would not be returning to the office that evening. He was at Madelaine's.

A long frustrating day had Heloise in a rare, bad mood.

6:30 to 10:00 PM, she had been alone, working on the Jordan estate. Her only company had been the telephone, and it was a foul-mouthed, inconsiderate companion. It conveyed nothing but bad news, disruption, delay and finally death.

Her husband, J.J., had failed to call from the doctors' as he had promised. The check-up was an important one to them both, pertaining as it did to the recovery of the use of his right leg. Ever since his accident, five years before, J.J. had been struggling bravely to restore his once-athletic mobility.

It had tied her, them, down for what seemed a lifetime. J.J. had been unable go work and his beautiful temperament had eroded to near-bitterness Heloise had devoted those five years go earning the money and, much more difficult, buoying her husband's flagging spirits. Without Rick, neither of them would have survived.

The time, she felt, was coming when everything would change. By a recent stroke of luck, if J.J. cleared his physical, he could start work in three months with his old employer, Speyer Refining. Rick's practice was falling apart and, if the tenants continued go terminate their leases in the Haller Building, he would not be able go keep going.

Her worst fear, however, was that Rick had become completely dependent on Madelaine Jordan to keep afloat. Josh Einberg, calling during the day over the changing attitude of Francis DeJong, had been shocked at Rick's dilemma. Madelaine's opposition inside J & T, and particularly Einberg, looked at Rick as their lever, if not their leader. Einberg had nearly wailed on the phone when informed of Rick's financial trouble, which led go a late call from Susan Hill, the beautiful Vice President of Tylton Equipment. Rick's loyal surrogate on the Board of Directors of J &T, Susan Hill had demanded to know the status of the battle against Madelaine, which she would have to lead in any upcoming meeting. She had wanted to know if Einberg's fears had any validity.

If so, she had said unhappily, she would have to desert Rick for Madelaine and accept a proffered promotion to the doomed Einberg's position.

Heloise had listened in amazement as Susan Hill told of Madelaine's not-very-secret plan to fire Josh Einberg, her father's most trusted aide, and, Madelaine claimed, replace him with her worst, truest enemy, Susan Hill.

If Susan believed that, she was in for a shock.

Acknowledging that opinion, Susan Hill had promised to keep the coalition organized and cool. More importantly, Susan had put Heloise in touch with her investment department, from which a loan for the Haller Building could be made available. But only in a pinch.

Then came Rick's call. He had gotten tied up at Madelaine's, he had said, and could not make it back to the office as planned. His explanation that Madelaine had taken ill had a hollow ring to Heloise's ears. Not that she doubted him, but the thought of it bothered Heloise,

He had gratuitously wished her goodnight and rung off, after which Heloise, for some reason, had knocked the telephone off of the desk. When she left, it was still on the floor.

~ ~ ~

Madelaine's unending task of preparing the inventory of her father's assets was interrupted by a knock on her bedroom door. Behind the rap, she found George Bestral, a small box in hand, wearing a haggard, tentative expression. "What's wrong, George?" she demanded.

As he entered, George did not look at Madelaine, searching out instead the chair by her dressing table. He took the seat with the air of an old man expecting each movement to be his last. For several seconds, he just sat staring at the carved wooden box, his head drooping in a way Madelaine had never seen before.

She stood gazing at him with curiosity and concern. George alone, perhaps, could stir the emotion of concern. In place of her father, George had helped guide her through the tumultuous period of childhood. Unlike everyone else, George meant something to her.

When George looked up at her, finally, she looked paler than usual, less tall. The etched lines of her face had become more muted despite the harshly bright light of the room. The shadows of her deep-set eyes appeared darker, the depressions in her cheeks more severe

It was a confusing sight to George. "Do you mean the things you say, Madelaine?" he asked in a forced whisper.

Slowly she stretched back to full height, but her face remained unnaturally wan. "How do you mean, George?" With only a brief, rhetorical pause, she continued. "You refer, I take it, to what I said downstairs. About Father?"

George nodded. "You were wrong about your mother. I no longer know about you."

She smiled, a little disappointed. "Ah, but George, you are supposed to know me best of all."

"Sometimes," he said, swallowing his words. "Sometimes, I think that Rick Stapler has a better understanding of you. That's funny, isn't it? I've known you for each of your twenty-eight years."

Madelaine broke her pose and approached him. "It doesn't seem funny." In fact, it made her a little unhappy.

"Twenty-eight years," he repeated

"And for how many of those years did you like me?"

As though he had always expected that very question, asked so bluntly, George answered, "Not all of them. No. You were like my own, Maddy, but I couldn't honestly say that I always 'like' you. You didn't want that."

In one effortless movement, Madelaine sat on the floor beside him. From that position she looked up at him. He looked the same, older maybe, but the same as he had when she used to sit on his lap. "I don't mind," she said softly.

"You have made yourself very difficult, Maddy," he said sadly. He brushed the side of her head with his dry, stiff hand. "You made yourself whatever you are today. Your mother calls it a monster. Perhaps she is right."

Unconsciously, Madelaine leaned toward his hand as it caressed her cheek.

"We have always exchanged compliments, Mother and I," she said deliberately. "It's strange, George, but with all that there was here, to go around, we fought over every single thing. Large and small. And it's happening again." She thought a moment before adding, "We have always hated each other. My first thought was how much I hated her. Did you know that?"

"Sometimes," he said, "I think that hatred is your only human feature. It makes me sick, Madelaine. As it did your father."

She pulled away from him. "Oh, did it? Father was sick long before I got this way," she snapped. The sound of her voice shocked her and she relented. "I mean, he had plenty of other troubles to worry about besides me. I wasn't the worst of them, either."

"To him, to me," George replied, "yes, I believe you were."

His hand on her shoulder prevented her from getting up. She wanted to move, to stand up. His words made her nervous, she had to move. Standing, she could listen better to him. She was tall enough to withstand anything, smart enough. She had always been.

"It is time," George said firmly, his hand pressing down on her. "It is time for you to listen to me, if only for the last time."

Madelaine felt trapped. Her mother had always held her down, surrounded her with arms, grasped with hands, to trap her, to trap everyone. She had learned, Madelaine had: Those arms, more than the tears, the smiles, they were her mother's weapon.

"Your father and I used to talk about you," George went on. "No topic made him more unhappy. He shouldn't have expected, perhaps, that you would be like other daughters. You have never been like others your own age, or any age."

"Should I be?" Madelaine retorted.

He continued as though he had not heard her. "Your disdain for everything and everyone around you, it wasn't like that at first, but it grew to the point of ugliness, Madelaine. Even to those of us who loved you."

Her laugh was harsh. Ugliness, she thought. She hadn't had far to go for that. She had been born with it. As for love, well, that she had managed to avoid somewhere along the line. She did not want the horrible possessiveness that they called "love."

She had seen it: Her mother's grasping, clutching, so-called love for her brother, for her father. Madelaine, at least had been spared that "love." Her brother? He spent her first five years abusing Madelaine and the next fifteen fleeing her. She hadn't seen him in eight years.

And then there was her father, the loving husband and father, the loving business man. It hadn't taken long before she had seen through him. He had belonged to his company and his wife, wrapped in their arms not hers.

That was all right with Madelaine. She had herself and that would have to do. From an early age it was clear that only her own resources were available to her. Over the last twenty-three years she had made damn sure that those were enough.

"Go to hell, George," she suggested coldly.

The old man released her shoulder with a heavy sigh. Automatically, Madelaine sprang up. She stretched and walked to the door. Opening it for him, she felt regret stirring inside her. She stopped him before he went out.

Looking for something in his tired eyes, she said, "George, I'm sorry. You deserve better than me for a daughter."

George Bestral returned her gaze with sorrow for a moment, placed the strange wooden box in her hand and left the room.

When the door had closed, softly, Madelaine felt her knees weaken. She had obviously not recovered from her black-out at the University Club. Her eyes had gone bleary again and her hands shook. The box George had left behind shook, too, as she stared at it.

It was old, finely carved wood. Madelaine felt her stomach tighten as she opened it. The waltz it played filled her head, as the tiny wooden figures plied their instruments inside. Had she given it to her father, or had he given it to her? She could not remember. In either case, she had it back.

~ ~ ~

The scotch had been empty for over an hour; the Jack Daniel's had but a few ounces to go, but that would have ended up on the rug. Stapler and Montgomery elaborately mourned the passing of each bottle. It didn't seem proper that they be left without such good company at so early an hour.

"I should have warned you," Stapler admitted glumly. "Madelaine Jordan will drive you to drink."

Montgomery, his head propped up against Stapler's sofa, nodded. "Tardy, Ricky," he slurred. "Your warning is tardy."

"Sorry," Rick offered apologetically. "It is, however, your own fault. As we say."

"How does your intricate, little mind figure that?" Montgomery asked politely.

"You tackled too much woman, you clown of a detective."

"Is she a woman?" Montgomery wondered, as though the idea had not occurred to him before.

Stapler lifted his glass. "I can vouch for it!"

"How?" Montgomery summoned curiosity that he was not conscious of possessing. "Have you vouched on her yourself?"

"I have my sources," Rick replied, coyly. "Indirect, but very authoritative and sincere."

"Whom?" Monty asked, holding onto the "M".

"Whom else?" Stapler asked rhetorically. "Madelaine whom. That's whom."

Montgomery gargled when he meant to chuckle. "I believe it! Hermaphroditic! I noticed that she was all wrapped up in herself." He felt amusing only when drunk.

"No, no," Rick retorted. "Listen, you dumb cop. She used to tell me, really, that she was one. A woman, I mean. But she wouldn't let me touch her. Everyone else in town can, probably, but not me."

"Bullshit!" Montgomery commented.

"Oh, yeah? She's not as frigid as she looks, she tells me," Stapler replied.

"Do you believe that crap?"

"Nope."

Montgomery nodded hard for emphasis, too hard and slipped out of position. "Good," he said, lying flat on the floor. "I had a wife like that once."

Stapler could not visualize Montgomery with a woman at all. "You? A wife? Was she really frigid?"

"No, damn it," Montgomery explained. "Full of crap! She doesn't like my job."

"Tell her to quit."

"She already did," Montgomery stated before passing out.

Stapler glared at the unconscious detective. "Wake up, you son-of-a-bitch! I'm not through with Madelaine." He shook his guest very hard, with no success. Not wanting to be alone, he squeezed his eyes shut, pushed the room away and collapsed. It was better that way.

~ ~ ~

The strong arm enclosed her again, pressing her close to his body. The room was hazy and bright. Madelaine Jordan and her lawyer, Rick Stapler, sat at a table drawing up the papers to sign her grant. Madjerin meant to wave to them, but Hank did not free her arms and she didn't care.

Outside, a new car sat in front of a new apartment in a new building. Inside, wall-to-wall carpets spread out beneath them. Hank's new suit lay rumpled at the foot of the large luxurious bed. It was a suit of tails. A simple wedding dress lay beside the tails, brilliantly white.

Carleton was there, too. He began to look over the charts of the machines. Telling her that she had been right all along, that he was sorry for doubting her. Madjerin forgave him and told him to come back and work with her if he wanted. She had enough money now.

Something went wrong all of a sudden. Carleton pointed to a door opening under the carpet. With a terrible sound, like tearing flesh, the rug ripped open. A figure climbed out, wearing a satisfied expression. For quite a while, however, the figure was obscure and pulsating. As it took shape, Madjerin heard its name.

In her dreams she peered closely at the face of the shadow, and did not see anything. She recognized the name she heard floating about her head with the pain. It didn't seem right.

Carleton was there already, but... no, he was gone. Carleton, the voice told her, again.

Hello, Carleton, she dreamed. She didn't really welcome his intrusion. It wasn't right. He didn't belong. Not this Carleton was he doing there?

The word "kill" stood out among others jumbled and hissed.

He had come to kill her. Revenge? Justice? The faceless, amorphous Carleton began to move, haltingly at first, then surely, toward her. To kill her. She knew that much

Madjerin became frightened. She knew it was a dream, but she felt it was no longer her dream. She wanted to be happy not dead. She screamed as Carleton neared. She seized Hank lying with her and shook him. Wake up! Hank! Wake up!

~ ~ ~

Feeling Madjerin's tiny hands flailing at him, Hank awoke.

He had to grab her hands to keep her from blinding him. He tried to shake the sleep from his eyes. Poor Madj, he thought, she must be having a hell of a dream. Her clawing did not stop, however, when he tried to bring her out of her nightmare. She was clawing, suddenly at her own neck. The skin reddened and began to bleed as she proved too strong for Hank to control.

~ ~ ~

Carleton's hands were around her throat. Growing stronger and stronger. Madjerin's nails bit deep into his hands, but had no effect. He had a grim, determined expression. He would kill her. There was no escape. I want to wake up! Hank! Wake me up! She could feel that Hank was trying, but he said Hank would have no success. Carleton was only amused, and confident.

~ ~ ~

Hank began to fear that Madjerin would do herself real harm. Her hands were already covered with her own blood by the time he had restrained them. It took all of his strength to keep the tiny dark arms on her chest. He called louder to her, afraid to slap her, afraid to let go of an arm.

Hank, don't hold my hands down! she screamed. Now Carleton commanded her neck without any opposition. His fingers pressed hard and harder, and her head throbbed. Her head hurt, not her neck. She knew he was killing her. Like hunger, there was no escape. She would be dead in a matter of seconds.

With her frail body thrashing from side to side, Hank released her arms and hit her face very hard. Once, twice. Three times arms struck out now, not at Hank, but at the ceiling. Someone in her dream. The expression on her face was one of wild terror. Her mouth opened and shut like that of a human puppet, straining to cry out, able to emit only the sound of trying to scream. She was kicking as though seized by a fit. Whatever she was resisting, Hank knew then that it was horrible and deadly.

~ ~ ~

Carleton expressed some surprise that she took so long to subdue. His hands never changed position, only tightened with each passing minute. He withstood her wildest fury. Hank tried in vain to help. Somehow she knew the battle was hers alone and she was losing. He had compressed her neck to the size of a straw. She could no longer breathe. Please let me up!

~ ~ ~

When Madjerin started gulping helplessly, vainly, for air, Hank gave up trying to hold her down and went to the phone. As he dialed he watched her striking out viciously, leaping about the bed, in a mad struggle with nothing. The phone rang, long, forever. By the time

Hank got an answer, Madjerin had stopped moving. The hideous, desperate gasping had stopped.

Hank dropped the phone and rushed to the side of the bed over which her red, broken-fingered hand hung limply. Hank searched in vain for a pulse. Finally, he put his ear to her breast. The melodic thumping he had enjoyed a few hours before had disappeared. His shaking hands groped for a sign of life.

No breath came from her mouth, grotesquely gaping to reveal the cracked teeth within. Her temples, nearly bursting a minute before lay still. When he opened her eyelid to seep some life, Hank recoiled. He fell to the floor violently sick. By the time the police had broken down the door, Hank Washington had been in shock for five minutes.

CHAPTER ELEVEN

The cold water of the shower had made Stapler's head hurt in a way unlike any he could remember. The ringing of the telephone had cracked it open and the news had lodged deep inside, like a dull knife. As attorney for the Talbot, the police had chosen his enfeebled mind to receive the bludgeon first. He and Montgomery had been dead to the world for hours by the time the police made that decision.

It was 5:40 before he reached the hospital. Hank Washington was still in emergency as the staff struggled with a massive case of shock that had him hovering near death. Madjerin's blood covered corpse lay quietly on a stretcher awaiting the coroner. Stapler could not bear to look at the body, under the red and white cloth

He waited, leaning against the wall, until Montgomery came out of a nearby room. Stapler's daze did not allow him the luxury of observing details. Not until Monty was right next to him could Rick see the expression that bent the cop's face downward. Montgomery took him by the arm and led him into an empty waiting room.

"He'll live, Rick." Monty said, diffidently. "But he's got a problem. He was in her apartment. She has scratched the living daylights out of him and herself."

Stapler tried to look at him to understand what he was saying, if he was kidding. "Hank?"

"Our boys are talking rape and murder, Rick," he said, uncomfortably, having learned on the way to the hospital of Stapler's fondness for the black janitor. "I'll do what I can."

Stapler grabbed Montgomery's arm and squeezed it hard. "Monty, it is ridiculous. They've been mad about each other for months!"

"Yeah," Monty replied. The pit of his stomach was in constant pain these days and it tormented him even more, as he watched the coroner's Kline walk by. He left Rick alone and went to join the assistant coroner, who was examining the body.

The quizzical look on the newcomer's face told Montgomery's ulcer that something was wrong again. Horace Kline bent close to the neck and shook his head. He looked at the fingernails. Again he shook his head. After getting a nod from Hank's doctors, he went into the room in which Hank struggled to recover.

When Kline came back to Madjerin's corpse, Montgomery approached him. They shook hands, needing no introductions.

"Well, Monty," Kline began. "What's the story?" "I was going to ask you."

"Offhand?" Kline shrugged. "The boys around here say asphyxiation. I'll go along with that. Your boys say rape. And I'll go along with that. There was a pretty vicious struggle here."

"Let me take a look," Monty said. He figured he might as well get back into routine. The Jordan deaths had been affecting him too much. A normal murder might do him good, no matter who the characters were.

Kline was talking again as he went to lift the shroud. "They're talking broken fingers. Both knees disjointed. Separated shoulder. Maybe broken neck. The dude looks strong enough. What bugs me is that there's minimal bruising around the neck. Lacerations, plenty. But nothing to indicate significant hand pressure. Hyoid bone's intact. I don't like it, Monty. Tell me what you think,

Montgomery's immediate reaction to the neck region was one of agreement with Kline. He couldn't see the usual discoloration that accompanied strangulation. A fingernail lodged in the skin, yes. Plenty of blood. It was good to see blood again. Bloodless death had begun to haunt him in his sleep. The blood was almost refreshing.

He checked the fingers. Plenty of skin scraped under there.

It was dark, but not as dark as he remembered Hank Washington. Several fingers were broken, a nail missing. Blood remained the most obvious characteristic. Running his hands up her arms from the wrists he felt for the signs of knotted muscles

"We may have a torn muscle," Kline commented. "Pulled the muscle right out, Dr. Inver says. That's his guess."

Monty finally looked at the face. The mouth propped open. It was so twisted that the dark, clay-like face didn't look human, not even for a corpse. The nostrils looked permanently flared. Several surface blood vessels had popped. It reminded Monty too much of Melton. He felt his stomach convulsing. "Have you checked her eyes?" he asked, nagged by grotesque images racing through his throbbing head.

Kline laughed. "Sorry you asked," he said. "The way they're talking around here, I didn't want to take a look. I suppose I should."

They stood on either side of Madjerin's cold, dark head. Kline turned the head slightly toward him and lifted one eyelid. Monty saw a flash of white, before Kline let go, reeling backward. An experienced professional, he caught himself quickly, however, and shuddered off the effects.

Kline's own eyes bored into Montgomery's. The expression read out as suppressed disgust. He breathed deeply twice. "Were you expecting something, Monty?"

Monty lowered his stare to her face. He could see a bump in the eyelid. "I was hoping not," he said hoarsely. He knew he had to look to confirm his suspicions. With a careful, hesitant motion, Montgomery elevated the eyelid.

The jerk of his hand almost tore off the dry flap of skin.

As it happened, it caused the lid to stay partially open. Madjerin's right eye had turned completely around and sat in a pool of blood and clear fluid. Kline lifted the other, to give them an idea of the whole face. The other eye had torn its bindings, as Melton's had, from the side and had turned outward so that the iris was barely evident.

No mask of death, Montgomery thought. It wasn't death at all. It was a look that belonged in nightmares. Jordan, Melton and now a tiny Indian girl, too small to be an adult, too fragile to be painfully wrenched from life. What was happening? What in God's name did this to people?

Kline's expression asked the same question. For along, drawn moment, two hardened surveyors of death gazed at each other in a stupor, begging for some answer, even a lie. Finally, they walked slowly down the hall, in a deliberate, courageous gait to empty themselves of all that they could. The less of them that remained to remember, the better.

~ ~ ~

Preoccupied and tired, Madelaine had agreed to allow Josh Einberg drive her to the hospital. His call had followed Jean Skeffington's by a matter of seconds. Einberg was definitely a very worried man.

The brown and cream Cadillac proved more comfortable than Madelaine had expected. Perhaps she was just tired.

Einberg had spent several minutes explaining away the disastrous financial results at Tylton Machinery. Madelaine had hardly listened, for she was well acquainted with his problems. That was why she intended to fire him as soon as she could. And that would be soon enough, if she could convince him to go along with Francis DeJong in calling a board meeting.

Josh," she said firmly. "It's none of my business what you do over at Tylton. All I can say is that a 1.348 percent return on our investment is not very impressive. I can think of a couple dozen companies we could buy with triple that number."

"Like Speyer?" Einberg asked, defensively. Madelaine's attack on his performance at Tylton was nothing new, but it angered him all the same. And now, he understood, she was toying with Franklin Speyer's ailing petrochemical company.

She shot him a glance before answering. She had reasons for acquiring Speyer Refining that had nothing to do with its profit and loss. On the latter basis, she could not justify her move. "Speyer has potential," she said flatly.

Einberg nodded. "But it doesn't mix with Talbot Instruments," he said carefully. "Not with your recent acquisition policy, anyway." He laughed lightly. "That's the kind of thing that you're criticizing me for."

Madelaine said nothing. She had another idea, a good one, to spring on him at the right moment.

"I have been trying to diversify. The capital spending slump we've just come through almost killed us at Tylton," Einberg explained.

"You don't run a tight ship, Josh. Reorganize," she suggested, reiterating a theme of their past conversations. "And double duty is going to make it more difficult."

The aging executive could see it coming. Madelaine would attempt to threaten, cajole and blackmail him into staying out of the Chair at J & T. As Tom Jordan's closest adviser, Einberg and almost everyone else, considered himself best qualified to succeed his old friend. "Will you fire me if you win?" he asked simply. "And replace me with Susan?"

Madelaine watched the hospital approach. Suddenly, she didn't care what Einberg did for the time being. Except for one thing. "Josh, don't be silly. I want you to stay at J & T, in what capacity, I don't know," she said languidly. "But you are the only one who knows the whole corporation." She smiled to herself. "By the way," she added. "I was examining Tylton's investment portfolio."

"Really?" Einberg asked, surprised. Susan Hill took care of that kind of thing at Tylton, not him. How would Madelaine use it against him?

Madelaine opened the door, pausing before exiting. "Yes. You've gotten pretty deeply into Real Estate, Mortgages and the like. If I were you, I'd avoid any more."

Einberg shrugged. "I hadn't noticed." He decided to throw Madelaine a sop. "I'll order a hold on that kind of thing myself, if you think it's a good idea."

Her smile said what it was supposed to. "It's up to you, Josh. All I want is the J & T Board meeting." But not too soon

We'll see, Einberg thought, congratulating himself on stalling so successfully. "We'll see."

Madelaine strode away, into the hospital, tying up her thoughts on J & T. Stapler did not dare cross her so long as his building was in jeopardy. Since he could no longer get a loan from Tylton, she suspected, his position would get worse. Time was on her side now. Without Rick, and with DeJong wavering, Einberg would come around. She could have her meeting anytime and triumph.

With that to buoy her spirits, Madelaine proceeded to steel herself for the scene in the hospital. Why she had felt compelled to come, she did not know. Neither Madjerin nor Hank Washington were anything to her.

Madelaine spotted Montgomery and headed for him. The ashen-faced detective stood talking to a circle of doctors as she approached. He recognized her immediately and split away.

"Miss Jordan," he said, with cool politeness.

"Where is she?" Madelaine asked. "And where is Stapler?"

Montgomery wondered why she had come. Madelaine Jordan could not have been friendly with either the Indian girl or the janitor. She wasn't friendly with anyone, as far as he knew. Yet, she had come.

Leading her to Madjerin's body, Montgomery explained the few facts he knew. Madelaine's face reflected neither surprise nor concern. She simply continued walking, right up to the corpse. He pulled down the sheet, revealing the body, its eyes closed.

Madelaine had already guessed what she would see, the expression of the body's eyes. The pallor of the detective had told her enough. His body language had suggested that she not look at the dead woman's face.

The combined effect forced Madelaine back several steps. Her eyes shot to Montgomery's, fixed off in space somewhere. She remembered that Montgomery, a man who studied people, had not looked her in the eyes once since she had arrived.

"What do you think about Washington?" she asked calmly.

"He'll be Okay," Monty said. "His memory is shot for now, though. And I'm stuck with a murder/rape charge until it comes back."

She breathed in hard. "Is this the same as the others?"

"The same?" He shook his head. "Not really. Asphyxiation. Strangulation? But it looks the same to me. I don't give a shit what they tell me."

"Where's Rick?" she asked.

Grimly, Montgomery replied, "He's in a daze in the waiting room. He's not used to this kind of thing."

She stared hard at him. His eyes darted away. "Are you?" she demanded.

"Keep him company," Monty suggested harshly. "And don't ask me questions." With that he stomped away and into Hank Washington's room.

In the other direction, Madelaine found the waiting room and Stapler sitting, elbows on knees, looking at the tile floor. Madelaine took the space next to him, without disturbing him. For a few minutes he watched him staring at the floor.

The blank expression reminded her how easily some people become involved with other people. She touched his arm and asked in a low, throaty voice, "Are you all right, Ricky?" It didn't sound like her at all, she thought. Was she affected by all of this as well?

Stapler shuddered at the sound. He shook his head to clear the clutter gathered from the night before and the early morning. Massaging his forehead, he responded, "I'm Okay, Maddy. Thanks."

"Montgomery said that Washington will be all right," she informed him.

"She's not dead then?" he asked, confused.

Madelaine looked stern. "Madjerin? Yes, she is dead. Not even your friend Montgomery can change that. Though I think he'd like to."

Stapler dropped his head. "Madelaine," he said. "You are the smart one. Tell me, what's going on. Every time I look up, someone is dead."

"Death itself is not horrible, Rick." She sounded pontifical, even to herself. "It is the manner in which they are dying that is so dreadful."

He smiled at her, because she was always the same. "Maddy, Maddy. Sometimes, I absolutely love the way you talk. You seem to view us poor mortals from very, very far away." He took her hand. "If I were to drop dead just now, like everyone else, what would you say about me? The same damn thing?"

"Don't be morbid!" she snapped, angry with his presumption. Angry that he was right.

"Why not?" He looked at her for a while. "Seriously."

Madelaine felt decidedly cold. His demanding stare bothered her. She wanted it to stop. "You wouldn't, though, would you? It would be too easy for me, if you did."

"Drop dead?"

She nodded, her face slightly flushed with color.

"What would you say?" he asked again. "'He died. Everybody dies?' Something like that?"

"Probably," she agreed, wondering. What would she say? "Maybe I'd that I'd miss you a little, I think." Her emotionless voice sounded funny mouthing what was almost emotion.

Rick slapped his thighs, feeling restored. "And I think I would miss you, too, Madelaine." He helped her up and she let him. "You are the unchanging in an ever-changing world, Madelaine. You are my brilliant, towering beacon, flashing out your cold gray light to reassure me. Even though you will undoubtedly ruin my career and my life, I think that you are one of two women I would rather not live without."

Madelaine stood with her shoulders angled back and her eyes open in astonishment. He had gone honestly mad.

Stapler took her hand and pulled her after him. "Let's go have some coffee. You look tired."

~ ~ ~

By nine o'clock, Heloise had begun to feel lonely. The drawback of her boss' elaborate suite lay in its spaciousness. The rooms were large and beautifully marbled, but when she was alone in them, as she had been the last several days, Heloise felt a frightening isolation.

She had decorated the office originally in the most intimate way she could, considering Rick's tight budget. To some degree, plants, paintings and even the file cabinets helped mute the ancient formality of the penthouse.

That morning, however, none of her handiwork helped dispel her feeling. Since her arrival, early, at 7:30, Heloise had simply stared at the huge pot of coffee she was supposed to make. She didn't see any point to it, since she alone drank very little.

The day before had been bad, but after her fight with J.J., this day would be much worse. Upon her late return the previous evening, he had given her questioning glances of the most suspicious kind. Her lone question concerning his examination had touched off a tirade on several aspects of her relationship with Rick which did not exist. J.J. had insisted that Rick Stapler was scheming to get him back to work in less than two weeks and in New York. All through the "good offices" of Madelaine Jordan. "And you," he had said, nastily, "You will undoubtedly stay here."

She had gotten so upset that she had lost it. "If he needs me, you're damn right I will!" Which, of course, she couldn't have meant.

Everything had been so good for so long. Now, all she had was a bitter, suspicious husband, a huge, empty office and the overpowering presence of Madelaine Jordan for company.

And the Goddamn phone!

She took her time in answering. On the other end would be only other people's troubles. No one cared about hers.

"Hello, Mrs. Carpenter," Tim Hirsch said. She could tell that he would apologize next. "Sorry," he said without stopping. "But I guess you must have been right. Something is wrong with the system down here. I really must apologize."

"Not at all, Mr. Hirsch," she replied, thinking the contrary.

He laughed. "We've been getting this kind of thing all along for about a month and a half, it seems," he explained. "Other accounts apparently have also complained about the last month's billing. Each of them as ridiculous as Mr. Jordan's. The computer checks out, but our supervisor realizes that something is wrong. He told me to bill you only for the average billing over the last few months, if that's all right."

"Of course." Heloise did not feel communicative.

"I really am sorry, Mrs. Carpenter," Hirsch said, put off by her clipped responses. "It is very strange, really. Our service people insist that nothing is wrong, but there is nothing to account for that kind of power usage in a residential location. We have had about half a dozen complaints and we can't stick homes with bills fit for factories."

"I quite agree, Mr. Hirsch." She didn't much care anymore. Let Madelaine pay it. "Send me the new bill when you can. Good-bye."

At the moment she hung up, Rick and Madelaine, both looking as though they had spent the night half asleep, strolled into the office.

Heloise had to wonder how little they had slept. She had her own idea.

~ ~ ~

His eyes showed the strain of too many sleepless nights. The mirror revealed a general haggard look that aggravated Carleton's already bad mood. While the last two nights had been easy from the technical end, they had been brutal, both physically and psychologically. He intended to sleep the entire day.

Lying down on the thick, lumpy mattress, Carleton mulled over his accomplishments. He had squared accounts with everyone at the Talbot who had conspired against him earlier in the year. The six-man majority of the board of trustees, responsible as they were for the revocation of his grant, had, appropriately enough, learned the value of the very project they had spurned. Madjerin, their selfish, dimwitted accomplice who had survived at his expense, had been put in her proper place–and she wouldn't even have to go back to India.

Carleton did not think of himself as a monster. Quite the contrary, he felt sorry for those whose underestimation of him had doubled back on them. Sometimes life was cruel, but it was always just. If you commit a wrong, he thought, you must pay for it. Your mistakes will always do you in. It had happened to him when he was young, when he had made mistakes.

Perhaps, it was just, he confessed, that he, who had abused sleep, was now denied it. His mind was too full of the people who had never awakened. He feared that he, too, might fail to survive his dreams

They would all be there again, he knew that from experience. As good as the system was, it had one failing: Feedback. He had invaded sleeping minds, but so had theirs invaded his.

As he had for several weeks, Carleton lay stone dead awake, trying to devise some way of avoiding that reversal of his process that had proved so deadly to those who doubted its possibilities. The more power they had, the greater the amplification, the more important it became. Clever as he was, he still could not do without it, the feedback and the control it gave him over their dreams. And, yet, it cost him control over his own.

Now that he had concluded his campaign of retribution, he hoped to forget all the images that had been ground into his mind since springtime. It was necessary. It gave him a feel for their dreams that enabled him to incorporate his thoughts to the scenes swirling about in their heads. To become, for a moment, a part of them. But he paid the price. The last one, Madjerin, had been so difficult, had taken so long. Despite all of his refinements of the system, it had proven an increasingly arduous task to use it.

Not even wanting to fall asleep unaided, Carleton jumped from the bed and seized his cassette tape recorder. He played the tape to see what remained on the side, the one not used the night before. "Tonight, Mr. Jordan," it said in a voice that didn't sound like his. It seemed so angry and cold. "You have all of the directions you will need. This tape will give you each step, which you will follow completely. You will not awaken until reception from Mr. Jordan ceases."

All of that was useless, he thought. The deed done, his keeping the tape was childish. He had forgotten somehow, to reuse it. Since he now had a use for the tape, Carleton pushed the button.

"Good evening, Carleton," he said into the mike, consciously pleasant. "I am going to help you sleep. I am going to count to ten and when I say ten, I want you to sleep. You will hear my voice and I will give you some instructions, which you will follow completely." His standard beginning, at least, was still effective enough. He counted to ten with a special emphasis on the ten. "Now, Carleton," he continued, "you are asleep. Today, I just want you to sleep. There will be no need for you to concentrate or run the machines or anything else. Just sleep. Only one thing, Carleton, I want you to forget what happened in your previous states of suggestion while you are asleep. Do not dream about anything that has happened in the past two months. You will awaken when the alarm goes off at 6:00 tonight. Turn the machine, the tape recorder, off in a minute and when you hear it click, lie down and go into a deep, normal sleep."

Carleton sighed at his need to resort to hypnotism to refresh himself. At one point, he had used it to give him the equivalent of a full night's sleep in a very much shorter period than eight hours. That convenience had progressively deteriorated until now his trances could not even give him sleep, only fearsome headaches. To undo that conditioning, he realized, would require time, even with hypnosis.

He set his alarm clock for 6:00 and set it beside his bed. He got out of his crumpled pants and dirty shirt. He placed the recorder at the side of the bed abutting the wall. Before rewinding and playing the new message, Carleton glanced quickly about the room. He reassured himself that it would still be there when he woke.

His preparations made, the exhausted young man turned on the tape recorder beside him. "Good evening, Carleton," the strained voice intoned.

It always still sounded so foreign, so unreal, to him. To some extent, of course, he did it that way on purpose. He had always hated his little-boy voice, and he hated to take orders usually. At least, this voice didn't really tell him to do anything he didn't want to. It didn't patronize him. All it said, usually, was "concentrate" and "think", both of which he did anyway.

By the time the voice hit "ten", Carleton had fallen into the state of unconsciousness, or semi-consciousness. His fatigue retarded his concentration, even in this state. Unfortunately, Carleton was too tired to be fully responsive to his voice's commands. When he fell asleep, finally, really asleep, he disobeyed one command. All he could dream about was what had flooded his mind for two months. The fists he was making would hurt at 6:00, so would the tightly clenched teeth. Worse, Carleton would not feel refreshed when he finally awoke. A grim parade of seven vengeful dreamers would see to that.

~ ~ ~

After checking up on three other cases, Montgomery called it a day at 10:30 AM. The routine matters, a shooting and two knifings, only reminded him of the Jordan case. Finally, he decided that he had to get some real sleep, that he had to break the debilitating grip of complete fatigue.

He stared at his comfortable double bed for a minute before yielding to its temptation. It was a lonely place, that bed, lonely and recently, frightening. His dreams contrived to rob him of needed sleep. It was as his wife had once told him: Your dreams can make you dread going to sleep.

But awake, he felt miserable as well. He had begun to feel uncomfortable, no, useless, in his job. The collapse of reason undercut his satisfaction derived of the struggle to hunt people, simple people, and bring them to justice. What would he save the victims for? Save them for the much worse, far uglier fate of sleep?

~ ~ ~

Montgomery's mind was detached from his body. It floated over the beds of three dry, stiff bodies. Naked, only their heads were covered. He knew why. He knew what lay under those shrouds: Faces, staring out at something, screaming in silent agony.

A kindly, motherly figure hovered around the three corpses. She identified the three of them as her own children and blessed them with a sprinkling of a fine white powder. Montgomery demanded to know her and what she had done to her children. She smiled benignly and pointed to a fourth table.

Moving effortlessly to the fourth table, she caressed its head. She bent low to it, cooing in its ear. Then she picked it up, singing and rocking it in her gentle arms. She let the shroud drop and Montgomery saw his own face, the white powder she sprinkled settling in his eyes.

All the while, crooning softly and moving him back and forth in her arms, she began to tear his face apart with her horrible, long teeth. Her face covered in his blood, she paused occasionally to watch his feet and arms fly wildly about. Long fingernails cutting his chest, she smiled again and began to eat the throbbing, purple glob that was his heart.

~ ~ ~

Montgomery stared at the ceiling, stiff and soaking wet. Like small insects running over his forehead, beads of sweat crawled down to the pillow. His hand swept the feeling away and he sat up.

The bedroom was as empty as usual. Only his bed and his dresser, Rising, his legs shaky, Montgomery headed for the bathroom. He had been wrong, he had been betrayed. His wife, long ago, in Philadelphia, had been right. Death was a fraud.

CHAPTER TWELVE

Heloise brought the coffee into Rick's office just in time to hear Madelaine insist that "life goes on, Rick."

He looked at Heloise gratefully. "Thank you, Hel. I hope you won't feel degraded if I ask you to pour. We're shot to hell."

Madelaine lied. "I feel quite all right, Counselor."

"Pour for Madelaine anyway," he said. "She is a paying client. For the time being, eh, Maddy?"

Heloise went about her chore mechanically. She did not feel like pouring coffee for either of them. With resentment building, Heloise could not resist asking, "Is she tired of your company, too?"

Wisecracks from Heloise came so infrequently that Rick was not sure if she were kidding. "I doubt it. But she has a horribly low opinion of my talents."

"Not at all, Rick," Madelaine said firmly. "I recognize talent when I locate it. Yours just does not fit my future needs. I need a business-oriented attorney, not an estate lawyer."

"I can learn," he said eagerly enough. "You and I work so well together."

Madelaine grew tired of chatting quickly. "Perhaps we can. I want to get some of these matters out of the way. Simply because you are worried about your janitor friend, I cannot wait."

Seeing Heloise's questioning expression, Rick explained, "Hank Washington, you remember? The janitor at the Talbot?"

"We handled something for him," Heloise recalled. "What's happened?"

"We got a call last night," he said, referring to Montgomery and himself. "About 3:30, Madjerin, the Indian-girl? She died of God knows what and Hank was in her apartment. It is another mess."

Horrified, Heloise tried to conjure an image of friendly, contented Hank Washington assaulting a frail, harmless Madjerin. She failed. "What happened? I don't understand, Ricky."

Madelaine interjected her own clipped terminal remark. "Neither does anyone else, Mrs. Carpenter. That is why we have to finish some of these other problems. If Hank Washington is in trouble, your Ricky is going to have to help him. I can't afford to be kept waiting, even during so noble a crusade. We will call you when we need you further."

Had any other client spoken those words, Heloise would not have been insulted. Madelaine, however, managed to express herself in so matter-of-fact a fashion that Heloise balked. Madelaine was always so condescending or curt, unless someone had punched her in the nose. Out of habit, Heloise awaited Rick's short nod and his one-sided smile, a combination designed to reassure her. That morning, the smile only made Heloise angrier.

"Yes, Miss Jordan," she snapped. "I'll be ready." Heloise turned on her heel and left the room.

Madelaine did not bother to look at the retreating secretary. Instead she observed the puzzled expression on Stapler's face. Evidently Heloise's display of pique was directed mostly at him. "Did you do something wrong, Counselor?"

He laughed before he answered. "You are a marvel, Maddy," he said. "Does anything escape those beautiful eyes of yours?"

For a reason Madelaine could not pinpoint, his question struck her in a strange way. She did not, however, pause to analyze the feeling of vulnerability that rushed through her, rejecting it instead. "Things do, Rick," she said flatly.

It was Stapler's turn to feel an odd sensation about their conversation. He did not like the combination of a slap in the face from Heloise and a reflective comment from Madelaine. Deciding to let Madelaine continue her charge, he said nothing.

She understood his silence. "One of the things that do escape me is the status of the challenge by Mother. She is in under the will for half. She's lucky to get anything at all, in my opinion."

Feeling decidedly uncomfortable sitting opposite her suddenly probing, gray eyes, Stapler rose and paced about. "As you recall," he began, examining her hard -lined profile, "the separation agreement allowed her a one half share of the estate, as it stands at the time of death. The language of the agreement specifically excludes the assets of any trusts previously set up by your father, and the Talbot Research Foundation."

"As I read it," she said, "that leaves her out of those trusts."

"It should, Maddy. We cleared out his estate with four separate trusts. Unfortunately, she has herself a lawyer who insists that she can avoid all our cleverness by calling all transfers after separation a fraud against her right to the assets of the estate," he explained. "Their gimmick, of course, is that the transfers for the trusts were made to deplete the estate. If the court can determine that, then those post-separation transfers to the trust, and that is a bundle, will be included in the estate. And you'll get blasted."

Madelaine rubbed her nose and tried to follow his movement. "What are her chances?"

"Not too good," he replied. "I anticipated this problem as much as I could in drawing up the agreement and the trusts, but you never know."

"And you don't have enough insurance to cover the malpractice claims, do you?" she asked clinically.

Leaning on the arms of her chair, he smiled right into her face. "My insurance and my very life wouldn't even cover the state taxes."

She shrugged back at him, her huge eyes fixed on his. "I didn't think so," she said

Half of him wondered if she realized how powerless people became she looked at them the way she did. 'Mesmerize' was the only word that he could think of. He didn't care that she would sue him if she thought it would pay; for the moment, at least, he couldn't consider it. The mercurial gray seemed infinitely deep. Its undertow swept things under the surface, pulled them into the vastness of her mind. Only the few colored fragments, remnants of earlier victims, remained, floating forsaken on the surface. After an age, she blinked and Stapler straightened.

"Besides," she was saying, "I think the documents were well drafted. We won't settle, even when they ask."

Breathing deeply to refill his lungs, Stapler said thinly, "He'll ask, all right. He knows the odds as well as I do."

Madelaine wondered if the way he looked at her meant something. That he knew she was trying to destroy his independence from her. "What about Mother? What do you think she is after?" She asked, only half interested.

He watched her stare into the distance. "Money?" he asked rhetorically. "She has plenty of that. I was hoping that you could tell me. It might help us fight her."

Why she had chosen the cathedral, standing so solitary on the hill, Madelaine did not know. Even in miniature, in the distance, it looked strong and comforting. She had seen it up close many times with her father when she was very young, and she knew how grand and high it soared. From a distance, she saw it now, only from a distance.

Without taking her eyes from the church, Madelaine answered Rick's question. "She doesn't want me to have it." Madelaine knew that was true. It had always been true.

"Christ," Stapler retorted. "The estate is big enough for both of you, Madelaine." He could not be sure that she was listening.

Lately, he sensed that she had been that way, not always listening to what he said, not concentrating. In Madelaine, who devoured ideas as they issued from one's mouth, lack of focus was unheard of. Suddenly, the sense condensed into worry. He actually began to worry about her. "You don't need it, anyway, Maddy."

As if the haze nestled into the valley were inside her head, Madelaine heard his words drift to her. Without a conscious thought, she said, "It's all I have, Rick."

~ ~ ~

"And all I want," Montgomery told his reflection, "is some God damned sleep."

The mirror did not have any response other than the despondent, resigned look it returned. They both knew that Detective Sergeant Montgomery would not have an opportunity to get the kind of sleep he needed. It had taken him a long bath and a longer lunch to face the unsympathetic glass. He was still afraid to close his eyes.

He took the seat behind his crowded desk. Paperwork had piled up endlessly. Even though he had no recollection of working on anything but the Jordan case, Monty faced a mountain of forms and reports on other matters. Why could not the world stop when he was involved in something this? Something he had to work out.

That was what worried him. After so damned many years on the police force, he had gotten involved in this kind of thing. What kind of thing? He had never seen anything like this mess before. Death shouldn't bother him. Homicide was, after all, his business. Not directly, he never got into death directly. He couldn't stop it, just sweep up after. What good was it?

"Jesus Goddamn Christ," he said, addressing the tiny plastic bottle of Sweet Tooth. "What a way to die." It made sense to him that afternoon to hassle with the minuscule agent of long, long, interminable sleep.

"Why do you put people to sleep? Silly question," he continued, not feeling at all ridiculous: This bottle, after all, held the answer. "I couldn't get to sleep myself today, could I?" The Sweet Tooth remained inscrutable.

"Well, actually, I did get to sleep, but I needed something to make me stay that way. You seem to have an uncanny way of helping people remain asleep, my little friend."

When the bottle refused comment, Monty picked it up and fired it across the room. Initially, he chided himself for throwing evidence about, but then apologized. That rotten little bottle contained nothing but a false sense of sweetness, and a real sleeping powder. It kept you asleep–not dead. It didn't make anyone have a heart attack. He had almost had one himself without it.

He had almost had one without it! What if he had taken some of that sweetener in his coffee before he had lain down? Simple answer!

He would not have awakened during his nightmare. Of course! The powder was to keep people asleep–not get them there. "Nobody's strong enough to face that!" he yelled at the distant bottle. "And you know it."

~ ~ ~

Madelaine was a stenographer's dream. Her voice was so even, so beautifully paced that the symbols flowed onto the pad. Heloise lost all consciousness of her task. Detached, she watched her hands fly over the paper creating hieroglyphics fit for a sphinx. Rick, she thought, didn't dictate like this. He was so stop-and-start, on-again-off-again, a joke, an aside and a sigh.

The flow was interrupted by Stapler's first sigh in half an hour. "Madelaine?" he asked.

She stopped speaking and looked at him. He had entered the room carrying volume 379 of the Pennsylvania Reporter. The legal reference book lay open across his hands. "Have you found anything?"

His face glowed with triumph. "This case gives a string of precedents on that charitable deduction issue. The IRS may have to eat this one whole." He knew that when he put his mind to it, he could read cases as well as anyone. "Give me another half an hour while I check these things over. How's it coming?"

Madelaine had to pause for a moment to figure out how many letters she had dictated. "Pretty well, Counselor," she said. "I'm going to get to the grant denials in a minute."

He shook his head. "Maddy, you're moving pretty damn quick on those things. I hope you are considering them seriously. They were terribly important to your father."

Standing up and stretching, Madelaine said, "Listen, Rick, we must have made a mistake. That absurd list did not have the top quality on it. Considering all of the people released by the Board of Trustees and the talent available, I can't believe that Father wanted me to limit my choices to this group."

"Well, we didn't have any instructions on it, Madelaine. You aren't bound by it," he admitted. "George just gave it to me and said that your father had been working on it for a week before he died. It could be candidates for washing the floors for all I know."

"I have checked records of the others who left the Talbot," Madelaine said, "and a lot of good people are not included on this list. I even recognize some of the names as people Father originally sponsored himself."

Stapler hated to agree, but she was right. One thing that had nagged him was the date of the dismissals of the listed candidates. Each had had his funds cut off at the spring meeting. While many of the best went last, plenty of others had been axed earlier, in the late winter. "All I know is that he was considering them for something," Rick said, unconvinced. "He marked them in that characteristic way. With the x's and asterisks."

Even an inattentive Heloise was struck by his mistake. "Stars and crosses, Rick." she said, petulantly.

"I use the x's and asterisks, Madelaine said stiffly. The statement sounded horribly silly to her ears.

Grinning sheepishly, Rick apologized. "I am sorry, Maddy," he said. "I guess I have been too devoted to you lately. I must have lost all track of what's right in the world."

Madelaine frowned, her pale cheeks glowing pink. "I'm not very original, am I?"

"Original? You are the original, Maddy," Stapler said. "Nobody can be original in everything."

The whole conversation galled Heloise. She tried to get it back on the track. "What's wrong with the list?"

Everybody felt more relaxed when Madelaine returned to her theme. "The idea of it is wrong. Father knew quality when he saw it. He also liked stability, yet the most solid researchers on the list got no mark at all." A solution came to her. "How did father vote on these people when their finding came up in the spring?"

Heloise and Stapler offered embarrassed expressions. As secretary and assistant secretary of the Board, they should have had the information ready for Madelaine from the outset. Neither had thought that she would be interested in how her father really felt about the candidates.

"Surely, there is some record," Madelaine insisted.

"Oh, yes, Madelaine," Rick replied. "There is. The minutes. But, quite frankly, I don't know where they are."

Madelaine would have been disgusted with him if she had not remembered where she had seen them. "I do. Father had them at the Talbot, Skeffington must have them."

Stapler sighed relief. Too many people had died lately and he did not see any point in joining the ranks. He could not afford to have Madelaine Jordan upset with him now.

~ ~ ~

The second time Henry Washington regained consciousness; there wasn't a single doctor, nurse or cop around. The
room remained sterile and uncomfortable, as it had been
the first time he had seen it. Hank did not feel particularly
sick, though a strange weakness warned him that rising
would not be a good idea.

Passing the time by surveying his room, Hank examined
each corner for dust and the floors for wax. Ill kept, he
thought. The hospital was old and had very nice tile floors,
but apparently no one took any care to keep them up. Not
like the Talbot, where the linoleum looked like glass.

Remembering the Talbot upset him, though he could not
divine why it should He enjoyed his work there because the
constant activity displayed its results immediately and to
everyone who entered, it was basic and obvious. He wondered who held the night shift now that he was in the hospital.

For that matter, he wondered why he was in the hospital.
Never sick a day in his life, Hank had not seen a hospital as
a patient before.

He did not like it and would have left had his body not so
strongly resisted the idea. Stuck on his back for the time being, Hank decided to figure out how he had gotten there.
After some effort, he gave up because he could not remember anything after his dinner with Madjerin. Perhaps that
was it, he had gotten too drunk.

He recognized that he should have had coffee with Madj
and Carleton, who had come to share the celebration, however briefly. Like a fool, Hank had opted for a brandy. When
money was scarce, so was brandy and Hank had not had
foolish-money in years.

He could, at least, recall how the two silly researchers
praised each other. Carleton had never impressed Hank as
the kind of fellow who was able to appreciate anyone, including himself. To hear that guy lauding his little Madjerin

struck Hank as unusual and even ridiculous. Carleton was like the rest, worse; he had ridiculed Madjerin as had the other staff members, but to her face.

Madj, for her part, had eaten the flattery without gagging. In her ebullience, she would have swallowed a pig's ear. She was only looking forward. Forward. He remembered they were going to get married. Was that true? Hank could not really remember. Everything after they had left the restaurant felt so hazy.

Hank's entire body shook. At first, he didn't understand why. As he watched, however, his head began to spin and his memory returned in bits.

Like snapshots, visions of Madjerin flashed before him, as though someone did not want him to catch the details of the picture. He concentrated until he could see her on the bed. His stomach revolted and covered the floor with a pale green syrup.

Suddenly everything fell into sharp relief. The entire episode stood before him as though burned into rock. Madjerin was dead, dead of something horrible. A fit of some kind had destroyed her completely as he watched. Hank Washington was a strong man, but he felt a nearly physical pain as he relived the previous night. And thought about the next day, alone.

He was used to being alone, he could get used to it again. More importantly, he wondered if he could ever look back on that final day. That day was important. Very important.

That was the day on which he had everything. He knew that it was not significant what he missed, only that he had missed it. His whole life, like everyone else's, was a dull mosaic of lost opportunities, small accomplishments and petty disappointments, setting off a few brilliantly painted moments. It didn't look like much close up, perhaps, but if he half closed his eyes, he could make it look like a rainbow.

CHAPTER THIRTEEN

By the time Jean Skeffington arrived at the Haller Building, Stapler had departed for a meeting with Montgomery. To a reluctant Heloise he had left the task of keeping Madelaine Jordan occupied and Jean Skeffington away from Madelaine's throat. His secretary, nonetheless, had little interest in either job.

Skeffington, with her rounded figure and Main Line accent, arrived bustling with her most officious manner. Her soft jaw seemed set but inadequate for the confrontation with the woman she had instinctively despised.

"Sit down, Miss Skeffington," Madelaine said, from behind Rick's desk. "Do you have the minutes?"

The acting head of the Talbot shook her head in disgust. "Of course, Ms. Jordan. I also brought some of the other papers you asked for."

Taking the minutes book, Madelaine ignored the nasty edge in Skeffington's voice. She paged backward through the book. The very first name jumped out at her. "What do you think of Raymond Carleton, Miss Skeffington?"

"He's a greasy little monkey whom your father despised," Skeffington declared. "And so did everyone else."

Madelaine read over the notes on the meeting. "There is some pretty harsh language here. Is any of this verbatim, Heloise?"

Heloise frowned. Madelaine's tone of voice was becoming more and more offensive to her. "Not quotes, but some of the words are the same. Mr. Jordan wanted everyone's comments recorded, more or less."

"Six to three," Madelaine said. "Madjerin fared better. Five to four."

"And," Skeffington commented, "your father almost turned that one around. As it was, he allowed her to keep her lab and computer time."

Madelaine sat back in the chair. Carleton haunted her. Something about him stood out. He was too tiny to have any physical impact, yet she had an impression of his mouth, his down-turned mouth, spitting words at her.

"Let me ask you, Skeffington," she began, "who do you think my father would have wanted restored if the Talbot were to get additional funds? Look at this list before you answer."

The plump administrator examined the list handed her. "Who are these people? I mean, why are they on a list?"

"That, Miss Skeffington, is the question."

Poring over the names, Skeffington laughed. "Is this your list, Ms. Jordan? It can't be Mr. Jordan's."

"No?" Madelaine was annoyed by the woman's manner but interested in her information.

Jean Skeffington could hardly look Madelaine in the face. She had heard too much bad about her. "You certainly can't stock the Talbot with these people!" she insisted. "Half of them are crackpots. The other half, idiots."

Drawing her mouth tight, Madelaine said, "I have no intention of stocking the Talbot with anyone. At least, not in the research department." Her eyes glowed with anger. "Where did this list come from?"

The harsh tone angered Skeffington. "How the hell should I know? And what business is it of yours? The Talbot belongs to us, the people who poured our lives into it," she cried. "Not to you. I don't care what you've inherited from your father, because you didn't get very much!"

Without pushing herself up, Madelaine rose from the chair. Her eyes were glued to the raging Skeffington. "Miss Skeffington," she retorted, "I have the power to dismantle the Talbot, if I so desire. Or to stock it with crackpots and idiots, if that is necessary, which I doubt. Your place is to do what I tell you to do, when I tell you to do it, or run back home to Philadelphia."

Skeffington wanted to leave, but Madelaine's gaze held her in place. "In spite of what you obviously think, Miss Skeffington, Thomas Jordan left the Talbot in my control, not yours. And he was my father," she added, "not yours."

"And regretted it!" Skeffington countered.

Madelaine bent forward, like a young tree in the wind. "I have what I want for now, Miss Skeffington. I suggest that for now, you return to your position at the Talbot. Thank you for coming."

Blue with fury, Jean Skeffington stammered a "good-bye," and left the room. Heloise tried to escort Skeffington to the elevator, but was severely rebuffed. When she returned, Madelaine was staring out the window.

"What did you think of that, Mrs. Carpenter?" she asked.

Heloise chose her words with care. "I think it was unfortunate."

Madelaine laughed. "You know what?" she asked. "Jean Skeffington reminds me of someone. Maybe that was why I was impolite."

"Does she?"

"Yes. My mother," Madelaine remarked. "Why don't you and I have a little drink, Heloise?"

The suggestion repelled Heloise. "No, thank you," she replied. The taller woman ignored her refusal and found a bottle of Scotch in one of Rick's closets. "Rick won't mind."

"No," Heloise agreed. Why shouldn't she? Who cares if he minded?

"Why don't you tell me something?" Madelaine asked. "Tell me how you seem to know the thoughts of a man who never thinks along a straight line?"

"You mean Rick?"

Madelaine sat down in Stapler's chair again, and leaned back. "Yes, I am interested," she said, "because I have to master the art of understanding him." In the short run, at least, she thought.

Heloise's mind raced. What had Madelaine in mind? Had something happened the night before? "Why?" she asked mildly.

"Because I don't," Madelaine explained.

"Neither do I," Heloise replied. She could not understand what Rick saw in Madelaine.

"Yes, you do," Madelaine insisted. "Of course, you were in love with him once. That probably helps, doesn't it?"

No, Heloise thought, it hurts if anything. "That was over a long time ago." If it had ever really been, in the first place

Madelaine became interested, as Heloise's blush deepened. "What was he like than? The way he is now?"

The memory of her "romance" with Rick Stapler could not bear examination, Heloise decided. Certainly, not by Madelaine. "The same."

Madelaine shrugged, accepting the dead-end. "Well, if one has to love him to understand him, then I'll have to give it up."

"You mean you don't?" Heloise blurted out. She had become certain that Madelaine did.

The words of Heloise's question rocked Madelaine. You mean you don't? she asked herself. It made her laugh out loud. "No, Heloise," she said reassuringly. "I suppose it would be interesting, but as one journalist put it, 'Madelaine Jordan has been too hardened by life to soften even at the thought of a diamond.' Not very well worded, but not inaccurate."

"But what about last night?" Heloise demanded, confused and embarrassed. She didn't like the look of amusement in Madelaine's eyes. "Weren't you together last night?"

Rising, Madelaine said, "Last night, Heloise, I ended up as alone as ever. Where your Rick was, I can't say. Supposedly, he and Montgomery got drunk together." She poured herself more scotch. "I could have used him, though. Don't tell anyone, Heloise, but this perfect machine you see before you is malfunctioning at the present."

"Last night," she continued, feeling relaxed, yet burdened, "Last night, I blacked out completely. Head on the table, the works. He was there at the time, trying to help. Holding my hand, as a matter of fact." That hadn't happened in years, someone holding her hand. "It was rather kind of him."

An unsettling feeling of guilt gathered in Madelaine's throat. Could she betray him, too, so easily, so completely? Yet she had to.

The conflict worked its way to the surface. "I have never really appreciated the man's better qualities until this minute. Isn't that awful?"

When Heloise said nothing, Madelaine spoke again, more evenly. "Perhaps I am a terrible person. Yes, I am. Do you know that at this very moment I have people negotiating with some law firm downstairs to get them to move over to my building next door?"

Heloise was horrified. "Yours? That is yours?"

Madelaine nodded. "I'm so used to fighting him, Heloise, I wouldn't know when to stop," she admitted.

"You are destroying him," Heloise said breathlessly. The wickedness of Madelaine Jordan escaped her. No wonder Rick had become her slave, she was evil.

Walking around the room compulsively, Madelaine agreed. "That was the idea."

Heloise grew red in the face and her mouth hardly worked. "You are a monster! You really are! Do you hate everything?"

A grimace betrayed Madelaine's dislike of the accusation. She had to regain control of herself. After a pause she asked, "Do you think so?"

"I do now," Heloise replied, not quite as angry. "You don't seem to have any feeling at all!"

The broad shoulders rose and fell. "Heloise, when I was young...," she tried to explain, "I didn't have any contact with it. I learned very early that I didn't have the looks to win hearts, so I started going for the head. Girls like you, with your face and your figure, you can have your choice, can't you?"

"Hardly, Madelaine," Heloise denied, starting to relive her own rebuttal. "You don't know anything."

"Any heart still pumping," Madelaine went on, not hearing. "Male, female. Young, old. Maybe dog or cat."

"It's not that easy." Heloise felt the old wound rupturing, threatening a flow that, once sensed, would inflame her adversary.

"If I had half what you have..." Madelaine stopped. Could it matter that much? "Who knows, maybe when I'm finished, I'll be irresistibly eligible."

"Finished with what?" Heloise asked, sensing a closing of the attack.

"Pardon?"

"When you've finished what?" Heloise asked again.

The phrase had slipped out and Madelaine could not remember where it had come from or what it meant. "Whatever it is I'm doing?"

"Ruining everybody's life?" Heloise asked, more conciliatory than anything else. "That's what you're doing."

Madelaine decided not to think about it. She had several individual tasks to do and she would finish them all. "Speaking of ruining people's lives, it's time to send out a few grant denials."

She returned to the desk and ran down her notes. "One thing I've found out," she said, striving to shift her mind to the work. "One of the many things I've been finding out," she corrected herself ruefully, "is that this list doesn't mean a thing. Several trustees Father really considered as having good judgment voted against all of them. To some extent this is a negative list, not a positive list."

Her eyes ran up and down the list again. "In fact, Father voted against most of them, except those with the crosses by their names. If you eliminate those people," she said, "you get a list of people down by at least a five-four vote."

"Any consistency in the voting?" Heloise asked, her balance regained. "Maybe these were to be excluded."

Madelaine's hand tore through the pages of the minutes book. When she had seen what she wanted to see, she sat back again. "This list, with the crosses, is a list of those voted down at the spring meeting by the four men who died before Father."

Heloise was stunned. "Was he becoming superstitious?"

"No," Madelaine said, "paranoid. Let's see. The people with crosses by their names were voted up by my father. How about that?"

"What does it mean?"

"Probably nothing, Heloise. But I am quite sure that Father would not want money to go to those with these stars," Madelaine said. "And no matter what else I do, I'll grant him that."

Madelaine underlined the names of those to be rejected without further consideration. She hesitated a moment when she reached the name Raymond Carleton. He had intrigued her, but he was probably too unstable to be useful anyway.

"Heloise," she said completing her task, "Call these people and give them the bad news. Be prepared though," she added, "Some of them will be upset."

~ ~ ~

If the call from Heloise Carpenter had awakened Carleton from a raging nightmare, its message awakened a rage in him even more violent. It was worse than the fit of anger that had seized him in the spring, when they told him of the vote. He had, once again, been spurned by them. Those who deserved only obliteration had rejected him again. Madelaine Jordan, like all of them, so proud of her physical stature, had proven herself a mental pygmy. And he had actually expected her to appreciate him. That was partly why he had so raised his expectations. He should have known better. No one had ever really appreciated him. Perhaps no one ever would.

The text of the call also contributed to his choler. "Dr. Carleton," she had said. "With the limited funds allocated, only a very few applicants, the most deserving projects, may be considered. Without Dr. Madjerin, the brain wave project is not sufficiently likely to succeed. Miss Jordan thanks you for your time and conveys her regrets."

Without Madjerin. Didn't that foolish hulk know that Madjerin was better dead. Christ, God damn it, he thought wildly, the damned girl was dead precisely because he had succeeded better than she! They all were!

Madjerin was an idiot next to Carleton. But, of course, that was precisely the problem. People of limited intelligence always preferred their lowly equals, fearing genius. Rightly so, too, he began to realize. In his struggle the force of the mind was certain to dominate. The strongest mind deserved to and would win out. They had all learned that lesson, albeit too well to benefit by it. Soon, Madelaine Jordan would understand, too.

Plans ran through Carleton's mind, his plan of attack. He knew how to gain access to the estate. He had already gained access to Madjerin's small domain in the Talbot without any of the difficulty for which he had been prepared. Before him lay the disheveled desk she had left behind, in her haste to celebrate her temporary victory over him.

Dozens of brain-wave printouts produced by a TI printing unit stood between Carleton and his object. Somewhere

in the mess around him he would find the personality function graphing of Madelaine Jordan. He had been able to take
the others with him when he had left in April.

Melton, Carstairs, Jordan, even that stupid lawyer's. The
great demonstration he and Madjerin had done for them.
All of the Trustees had conveniently put their personalities
onto paper. Madjerin, too.

Madjerin's little public relations ploy had enabled him to
prove conclusively to those who thought him unworthy of
their attention that he had succeeded. In the end, it was
each of them against him. With his creation and his mind,
he had shown them, all the doubters. Now, of course, he
would take on Madelaine Jordan.

He cast the various papers carelessly about, seeking the
one recorded personality he needed. His anger grew as the
mindless printout evaded his eye. He began to tear the un-
wanted materials into confetti.

Finally, he spotted a graph, undoubtedly Madelaine Jordan's, still in the printer. He seized the end of the paper and
ripped it out of the machine. Eying it quickly, he ripped off
the last few cycles, sufficient for his purpose.

Clutching Madelaine Jordan's graph printout, Carleton
stole into the laboratory unit once used by the memory expert, Alfonse Corbett. Corbett had been one of the few
whose work had required the sophisticated device Carleton
needed to prepare his program for Madelaine Jordan, at TI
875 reader.

Hooked to a huge TI computer in the Talbot's main computer room, the 875 gave him programming access he
could not do without. For months, he had used his building
privileges to use the 875 and, of course, to keep up his
Sweet Tooth supply.

Once the TI 875 was ready, Carleton placed the section of
graphing into position. The magnetic tape cartridge he had
brought with him contained the functions program, ironi-

cally of Thomas Jordan. That program, like Thomas Jordan's memory, would soon be wiped clean, replaced temporarily by that of his daughter. Carleton chuckled to himself, appreciating the fitting quality of it all.

Carefully typing into the keyboard of the TI 875, Carleton called forth the recording program he had used often before. When he typed the final command, "RUN", the cartridge began to spin, the printed graph being transformed into a magnetic record that he could more easily use in his own TI 125.

With his newly prepared Madelaine Jordan brain-function recording, Carleton stole his way toward the exit. There were still some of the staff workers in the building, and he did not want to be seen. Not that it mattered, but he despised them all so that he loathed speaking to them.

In any case, he was too excited. He had Madelaine Jordan in his shirt pocket.

~ ~ ~

Montgomery felt uncomfortable sitting all by himself at the University Club table. It seemed as though everyone around him remembered the ruckus he had kicked up just a day earlier. With Stapler on the telephone, Monty felt very much out of place. He doubted that he could even have gotten in the door on his own.

Rick had gone to the phone to inform the women at his office that he would be eating dinner with Montgomery at the Club and that they should join them if they wished. He had said that he wanted to discuss something important with Madelaine, "Real estate," he had said slyly.

Montgomery dreaded that Madelaine would accept the invitation. His day had already been remarkably unpleasant. First the Madjerin thing. Then his office and mounds of paper work; a sudden burst of normal homicide; and a late afternoon upbraiding by his superiors for his wasted time on the Jordan "non-case". The lousy, unproductive interrogation of Henry Washington and his lousy, uncooperative lawyer, Stapler, had been the easiest part of the whole damned day.

Washington had wanted to go home. So what, he thought, who didn't? Washington had even laughed when Montgomery had told him that they were holding him on suspicion of rape and murder. It was not a very pleasant laugh and it stayed with Montgomery. The laughter of a hopelessly drained man, trying to make the best of what little was left of his life. Montgomery did not like the sound at all.

Stapler, like a typical lawyer, instructed the edgy, black janitor to keep his mouth shut. To keep his stupid mouth shut! Naturally, Montgomery had gotten absolutely nothing from him. He didn't want to hang the bastard, but he was helpless unless Washington told him what had happened.

Rick had demanded a chance to talk to Washington in private before Montgomery could interrogate him. Perhaps he hadn't actually demanded it, but Montgomery had felt as though he had. Consequently, Rick had argued with his disgruntled friend for half an hour before receiving permission to see Hank.

The private meeting out of the way, the pair had adjourned to the Club for dinner before a joint interview with Hank at nine o'clock. Upon his return from the phone, Rick had promised he would fill Montgomery in on what Hank had told him. Since Montgomery was technically off duty, he finished both his and Rick's Chivas before the call was completed.

"You son of a bitch," Stapler said, sitting. "I needed the damn thing as much as you did."

Monty sneered. "Tell me."

Rick decided to pass that opportunity and waved to the waitress for two more. His phone call had produced unsatisfactory results. Heloise's gentle voice told him that Madelaine and she had gone to have dinner at the Jordan house.

After a tough day, he liked to have more of her than a taped voice to restore him. A second call had confirmed the name of the party who controlled the real estate owning a certain building.

"They coming?" Monty anxiously asked.

"No," Rick said. "They went to Madelaine's, where she'll probably contaminate Hel."

"You know," Monty began. "I don't much care. All I want to know is what my suspect told you."

Stapler felt vaguely victimized. He had too much on his mind to be beset by Montgomery's harangues. "Shit, Montgomery!" he barked. "Will you take it easy for once? What's wrong with you? You know damn well I'm not going to shut you out of this." He sighed, calming down himself. "You're the man most likely to help Hank."

"Alright, alright," the detective relented, disgustedly. In a day when nothing went right, he could not muster the strength to argue anymore. "Okay. You're the hero and I'm the heel. That's the way it's supposed to go anyway, isn't it?"

The lawyer shrugged. "You're not the only guy in this town who had a bad day," he said. Of course, neither was he, but it felt like it, "Want to hear something funny?"

"Nope."

"Do you remember that office building I told you about?" Stapler asked, ignoring the response.

Montgomery did, vaguely. "The one stealing your big tenants?"

"Madelaine owns it," Stapler informed him. Montgomery started to laugh uncontrollably. "It isn't that funny!

"Son of a bitch," Montgomery said, in between guffaws. "She's a good one."

Stapler nodded. "She's terrific, Monty. Cruel, rotten, clever to a fault," he agreed almost cheerfully. "I'll get even if it costs me my own building. She'd better find another sucker."

Hungrily, they grabbed their double scotches from the waiter's tray before he could set them down. Half of each glass was empty before Montgomery changed the subject. "Tell me, Counselor," he said. "What did your black pal have to say?"

His face growing serious, Stapler culled his memory for the details. The picture Hank remembered had been an ugly one. "He said that they were out celebrating. They thought she had her grant from the estate cold Hank got too drunk to drive, so he stayed with Madjerin."

Montgomery growled. "He wasn't all that drunk."

"True. They did go to bed together," he agreed, pausing for another sip of alcohol. "But he says he fell asleep, his head on her chest. He woke up at one point, hearing a buzzing, as he put it. Rolled over and went back to sleep. A bit later, he woke up again. This time, she was having a dandy of a nightmare. He told me that he got those scratches trying to keep her hands off of her own throat!"

Montgomery's skepticism gave way to gnawing interest. "Uh oh."

"The rest of his story," Rick continued, "sounds more bizarre, but not less familiar. She was apparently thrashing out and kicking at the air. He couldn't hold her, so he tried to call for help. She was dead before he got anywhere."

"I don't like the god damned sound of it," Monty snapped.

"The last thing he mentioned were her eyes," Rick concluded. "Then they had to sedate him."

Montgomery finished his drink in a desperate gulp. "But this wasn't a heart attack, Rick. If it were, I'd leave the poor bastard alone."

"I know."

"She strangled or was strangled," Montgomery stated. "What am I supposed to make of that?"

"What are you making of the other stuff?" Stapler demanded, irritated.

The haze hung before Montgomery's eyes as he reviewed his theories on the Jordan case and its counterparts. "Do you want to know?"

"I might as well," Stapler said grimly. "You and I are in this together one way or another."

"Then listen, listen first," Montgomery warned. "Give me the shit later." After he had the attorney's agreement, he went on. "That sweetener garbage was laced with enough chemical to keep a man asleep through anything. Note that I say 'to keep.' Not to put them to sleep, not to OD them."

Considering the emphasis, Stapler rubbed his chin. "Okay."

"All this occurred to me the other day," Monty said. "This morning, I tried to sleep off the effects of that little party we had last night. Well, I had a screamer of a nightmare. Believe me, I have them all the time and I'm still pretty young, but when I woke up, I thought my chest would bust wide open. My head was pounding. I checked with the doctor and he said my blood pressure had really shot up. I won't pass my next physical if it stays that high."

"I don't get it. You didn't have a heart attack."

"Right. But I woke up," Monty stressed. "What if I had stayed asleep?"

"Are you talking about a nightmare scaring a man to death?" Rick asked, incredulous.

"Have you ever heard the superstition that if you dream of falling and you don't wake up before you hit the ground?" Monty asked, glaring intensely at Stapler.

"You're dead."

"Exactly!"

Rick bit his lip, looking into space for a better explanation. "It's pretty far-fetched."

The sound of the theory, voiced out loud, didn't please the detective. It sounded like a last grasp at a fantastic straw. "Yeah. And Madjerin's death? That wasn't a heart attack. Shit."

"'She was grabbing at her throat, like someone had his hands on it,'" Rick said, repeating the words Hank Washington had forced out of his memory "What if she stopped breathing because, for some reason, she thought she already had?"

"Christ!" Montgomery groaned. "What a grisly way to die."

They had an hour until Hank's sedation would wear off. Too much crawling time to sit and think. If they weren't hungry, both men felt terribly dry. Without deciding, they began to drink the extra minutes away.

~ ~ ~

Madelaine glared across the desk at Carleton. She did not appreciate the rejected researcher's personal attempt to win a reversal of her verdict. Even less, had she expected that a man like Carleton would present himself to grovel at her feet. She decided that the least she could do was allow him time to degrade himself and have the coffee he had requested.

"Miss Jordan," he pleaded, "you have no idea how I need this money. I know that I can do as well as anyone at the Talbot. Just give me a chance."

Heloise brought in the coffee before Madelaine could reply. That was fortunate for Carleton, for Madelaine was tiring of the courtesy she had extended. Heloise's company, though subdued and a bit resentful, had begun to have a tonic effect on Madelaine's deteriorating nerves.

"How would you like this, Dr. Carleton?" Heloise asked in her automatically polite voice.

Carleton's mouth twisted into a smile. "I take mine with cream," he said. "And I use some of that great sweetener that Mr. Jordan gave me.

"Sweet Tooth?" Madelaine said, coldly. "I've heard bad things about it."

His smile broadened, as though he preferred the bad aspect of anything. "You mean you haven't tried any?" he asked, astonished, implying that a heinous crime had been committed. "You really ought to, Miss Jordan. I mean it was your father's concoction."

Madelaine fired her own deadly smile. "My father also formulated a popular oil additive," she said. "And I don't use that in my coffee."

Heloise interrupted, helpfully. "George says that he threw out the last bit of it anyway."

"Sorry, Dr. Carleton," Madelaine said, without regret.

Waving his hand generously, Carleton replied, "I always carry my own. I drink so much coffee that I need my own supply. Come on, Miss Jordan, try some."

Though Madelaine did not like coffee without sugar, she had no intention of trying the Sweet Tooth. If nothing else, she felt somewhat uneasy about the role it had played in both her father's and Red Melton's deaths. Before she could say anything negative, however, Carleton had infected her cup of coffee with the fine, white powder from a small plastic bottle. She did not intend to make a fuss out of the matter, for she had the feeling that Carleton rather hoped that she would.

As he watched Madelaine Jordan take the cup to her lips without comment, Carleton felt satisfied. The rest would be downhill. It had taken all of his will to present himself, begging as he had. He had had no choice, however, if his counter-attack were to be swift. He put the bottle of Sweet Tooth over his coffee cup, one finger on a tiny lever–his own creation–that released the unadulterated Sweet Tooth from its separate reservoir in the small plastic bottle. To each his own, he thought.

The taste of Sweet Tooth proved slightly better than Madelaine had expected, but slightly worse than her father had repeatedly insisted it would. It left a bitter taste in her mouth that, she suspected, would linger long into the night. Her eyes fixed on her visitor, she finished half of the cup.

"Dr. Carleton," she began, "As far as I am concerned, and for that matter, for your part as well, the question is closed. I am directed by the express terms of my Father's will to decide which former staffers of the Talbot merit these generous grants. He left me sufficient standards and guidance to tell me that you were not the kind of man he would have chosen or would have wanted me to choose."

"But, Miss Jordan," Carleton protested, to make his scene convincing, "with Madjerin dead, there is no one to complete her work. I'm the only one who can."

"That I considered giving that unfortunate young lady a grant, Dr. Carleton, is no concern of yours," Madelaine explained coldly. "I judged her on her individual merits, not on the merits of her project, which I think is, ultimately, useless or even dangerous. I also judged you on your individual merits. Nothing you can say at this point will convince me that you deserve any part of the estate my Father spent his lifetime accumulating."

Even though he did not care to change her mind, Carleton found the brazen behemoth's words intolerable. "I can prove otherwise!" he shouted. "You are so damned stupid. I have made one of the greatest developments in biological science in history! And you don't see any merit in it or in me. Well, you are even more ridiculous than I thought you were."

"And you," she retorted calmly, "are as I thought you were."

"Never," he said softly, each word more venomous for his hushed tone, "never in your wildest dreams will you understand what I can do. Soon enough," he continued, spitting each syllable out quietly, "Soon you will appreciate my genius. But you won't understand it."

As her guest rose, Madelaine stood. She did not move from her position, towering over the desk. Her face showed no expression and her voice betrayed no emotion. "I shall never appreciate a base genius such as yours, Dr. Carleton. I certainly have no need of it. It is my opinion that no one else has need of it either. Good night."

Carleton had stopped at the door long enough to absorb her words and glower back at Madelaine's deep-set, gray eyes. His consolation was that she would close them only one night more. "Good night, Miss Jordan," he snapped. "I hope you can sleep well tonight after what you have said to me."

Madelaine said nothing as he shot a glance at Heloise who still stood near the coffee tray. He even gave her a stiff, angry bow. Not bothering to look back at Madelaine, Dr. Carleton stormed out of the study and the house

Heloise first stared after him and then looked at Madelaine, whose eyes had followed his exit from the house. Madelaine's face seemed like a pale mask to Heloise, punctured only by her huge, steel eyes, which eventually returned Heloise's gaze.

"Well, Mrs. Carpenter," Madelaine said. "I think I will have some more coffee. With sugar this time."

CHAPTER FOURTEEN

"Sugar," Hank repeated dumbly. The question perplexed him. "Should I remember if she used sugar?"

"Shit!" Montgomery said.

Stapler tried to hide his growing exasperation. Hank Washington had not recovered enough to remember anything about the previous night. Gently, he and Montgomery had tried to lead Hank back to his senses, but each time during the draining two hour stint Hank had fallen back into a semi-stupor. "There must have been sometime," Rick suggested "when you noticed."

Hank's face went blank and then compressed into an expression of agonized inadequacy. "I can't remember, Mr. Stapler. I'm doing my best but I can't think back. Why don't you ask Carleton?"

Montgomery exploded, "We're asking you, you dumb bastard!"

"Why Carleton?" Rick asked, hoping to glaze over Montgomery's outburst.

If Hank had heard Montgomery's insult, his eyes did not show it. His voice became hollow, distant as he replied, "He used to drink coffee with her. All the time. When they worked together. All the time. Last night." It was such an incredible fog to him. The harder he tried, the more dense the fog became. The closer he looked, the farther away he got. It was a queer, frightening feeling. "Leave me alone," he cried.

Rising with uncontrollable frustration, Montgomery growled, "If you weren't so damned stupid, you cocksucker!"

Stapler worked his neck to relieve the knots that had developed in the hours of patient questioning. He knew Hank did not hear Montgomery. "Take it easy, Monty," he said, "Hank can't even hear you."

Monty spat on the floor. Everything had gone wrong since the beginning. His nerves had frayed and he knew it. The monstrosity of the Jordan case lay in its unrelenting attack on his nerves. "Shit," he responded.

"We have to get somewhere" Rick stated. "Neither of us will get any sleep until we can make something of this. Sit down, Monty. For Christ's sake."

His stomach aching, Montgomery took the chair to the corner of the room and sat down. The farther away he got from the whole damn thing, the better he would like it.

Stapler waited until he thought Montgomery had calmed down. He hadn't known the detective very long, but he realized that Montgomery was in bad shape. Perhaps they all were. He could see that Hank Washington had little left to give. The constant good cheer had been wiped clean from his face. All that remained was an impenetrable daze.

"Hank" he began again, "You have told us that you and Madj had dinner last night."

"I did?" Hank asked. "I guess so."

Stapler sighed at the repeating of the pattern. Hank couldn't even remember what he had said minutes before. "Okay. Now at dinner, you had brandy and Madj had coffee. When she drank it, was it black?"

Hopelessness wrapped each word Hank spoke. "Black? No, not black. She didn't like it black. I made it that way once to wake her up. But she didn't like it that way."

"It wasn't black, then" Stapler said nodding. "When she put in the cream, did she do anything else?"

Hank closed his eyes tight trying to visualize the previous evening. When he conjured the scene and saw Madjerin in his mind, he let out a whimper and lost the whole picture. "I can't!" he cried. "I'd tell you if I could, but I just can't. I didn't pay any attention to it. I had my brandy and I didn't care what they put in their coffee."

"They?" Montgomery demanded, out of his chair again. "They who?"

"Who else was there, Hank?" Rick asked calmly, though his mind raced. "Who else?"

Hank looked for the first time in half an hour at Montgomery. "Carleton."

"Carleton?" the other two asked in unison. Rick and Monty exchanged quizzical glances.

Montgomery demanded of Rick, "Who is this Carleton, anyway?"

Rick shook his head and pursued the thread. "When did Carleton come? How long was he with you?"

"A little while," Hank said, slipping back into the mist. "Just for coffee."

Stapler turned the name Carleton around in his mind several times as he stared at Hank's vacant expression. Carleton was one of the very few people that Madjerin had had any real contact with while she was alive. It made sense that he had some connection with her death. At least, he might give them a direction in which to look.

"Hold on a second," Rick said heading for the door. "We'll just have to find out what Carleton can tell us."

Montgomery intercepted him at the door. "Where are you going?"

"I'm going to phone him," Stapler explained. "I think we should go out there and talk to him."

The idea of chasing about the night depressed the weary detective. Still, he knew he had no choice. "Don't give us away."

With a nod Rick left the room. Montgomery turned his attention to his exhausted suspect. Hank Washington just lay on his bed staring at the ceiling. His face seemed a shade lighter and his lips were almost white. The nightmare he had seen had almost killed Hank Washington and certainly had devastated him. Montgomery felt it was having the same effect on him, more slowly, less dramatically, but just as surely. He could hardly bear to look himself in the mirror.

"Listen," he addressed Hank quietly. "I'm sorry about what happened and how I've pressed you, Washington."

Ponderously, Hank lowered his gaze from the ceiling to Montgomery's face. Some life had returned to his eyes. "Sergeant Montgomery, it doesn't matter to me," he replied. "Half the time I don't even know what to say."

Montgomery had to look away, to hide the shame he felt. "Yeah. I guess I'm a damn fool not to allow for what's happened to you. A good cop wouldn't ignore the effect it's had on you," he said. "Or on himself for that matter."

Hank's sigh emptied his body. "I don't remember what happened, Sergeant. I hope I don't. Ever." He tried to lift his shoulders in a shrug, but didn't have the strength. "I am alone again. I always have been. Except for her, I mean. I've never been one to look at what's past. Or to expect what's coming. For me, either's very special. Maybe a man doesn't deserve more than I had. Maybe I didn't deserve that much."

"Yeah," Montgomery agreed. "I guess I can't really appreciate what you lost."

A weak smile came to Hank's drawn face. "You got to have someone to lose, to understand, I guess. Comes as a surprise when you do."

Before Montgomery could put his thoughts together to form an answer, Stapler came back into the room.

"No answer," Rick announced grimly. "Let's take a run out there. He's got to be home."

Heaviness dropped over Monty's eyes. He felt he had to sleep. "It's getting mighty damned late, Stapler," he objected.

"It won't take long. He doesn't live all that far from here."

Montgomery looked at Washington, staring back at him with almost unseeing eyes. He would be the same way himself soon. "Shit," he cursed under his breath. "Okay, damn it." He stormed out of the room.

With his hand on the call button, Stapler smiled at Hank. "Take it easy, Henry. Okay?"

Hank nodded his head in a dream-like way and let his head fall to the pillows. Rick stared at him for a few moments more before quietly closing the door.

~ ~ ~

Carolyn Jordan returned from the hairdressers to find George entertaining Heloise Carpenter in the gloom of the study. Tired from the ordeal of forcing her brittle hair into an acceptable arrangement, Carolyn hesitated to make her arrival obvious. The sound of voices, however, had become so rare in the house, that she was drawn to it.

George and Heloise were locked in an intense conversation of some sort, the words were not important to Carolyn. She heard Madelaine's name then her own. It didn't matter that they discussed her. They had dissected her in the study often enough in the past. She stood in the hall, just beyond the door simply drinking in the murmur of voices. Since she had arrived, it seemed, no one had spoken in the house.

"Mrs. Jordan" Carolyn heard Heloise say. "Would you like some coffee?"

A moment passed before Carolyn realized that she had entered the study and that Heloise addressed her. She had been thinking of similar scenes in the past. Madelaine, as a little girl, had always been allowed to invade the study to talk for hours with her father. In that same room where she had been so unwelcome. Even now, she lingered at the doorway, reluctant to intrude into her husband's room.

"No, thank you," she said finally. She could feel each step she took as she walked to the desk. She lifted herself onto

232 | John Nicholas Datesh

the desk top, the only seat in which she felt remotely comfortable in that room. "Don't let me interrupt." she said.

George spoke casually, but his tone indicated that the conversation was over. "We were just chatting about Madelaine." He knew that Mrs. Jordan avoided that subject if possible.

Carolyn looked around the room. "Where is she, George?"

Heloise answered so quickly as to suggest embarrassment. "She went to bed a little while ago, Mrs. Jordan," she stated. "She's been working so hard lately."

"She inherited that trait from her father," Carolyn replied, examining Heloise's unlined prettiness. Shouldn't her daughter have been more like Heloise than Madelaine? Heloise seemed so human, so female. Not like Madelaine. Not an unloving, five foot eleven inch accounting machine."

"She inherited everything from her father," Carolyn elaborated. "Everything. I got nothing."

Innocently, Heloise agreed, "She does look a little like Mr. Jordan. Especially now."

Carolyn laughed bitterly. "Now that he is dead?" she asked. "Or now that Maddy has fixed her nose. I hadn't thought of it, but she does look more like Tom now. She chose his nose for her own. How like her."

"Really?" Heloise asked, surprised.

"Oh yes," Carolyn went on. "And I'll bet the silly damn girl doesn't even realize it."

"I think she can look attractive if she would fix herself up," Heloise said reassuringly. "Why does she insist on looking the way she does?"

It was Madelaine's way of getting even, Carolyn mused. Or perhaps it was more than that. Madelaine avoided gloss in almost everything. "Dressing up never helped her, Heloise," Carolyn explained as much to herself as to her listeners. "Make up only made her look more ridiculous. Pretty clothes were useless to her and I used to buy her very nice things," she added, savoring the delicious memories of

Madelaine's torment. It made her feel suddenly guilty. "She came to realize that it was a waste of her time, I think. She never really dresses up. Stripping down is much more her style."

Heloise flushed. The thought of Madelaine as a sexual creature reminded Heloise of Rick's relationship with her. Heloise had never before thought of Madelaine in that way, but increasingly, she had begun to realize that Rick and Madelaine were more than business partners.

"You misunderstand me, young lady," Carolyn said, amused by the flattering glow of natural rouge on Heloise's cheeks. "Madelaine abhors physical contact. In spite of what you may have read about her, Madelaine has no real sexual desire. What I meant was that Maddy prefers to look at all of us stripped naked, figuratively," she explained. "When she looks at you with those frightening eyes of hers, don't you feel she is ripping away the layers to get to your soul?"

Carolyn was becoming caught up in her thoughts. "'Sweep all the clutter away,' she once said to me," Carolyn continued. "What a fraud! I'll bet she's a hell of a lot more cluttered than you or I."

~ ~ ~

The junkyard looked familiar to Madelaine. She recognized most of the objects strewn about her. She knew the vague, distant walls towering above the piles of trash. Many times she had wandered through the place. And every time, she had spent her entire dream looking for something, she didn't know what, purposely lost amid the debris of so many other people's lives.

Madelaine understood that she was having another in a series of dreams with the same theme. Over the years she had dozens of dreams very much like the present one, not always about junkyards. The dreams had in common her searching for that 'something' that she did not know. Lately, however, the dreams had been more frequent, and more violent. Madelaine let her quest grow into a mad ransacking of some building. She would become wild with frustration at failing to locate the mysterious prize and leave nothing, no matter how valuable or dear, unbroken in her rage.

The same pattern had already begun in the dream junkyard. Having looked over the area several times for clues, Madelaine plunged into an intense rummage. Vainly she called for the junk-man to guide her, but he did not respond. He had abandoned the yard, she knew, as well as the small hut that commanded the dump. His absence incited her all the more. She strode about the yard kicking anything she saw, or throwing it against the hut if it were small enough. No piece was too important, old or broken to avoid her rampage.

As always, Madelaine would brook no interference during her dream. Characters had already entered the walls surrounding the yard, only to be sent fleeing by missiles from Madelaine's hands. She allowed them to enter quite far in this dream, tacitly inviting aid. Heloise Carpenter had been the first, fresh from a chatty dinner. Heloise had gotten remarkably close, before Madelaine showered her with projectiles of all descriptions. Heloise had gotten closer than anyone else and suffered all the more for it.

Rick had been there too, but he knew better than to get so close. He had vaulted to the top of the wall and happily mocked her futile efforts to dislodge him. She had tried everything, as usual. As usual she had failed to knock him from his perch. The debris she had thrown at him had merely piled up beside him and he sold it to passers-by on the outside, on Kingsfield.

Of course, her mother had laughed at her from beyond the walls. She was always beyond the stony enclosure, taunting Madelaine. Undoubtedly, the junk-man was with her mother, doing her bidding in every loathsome way. Incensed by the thought that her mother wanted the junkyard as a trophy, Madelaine resolved to leave nothing intact.

She turned her attention to the hut, a glorified out-house, in which the junk dealer had done his foul business. Anger streaming from her long, strong fingers, her hands ripped off the door with its sign that claimed, "Proprietor away." She smashed the thick oak against the shack's brick walls. Splinters flew in every direction, cutting her face, piercing her eyelids.

Unable to see, Madelaine seized whatever she could find in the building. Breakable things she smashed against the walls; other objects she crushed under foot or cast out the windows. She would empty the pissing place first, leaving only the layers of defecation. Then, kicking, scratching and pounding her fists and head against the plaster, Madelaine knocked out one wall. She collapsed with it, buried in the rubble.

Badly injured, Madelaine did not pause. She pulled herself out of the debris and rammed the second wall. Brick by brick she pulled it apart. Everyone was yelling at her. Her mother screamed and Rick goaded her on. She heard George begging her to stop. The owner, the junk man, said nothing all the while.

When the second wall finally succumbed to her fury, it inundated Madelaine with a ton of broken red stone. She lay under the weight, paralyzed temporarily by the damage. Above her she could hear the ceiling groan its warning. The roof would fall, crushing her, if she disturbed one more stone. Even if she moved, everything would cave in on top of her.

Madelaine had reached the usual climax of her dream. Absolute destruction awaited her slightest movement, yet she was compelled to continue. She began to rise from the pile of bricks and the building shook. It was then that she would awake.

Awake! Madelaine knew that she should have awakened. The roof trembled above her. Something was dreadfully wrong. This dream was different: She would not escape so easily. This time, Madelaine would not avoid the consequences of her actions by waking.

Carefully, Madelaine lowered herself back to the floor. She was in trouble, she realized, and suddenly, Madelaine was afraid.

~ ~ ~

The modified Volkswagen bus negotiated the last of the streets easily. Carleton knew the route perfectly, from his earlier visits to the Jordan house. He also knew the layout of the estate and that it suited his purposes very nicely. Well off to one side of the property sat the gardener's cottage. Fortunately, Kelly, the gardener, no longer worked full time and, therefore, no longer lived in the small building. It was just over the wall bordering the narrow dead end Kingsfield Place.

Due to the odd course of Kingsfield, Carleton could park his van in one of the street's bends and not be observed from Fifth Avenue. The last time he had used the site, Carleton had marveled at the fortunate design of the Jordan estate and Kingsfield place, giving him a hidden cul de sac in which to incubate his revenge.

He swung out of the cab without even bothering to look around him. Instead he proceeded directly to the rear of the Volkswagen to prepare himself. As compact as his equipment was, it had consumed almost all of the space in the rear of the vehicle. He had barely enough room beside the TI 125 desktop computer to sit during the session.

Jordan had trusted his fellow man enough to eschew security devices that would have complicated Carleton's work. The estate had no electronic warning equipment, no dogs, not even a guard to obstruct his access to the grounds. If the house were wired against entry, Carleton did not know or care. He would get inside the house in a way no one could stop.

Kelley's hut provided Carleton with the one raw material he could not carry with him. Without electricity in massive quantities, his deadly design would remain a harmless dream. As he was able to tap the 220 volt line at the cottage, however, Carleton did not have to worry about anything but a heavy duty, very long extension cord. Jordan had even been so kind as to install outlets in the exterior walls of the cottage for Kelley's electric garden tools.

Having surveyed the condition of his equipment, which had made the journey in fine shape, Carleton hoisted himself to the roof of the van. From that position he could leap to the top of the wall and lower himself down inside by means of a strong knotted rope. The darkness of the night and the density of the trees rendered his most casual movements unobservable.

Slung over his back, the wires and the small transceiver made him move awkwardly. In the open, he would have trouble moving with stealth enough to avoid detection. Among the trees of the Jordan estate, Carleton could relax as he prepared the transceiver for its task.

With the dangerous part of the job out of the way, Carleton struggled up the rope and over the wall to his bus. He found himself more easily tired by his preparations than usual, but did not worry as the physically taxing part of the execution was done. Inside the back of the Volkswagen, he paused to catch his breath.

Seated beside the TI 125, Carleton let his mind drift back to the first time he had tried his machine. He could admit that he had made several mistakes, not the least of which was placing his reliance on the cassette recorder to keep commands coming for the duration of the session. Because it had run out, Thomas Jordan had survived his first attack.

Jordan had been the first target for revenge, because Carleton knew that Jordan had been the force behind his treatment by the Talbot. Unfortunately, Jordan had resisted much longer than Carleton had anticipated and the reel of tape, with its essential instructions had finished before Jordan's heart gave out. Then and there, he had decided that hypnotic suggestion rather than an actual trance would provide the flexibility he needed in dealing with so many different people.

When he switched on the machine, Carleton immediately began to recall all of the instruction he had implanted several hours ago. He did his work without hesitation exactly as suggested in the earlier trance. He hooked up the communications interface to the TI 125 and put his remote telephone in position. He typed into the keyboard.

"53958-Phnnie. Communications."

The machine responded on the screen. "53958-Phnnie. Ready."

He ran two sample programs on the hook up to be certain that the link between the small TI 125 and the central computer at the Talbot was working properly. It was.

Next he placed the pick up next to his head, and typed, "Carl C 4." The screen responded with four narrow lines representing the output of his own brain. Then he did a final check on the hook ups at all stages of the equipment.

He flipped the switch controlling the transceiver and heard the familiar hum. The remote complement would bring him closer to his target, Madelaine Jordan. He lifted the magnetic tape cartridge from his pocket and put into the TI 125. The screen superimposed Madelaine Jordan's brain wave patterns on his.

His fingers went back to the keyboard of the TI 125. "Brain Functions Synchronize."

The screen showed the only activity required. Slowly the lines representing Carleton's mind began to fluctuate. They approached the lines of Madelaine Jordan until there were only four lines on the screen. Four discreet, bright lines, no longer eight. At that moment, a small red light on the transceiver went on.

Carleton closed his eyes and sat back. The computer had begun to do its job. Carleton's thoughts were being translated into the only form of thought Madelaine Jordan could accept. In a matter of minutes, only Carleton, through his equipment, would be generating thoughts based on that four function pattern. Madelaine Jordan would not.

CHAPTER FIFTEEN

The house where Carleton lived was dark by the time Stapler and Montgomery arrived. Shadows of the swaying trees hid the wooden, three story building and gave an eerie impression of movement.

Stapler's ring drew no response from Carleton's third floor apartment. Ringing the laboratory did no better. The partially deaf mistress of the place had let her own bell fall into disrepair. As the two men stood waiting for an indication of interest in their arrival, Montgomery quietly cursed his companion for dragging him out after midnight to ring doorbells.

"Let's get the hell out of here," he growled.

Stapler, finding the outer door open, ignored him and walked inside. He felt certain, as he had argued to Montgomery, that Carleton was too dedicated to his work to wander off late at night. He knew also that Carleton had neither girlfriend nor friends. He had no place else to be. If he were in his laboratory in the cellar, a knock on the door might bring him around.

Before he could knock, Stapler discovered that a door off the entryway was open, the one that led to Carleton's makeshift workshop. He looked in triumph at Montgomery who had followed him inside. Montgomery acknowledged the progress with a frown.

The stairs were completely dark and the descent treacherous on the antique wooden stairs. Not until they reached the dirt landing at the second cellar, did Montgomery sigh in relief.

"I'm too damn old for this," he whispered, lighting a match.

As if by invitation, Carleton's lab door hung open before them. In fact, the key remained in the lock. As the flickering light of the match died, Rick felt the wall for a switch.

"I'm afraid this place has a cord light," he said after a fruitless search. "Got anymore matches?"

Monty handed him the packet. "Burn your own fingers. It was your idea."

With the help of the matches, Stapler located the chain to Carleton's lights. When the small room flooded with light, Stapler started. "Christ Almighty!" he exclaimed. "He's cleaned it out!"

To Montgomery, the lab appeared less than cleaned out. If anything, the room had papers and wire strewn everywhere. A series of battered televisions occupied a bench in one corner. A couple of old radios half disassembled in another. Graph paper and computer paper covered the floor. Only one space in the entire room appeared to have been cleaned out: The desk.

The only object remaining on the desk where, Stapler recalled, the computer and its paraphernalia had sat, was a cheap, foreign made cassette tape recorder. Rick bent over it as though it contained some answer. Absently he hefted it in his hand. "The idiot left it on," he remarked disgusted. The play button was still depressed and the soft shirring indicated that only the ending of the reel had stopped the machine.

Stapler handed the machine to Montgomery, who glared at the tape recorder for several seconds before realizing that he had it in his hand. He was so tired that he had trouble focusing his attention on anything. He switched it off and proceeded to look over the room as a matter of habit.

For Carleton to be out at such an hour, Stapler felt, was unusual. That Carleton had removed almost all of his major equipment was vaguely unnerving. Stapler recalled that

Carleton had a habit of leaving notes for himself on any available slip of paper and then misplacing it. Rick began to search the paper on the floor near the desk. Much of that paper had been printed out by computer. Carleton's desktop model did not have a printing mechanism. Increasingly, Stapler felt the uncomfortable sensation that something was terribly wrong.

Poring over the printout material, Rick became convinced that it came from the Talbot. Most of the readings were of the kind Madjerin had produced during her demonstration, the graphs like those her project cranked out.

Montgomery grumbling in the background let out a "harrumph" and tossed a manila folder Stapler's way. "What is this crap?"

The folder contained photocopies of the brain wave readings taken from the Talbot Board of Trustees during a demonstration of the Madjerin-Carleton project in better days. Rick's pattern was there, of course. Carleton had used it earlier and he had a copy of it himself somewhere at his office. Madjerin had been so proud of that first demonstration.

"These are what make each of us unique," Stapler replied without clarification.

Montgomery, not feeling particularly philosophical, let the attorney's comment pass. Rick had already returned to his rummaging through the debris of Carleton's work. His eyes settled on a graph, very much like those in the folder, except that it had been torn at both ends, and the graph line began at the top of the page instead of the bottom. Stapler turned it upside down, but that did not help. The lines formed a very familiar pattern but he did not recognize for ten minutes that he was staring at the brain wave functions of Madelaine Jordan.

~ ~ ~

Heloise accepted the third brandy of the evening with re-luctance. She desperately wanted to go home. It was late and she was tired, psychologically as well as physically. Heloise did not have the stamina of most people and certainly not that of Mrs. Jordan.

Carolyn's smile of triumph softened when she saw that Heloise was close to tears. "I think I would have been happy if Maddy were like you, Heloise," she said, her hand on Heloise's arm. "Tom used to tell me about you sometimes. I think he was jealous of your Rick."

"Rick?" Heloise repeated wide-eyed.

"Yes. Your Rick and my Tom were very much alike in some ways, Heloise," she explained. "Their affection for you is one. Their fascination with Madelaine is another."

The words caught Heloise off guard. "Ricky hates her," she blurted.

"Don't be jealous of Madelaine," Carolyn said gently.

Heloise stood up abruptly. "Jealous!"

Carolyn seemed to ignore her outburst. "You and I are possessive, my dear," she said. "In our way. So is Madelaine, but she's not after what we're after."

Feeling awkward and abashed, Heloise returned to her seat. She could admit that she had something of a jealous streak, but of Madelaine? And over Rick?

Carolyn went on. "When Tom and I were first married, I objected to every minute he spent on anything other than me. And he spent whole days at J & T. Not at first. No, not at first, but even before Johnny was born, he was back at it. I had hoped that Johnny would bring him back home, but it made him worse. My God, I never saw him. All I had was Johnny," she sighed and shrugged her narrow shoulders. "I don't think it did either of us any good."

"I had to spend hours with Johnny," she said. "He was premature and sickly for a long time. I loved it. He was such a part of me. We were even near death together the first weeks." she smiled slightly.

Carolyn did not notice Heloise's discomfort. She had someone to listen. "Then came Madelaine," she grimaced. "I wish to God she had not been so monstrous. I had wanted a girl. Just like me. I remember I was so happy when they told me. It was horrible." She shuddered as she spoke. "It was really a shock to see such an ugly baby. That is the kindest thing I can say about it. She was frightening, with a huge head and those horrible transparent eyes. And her nose seemed to be all twisted. My doctors wouldn't even guess at what had happened. I think I threw up."

The dream-like cadence of Carolyn's voice had drawn Heloise back to her senses. She took advantage of the opportunity to gulp more brandy.

Carolyn was staring into space as she continued. "You know how babies are. All soft and cuddly. Not Maddy. She was just the way she is now. Only smaller. She was long and thin with the same features, those stern unforgiving features. And she hated being held. At least by me. I suppose she could sense how I felt about her."

"Babies are like that," Heloise agreed quietly.

Carolyn sighed again. "People, my dear girl, people are like that." She stared up towards where Madelaine was sleeping. "It is a terrible responsibility, Heloise. Don't fret that you haven't faced it yet. I was too young, perhaps. I hate to admit," she said, feeling the weight of the truth of the revelations, "but a mother has to take some responsibility for the way her children turn out. Poor Maddy. I'm sorry."

"Tell her," Heloise said, her suggestion surprising even her.

If Heloise was surprised, Carolyn was appalled. "That it's my fault?" she asked, mortified. "Tell Madelaine?" The idea sounded preposterous. Madelaine already blamed her for everything. How could she agree? "I don't think she'd accept an apology from me. Besides, I've been humiliated enough by her."

"If you promise not to tell her I told you," Heloise said," she isn't feeling very well, Mrs. Jordan. She told me that she is afraid that something is wrong with her."

Carolyn Jordan laughed at the thought. "Madelaine thinks something is wrong with her? It's not like my Maddy to admit weakness." Was it, she wondered soberly, that Madelaine had been affected by her father's death? All along, Carolyn had known that Madelaine would suffer when her father died and that she would never admit it.

Heloise reflected on Madelaine's recent conversations with her. "She really doesn't seem the same." And Heloise wanted Madelaine stay the same.

Madelaine had had blackouts before, Carolyn thought, but something about the most recent one led her to feel that Heloise was right. "You astonish me," she said. "You have somehow cajoled me into attempting reconciliation with my fiercest enemy, my own daughter."

Together the two women mounted the arcing staircase and approached Madelaine's door. Carolyn's determination faded. She could not follow through. Madelaine hid always hated her, from the beginning. Could anything change that? she wondered. The one thing that bound them was gone.

"Go on," Heloise whispered.

Carolyn knocked softly. Eliciting no greater response thin a reproving glance from Heloise, she tried again, slightly harder. "She isn't having trouble sleeping it least," she said.

Impatiently, Heloise took matters into her own hinds and opened the door. Carolyn gave her a wide-eyed look of amazement. They entered together.

Before them on the bed lay Madelaine, eyes clamped shut. The bedding, tucked in tightly around her, fixed her to the bed. She looked strangely restrained beneath the stretched covers. Her short hair, always so neatly arranged, seemed to be flying from her head in ill of the directions her arms and legs could not go. The expression on her face was, incredibly, one of intense concentration.

Her eyelids squeezed together. The thin lips drew in almost invisible line across her face. Deep lines furrowed her usually smooth forehead is the facial muscles pulled taut under ashen pile skin.

Aghast at first and then concerned, Carolyn moved to the bedside and tried to stir her daughter from her frightful slumber. Madelaine did not respond except, perhaps, by tightening her face still further. Shaking her daughter's shoulders, Carolyn found that the tension reflected in Madelaine's face ran throughout her body.

Madelaine did not respond to loud entreaties to wake from her mother. Physical efforts to rouse her had no effect in bringing Madelaine out of what increasingly appeared to be a deathly deep sleep.

Only when the two women ceased their attempts did they get any response at all. They were standing at the bedside wondering what to do, when for a shadow of a second, Madelaine opened her eyes. Her mouth curled into a terrible sneer and issued a frightening growl. Surprise and pain were all that her face conveyed.

~ ~ ~

As though a needle had been thrust into her head, Madelaine felt the pain. Whatever it was, it felt horribly wrong. And it hurt. It forced her eyes open despite the splinter of wood still lodged in them, through the eyelids. The tearing of flesh should have hurt, too, but she felt only the eerie opening of her head.

She tightened still further, fearing that any movement would destroy the fragile balance that kept her from being crushed by the tenuously suspended roof. Moments before the pain began she had heard her mother, felt her trying to shake the walls. Wasn't she off with the junk dealer again? Madelaine had tried to ignore her mother, not even bothering to tell her to leave her dream. Now, with the pain, Madelaine hoped she would stay.

But it was not her mother who was suddenly walking toward her. A bizarre blur, independent of her, it came in her direction with determination and confidence. He had a look of purpose. Hello, he said. It's Carleton. I've come into your dream, Miss Jordan, to kill you.

His words rang true. Madelaine was dreaming and she knew it. She was in danger and she knew that too. Defenseless, she was trapped in a perilously frail building that could collapse on top of her at any moment. And one thing was clear: Carleton, in sharp focus now, meant exactly what he said.

~ ~ ~

Montgomery absently searched through various, dusty preserve closets in the former fruit cellar, leaving Stapler to pore over the reams of paper scattered about the laboratory. Neither had found anything that appeased their growing frustration.

"Let's get the hell out of here," Montgomery exclaimed.

Stapler threw the papers he had been examining into the air. "Yeah," he agreed. "I don't know why we've been here this long."

Disgusted, Montgomery sat on the desk next to Stapler. He had spent several minutes in a compulsive search for nothing. While Stapler organized the stacks of papers he had gathered, Montgomery toyed with Carleton's tape recorder. The cassette leaped out of its pocket. "Shit!" he remarked. Having returned it to the recorder, Monty pressed the start button.

"Good evening, Carleton," the tape said. Monty immediately turned off the machine. The voice had sounded so unearthly as to startle him, despite its low, whispering tone.

When Monty looked up he found Rick gaping at him. It was a look of amazement.

His voice breaking, Rick said "That's Carleton."

"Huh?" Montgomery asked, dumbly.

Grabbing the machine Rick repeated, "That's Carleton. That's his voice." He turned the machine on again.

"You have work to do again tonight," the player continued. "As usual, all of the instructions you need will be on this tape. You will play this tape and remember all of the instructions. In detail."

While the voice cooed directions the two listeners stared at the tiny spinning reels. "You will now go to sleep, Carleton. You will go to sleep when I have counted to ten. It will be a deep, deep trance, the sleep-learning trance. You will recall every command given during this trance."

The strangely melodic voice began to count. Having reached the number ten, repeating it for emphasis, the voice said, "You are now asleep, Carleton. I have instructions for you. The commands will be largely familiar. Your task is not new and you will have no difficulty carrying it out. I shall make 'reference commands', those given you in past sessions, and you will remember all of those 'reference commands.'"

Stapler hissed the obvious. "Hypnosis."

Montgomery nodded. "He's some kind of nut."

The tape ran on. "You will remove your equipment to your van and install it as per 'reference command' one. The computer is programmed and you will operate it as per reference command 5. The input, of course, will be different, as the individual is different. You will then drive to Kingsfield Place as per reference command... No, that is not a reference command, but you have done it before. You will recall it. You drove there just several hours ago. Kingsfield Place."

Kingsfield Place. The name rang its alarm in Stapler's ears. It was incredibly familiar, yet he could not remember where he had seen it so recently. Kingsfield? Where else had he been? He always seemed tied up with Jordan estate matters.

"Christ Almighty!" he cried. "The Jordan house!"

Monty shut off the recorder. "What about it?"

"Kingsfield Place," Rick explained. "It's somewhere around Maddy's place. Only I can't remember where."

Montgomery nodded and let the recorder continue.

"You must set up the equipment properly as per reference command 4, Carleton," Carleton's voice said. "Everything will be the same. You will recall the setting of the transceiver from Mr. Jordan's session."

"What is he talking about?" Monty demanded.

"Don't look at me," Stapler snapped back.

"Return to the van, after placing the transceiver," the voice droned on. "Hook up the receiver for yourself and check the system and terminal hook-ups. As per reference command 6." With chilling assurance the strange instructions flowed off the tape, filling the cellar with a hushed urgency. "As usual, the transmitter will begin sending out only its general signals. Once you have made certain that all is functioning properly, type the following: 'Brain Functions Synchronize', and proceed to reference command No. 7. Once the program is in place and functioning, the small receiver light will begin to glow red. At that point you will type the word 'run' into the keyboard and enter into the operative trance."

The voice paused and then added, "The reel is about to end. Turn off the machine and flip the cassette to the other side. Now." The speaking stopped as the reel ended.

Neither Rick nor Monty moved or spoke. For a full minute, they remained transfixed by the voice they no longer heard.

Montgomery finally leaned forward and turned the cassette over. His voice was hoarse when he said, "Let's see what else he has to say."

Immediately, Carleton's disembodied voice began again. "When you enter the operative trance, you will have one task and one task only. You will not deviate from that task no matter what distraction. You will use your mind. You will direct all of your thought, all of your concentration to only one purpose. You will enter Madelaine Jordan's mind, you will invade her dreams and you will add your thoughts to hers. You will impose your thought on her mind. And you will think one thing only. You will think that you have entered her dreams for the sole purpose of revenge. You will tell her who you are and why you are there."

"Christ Almighty," Rick said in an incredulous whisper. "Turn that son of a bitch off."

"Let's get out of here," Montgomery agreed, dropping the machine. In his haste to get to the door, he neglected to turn it off.

After they had left, Carleton's insistent voice went on. "Tell her over and over, 'I'm here to kill you,'" it said.

~ ~ ~

His face colored by the glow of a small red light mounted on the face of his equipment, Carleton sat stock upright in his van. His eyes were closed, his face blank. Occasionally he wrinkled his nose or creased his forehead in concentration. He had his hands folded in his lap waiting until the time came to switch off his machinery.

He was concentrating as he had been told to, but he felt pain in his head and the fatigue of seven previous nights and their aftermaths. Sweat dripped down his cheeks and his eyelids twitched. He was concentrating on Madelaine Jordan and what he had to tell her.

"I have come to kill you," he intoned mentally. "I had hoped you would be different. But you were a fool, like the others. They chose to ignore me. Deny me. Belittle me. For many years I put up with that kind of treatment. I don't have to anymore. You cannot put me out of your mind. You cannot ignore me. I will have my recognition, if only for a little while. And I will be satisfied. Your headstone will be a small monument to my genius."

CHAPTER SIXTEEN

Though she tried not to listen to him, Carleton's words reverberated through her head in the strangest way. Each syllable shook the rafters of the roof. With very little effort, she knew, Carleton could make his threat a reality.

She did not call out for help. The only one who could help, she knew, would not come. Madelaine wracked her pained head for an answer. As Carleton droned on, like an automaton, Madelaine carefully dragged her shattered body from the pile of broken bricks. Each movement caused the roof to shift a fraction, but Madelaine got clear without bringing it down.

I killed them all, Carleton boasted. Melton, Madjerin, Carstairs, the others and your father, too.

Dead? Her father was dead. She knew it was true.

Carleton walked casually around the building, hefting a large brick. He looked up at the roof teetering above Madelaine. Laughing, he tossed the brick underhand onto the roof. A chiseled wood beam tore loose and crashed down within inches of Madelaine's jerking head.

You are quick, he said, picking out another, larger brick. With little effort he propelled the huge brick against one of the two standing walls. The building shook violently and slabs of heavy slate thundered all around her.

You shouldn't have done it, Carleton chided her.

I will not be denied anything, not anymore. No one will ignore me again.

Stubbornly, Madelaine raised herself up, trying to pull herself out of the doomed shack. She could not find a way out no matter which way she crawled. Her hand felt something *hard, on the floor, under everything. Madelaine knew she had to stop long enough to dig it out of the ruins of the house. Even in the gloom and dust of the wreckage, it shone silver. A band, thin and fine, it had not been twisted, or even dented by the bombardment of destruction Madelaine had caused. Though a tiny thing, it was bigger than she was. The small letters inside it said something. It was in her father's handwriting, etched in the brilliant surface.*

I am Maddy's. Love Daddy, was all it said.

~ ~ ~

Morex stood with his hand raised to knock as he watched Montgomery's car fly up the drive. The dome light bathed the front of the Jordan mansion in an eerie, pulsating blue light. The transfixed doctor waited until the two men had run from the car to his side. "You've heard?"

"Yeah," Montgomery grunted. "Let's go."

The three men brushed past George the moment he opened the door.

Morex and Stapler headed for the stairs without a word. Montgomery grabbed George by the shoulders.

"I'm looking for Kingsfield Street," he declared breathlessly.

George, though alerted to Madelaine's seizure, was puzzled by the commotion and particularly put off by Montgomery's request. "Kingsfield?" he repeated.

"Where is it?" Montgomery bellowed.

"Over along the wall," he replied shaken. "The left hand wall."

In another second Montgomery had left the house. He paused a moment on the front porch, to get his bearings. He knew what he was looking for, an old Volkswagen bus. Inside he would find a hell of a lot of equipment and a man in a hypnotic trance. He didn't know what he would do when he found them. He was not dealing with a normal assault, that much at least he understood.

The lawn stretched before him a long way. Beyond that he saw the dense trees and the outline of Kelley's cottage. Farther away still he knew he would find a wall. He hoped he could scale it when he got there. No, he couldn't do that sort of thing so easily anymore. With that painful realization, Montgomery started to run to the front gate.

"The front gate?" Rick cried, rushing to join Heloise at the window in Madelaine's room. "What the hell for?"

Sure enough, he could see Monty running down the long drive to the front gate. The detective's achingly slow progress looked almost funny from Rick's perspective. Unfortunately, Madelaine's life could well be dependent on tired, forty year old legs.

"He could never climb the wall, Rick," George said from behind him.

Stapler turned at George's remark and looked to where Madelaine lay wriggling under her covers. Her face went through a whole range of expressions as he watched her. Morex stood beside the bed helpless.

He had already decided against risking drugs to stimulate her out of the sleeping fit.

"All we can do," Morex had said, quietly, "is hold her down when the time comes."

~ ~ ~

Carleton glowered at her as Madelaine drew herself through the silver ring. As she emerged, she was outside, the shack forgotten. Carleton scoffed at her new strength, but he had stopped smiling. The brick in his hand fell harmlessly to his feet. The junk man's hut had disappeared and Carleton would have to find another way.

Madelaine got to her feet.

~ ~ ~

In response, Carleton retreated a step and surveyed the new scene. Nothing but open ground surrounded them now.

Only the high stone walls looming in the distance defined their arena. He, and Madelaine too, knew that he would have to struggle. With that realization, he felt the weariness of his seven earlier battles. For this, at last, Carleton would have to summon all his resources.

~ ~ ~

Madelaine had room to flee, but she did not move. As Carleton approached cautiously, she raised herself on her toes and clenched her fists, but she did not run. With lead in his gloves, Carleton swung at her. Madelaine bobbed her head, but still caught a glance of the blow. It hurt terribly, and would have crushed her skull had it hit her full.

Carleton's next series of punches, she avoided, blocking some, ducking others. The wicked sweep of his hooks and the weight of his jabs allowed Madelaine time to counter each one he threw. She resigned herself to poking, and jabbing to wear him down. She could not afford to be hit solidly more than once.

The first jolt that Madelaine dealt Carleton's jaw rocked him back on his heels. Shock opened his eyes wide, and stood him straight up. Sensing her opening, Madelaine bore forward to capitalize on his daze. Even back-peddling, however, Carleton mustered a wild, vicious left cross that caught Madelaine's right cheek. The stunning force of the punch threw her back fifteen feet, leaving a trail of blood for Carleton to follow.

Staggered by the pain in her smashed face, Madelaine was saved only by the distance she had been thrown. Unable to see from her right side, Madelaine had lost her sense of depth perception and her balance. Carleton consumed precious minutes in regenerating his exhausted presence to complete the job, time enough for Madelaine to pull herself back together.

~ ~ ~

The weight of Carleton's gloves prevented him from ending Madelaine's life when next he swung. He had lost the strength to lift his hands very high. His hook, then, only thumped her midsection and knocked her to the ground, still half alive. Carleton smiled triumphantly as Madelaine lay flat on her back. After savoring his victory, he flung himself upon her intending to choke the life from her.

~ ~ ~

Pulsating pain was Madelaine's only sensation. The ache in her head had become so intense that she could hardly feel her other wounds. She could tell, at least, that she could not move her arms or legs. It was as though someone were holding her down. Carleton took advantage of her paralysis to pin her arms and legs to the ground, somehow keeping his hands free.

Carleton paused for breath and flexed his tired hands. He said good-bye to Madelaine as he leaned forward. She managed only to snarl at him as he placed his hands around her neck.

~ ~ ~

"I can't see him anymore." Heloise reported from her post at the window. "I think he's turned the corner."

Without knowing what else to do, Morex held Madelaine's feet down, while Rick restrained her arms. All they hoped for was to avoid self inflicted harm, the kind suffered by the others. All eyes were fixed on the sleeping Madelaine. Their ears strained to hear the tiny groans she emitted. Every muscle tensed with Madelaine's strange movements.

When Madelaine snarled up at Rick, he let her arms free by reflex. Even as he regained his composure, however, he did not grab them again. Her arms remained in the awkward position in which he had held them, as though still restrained. Morex released her legs in astonishment. The legs remained unnaturally twisted.

"Oh, my God," Morex said.

"Jesus Christ," Stapler breathed, his hand grinding at his face. He became certain she would die if she remained asleep. "Come on, Maddy:" he shouted shaking her violently. "Wake the hell up!"

Morex dropped into a chair exhausted. Heloise joined Rick and the frozen Carolyn Jordan at Madelaine's bedside. Carolyn began to scream when she saw the terrible expressions Madelaine's face assumed. Heloise reeled against Rick as Madelaine first bared her teeth, then gurgled and gasped in horrible desperation for air.

Stapler gently pushed Heloise to one side as she regained her senses. He was ready, therefore, to leap onto the bed and try to hold Madelaine's convulsing body. She was shaking her head from side to side so quickly and powerfully that he could not begin to stop it. His hands failing, he gripped her head between his knees, fearing she would snap her neck if she continued. It took every muscle straining to prevent her from whipping Rick off the bed.

In response to Rick's efforts, Madelaine began to arch her back and shake her entire frame in a series of rapid spasms.

George rushed over from the door and lay across Madelaine's waist. Carolyn, half recovered, seized Madelaine's hands, still stretched so strangely over her head.

The room suddenly fell silent and Madelaine's body went limp. No one breathed, including Madelaine. Her face reflected surprised agony and her throat went in and out. Morex had passed out in his chair.

Is this what Hank had seen, Rick wondered. Good God, Almighty, he hoped not.

~ ~ ~

The remarkable Carleton's hands were much stronger than they looked. They pressed so fiercely into Madelaine's neck that she felt admiration for him. She could hardly breathe anymore, as she felt the weight of a man on her vibrating chest. She twisted her head as much as she could to free her neck from the deadly grip.

She opened her eyes. Her mother stood beside her crying and squeezing her hand. Please, Maddy, she heard her mother say.

Carleton stiffened when he heard the sound. He continued his strangling hold, but his face contorted in agony.

Maddy, Maddy, she heard from Carleton. Her father's voice poured out of Carleton's head.

Then he was there, her father, beside Carleton. He was dressed for a party, but his head seemed so horribly beaten. Carleton released one hand and swept it wildly at the figure of Thomas Jordan. Go away! Carleton shouted. Go away!

Her father did not go away. Instead, others appeared. Madelaine knew them all, Jim Carstairs, Red Melton, Madjerin, the Indian girl. They all were ghastly distorted shapes of themselves, as she had never imagined them. Carleton screamed at them and waved both hands, to keep them away from him.

A look of pained concentration returned to Carleton's face and, with it, his hands to her throat. The images around him faded, as he repeated, I will kill you, I will kill you.

~ ~ ~

Concentrate! Concentrate! He said to himself.

~ ~ ~

Madelaine looked up at Carleton, at the concentration in his face. She understood his power and focused her mind on his eyes. Suddenly, she could see in them, then through them. Madelaine saw, through Carleton's eyes, a familiar face, a long thin face. She saw her own large gray eyes staring up into Carleton's like twin steel barrels. There was her mouth, a narrow line of determination.

Maddy, Maddy. Her father somehow was still there. She knew that he would stay.

~ ~ ~

Oh, my God. Carleton heard his own voice. He could not concentrate on repelling the force of Madelaine Jordan's mind. The others, the others he had destroyed, they were back. They wouldn't leave him alone. And she was too strong.

Another sound. A bang! Someone was outside. Carleton screamed. He couldn't hold her! He had to pull himself free. He couldn't stop her!

~ ~ ~

Madelaine saw her face and Carleton's through sets of eyes. The faces merged separated again, differently this time. Carleton's face was below hers. Then she saw only Carleton's face, twisted with a horrible revelation. It was Madelaine who now squeezed harder. Her fingers dug into his throat as Carleton's eyes bulged in uncontrollable terror.

In an instant, her hands were empty, as she knelt over the barren floor. Carleton, lying there only a moment before, had disappeared. So had the incredible pain in her head.

Madelaine collapsed, gulping for breath. With her last surge of energy she looked around her. People were there, but not Carleton. Not her father, either. But he had been there. When she needed him. She would not forget that.

~ ~ ~

Montgomery's chest heaved quietly as he sat back in the rich leather chair in Tom Jordan's study. Soaking wet and exhausted Montgomery knew he could not think straight. He had seen death in many faces in his life, but Raymond Carleton's had torn his mind from his head.

"I swear to God," he declared. "I never want to see anything like it again."

The others, still too numb to comment, only half-listened, trying mostly to forget what they had themselves just witnessed.

"I blew the door off and there he was," Monty continued, compulsively unloading his burden on the others. "Sitting there, surrounded by all this electronic garbage. Carleton was just sitting there and suddenly he vaulted into the air and onto the floor with a scream I'll never forget." Montgomery shuddered at the memory of Carleton's last sounds. "For about ten seconds he wriggled on the floor of the van and that was it."

Stapler found some words. "He was dead?"

The detective bent his neck back and sighed. "I didn't check for a couple of minutes. Honest to God, I was afraid to touch him," he admitted. "But, yes, he was dead. If that is death."

A weak voice came from the corner of the room. "I'm afraid to go to sleep," Heloise said, her voice trembling.

As he entered the door, Morex, haggard and drained, said "Well, Madelaine still is. Her blood pressure is very low and so is her pulse, but not dangerously so. I would guess she's going to sleep well into the afternoon."

"At least now," Rick commented, "it won't hurt her."

Nodding gravely, the doctor agreed, "It should help, but after what's happened, I don't know."

The silence that followed as they recalled what each had seen. Finally Carolyn Jordan asked, "Will she be all right, Tony?"

"I don't know, Carolyn," Morex conceded. "I still don't really know what happened to her. From what Rick has told us, I can only believe that there will be great psychological damage. We don't know what happened in there," he said, tapping his forehead. "But we know it was terrible."

"How is she physically?" Monty asked.

The doctor laughed quietly. "She is a very strong young lady, Sergeant. There was nothing broken, but I imagine she damaged some muscle tissue at least. I would also guess that she has drained herself of almost all of her energy."

Montgomery snorted. "Not a very refreshing sleep."

"No," Morex agreed, with an ironic smile. "But the next few hours will help her. And I think they wouldn't hurt us either."

The strain of the morning and of the day before suddenly swept over Montgomery. The old reserve of drive had dissipated during his involvement in the Jordan case. Now that it was over, he realized that it would not return. From that moment on he would be an old cop, biding his time until retirement. He had never felt such emptiness. "Yeah," he said, pulling himself to his feet.

Montgomery and Morex left the room together, slowly, deliberately. The others prepared to follow them. Carolyn Jordan could hardly move and had to be helped to the door by Heloise, and Rick.

She shook them off lightly. "I'll be all right. I'll be all right."

Her voice was barely audible. "Thank God you were here," she said as she trudged up the stairs to where George kept Madelaine under his watchful eye.

Stapler took Heloise by the arm, back into the study. "I need a drink, Hel," he said. "How about you?"

Heloise did not answer. She watched him as he poured them both a drink. He moved so leisurely, she thought. She could barely stand up straight. She felt as though she were observing him from far away. "Rick?" she asked timidly.

He did not turn to face her. "Hmm?" He went on fixing his drink.

Once she had spoken, Heloise realized that she hadn't anything to say. "I guess I was wondering what it will be like when she wakes up."

Rick came over to her and placed a drink in her hand. He smiled in a way she did not like. "Madelaine? Oh, she'll be fine," he assured her. "She is the most remarkable woman I know. Christ, she'll be better than ever."

The confident cheer in his voice sent chills down Heloise's back. She detected more than the usual admiration in it. Everything would be different. She had known that by the way he pushed her aside in Madelaine's room. Her shivering went beyond her control.

"Heloise!" he exclaimed a concerned look on his face. "Are you Okay?"

"Of course," she replied without conviction.

Stapler took her by the shoulders. "Heloise, my God. You're shaking like mad. Are you sure you're all right?"

At first she could not look at him. Her eyes looked anywhere else. She hated that kindly worry in his voice and she could not bear to see it in his eyes. Her resistance was futile, she understood. She started to cry and wanted to get away from him.

Rick could feel her try to pull away, he wouldn't let her. "I've known you long enough, Heloise Carpenter, to know that you do not cry when everything is all right."

His firm grip felt foreign on her shoulders. Her crying became worse. Heloise did not want his kindness or his gentle concern. She knew him too well not to know what they meant, and she could not stand that. "I want you to love me, damn it," she cried. "All right."

Taken aback, Rick let her go. As she had when he first had known her, she frightened with her insistence. Still, it was different, somehow. "I always have, Heloise," he responded.

"You used to," she said.

"Don't be silly," he snapped aggravated at the implication that he had changed. He hadn't changed. "I still love you. I always will. You know that better than I do."

She knew him when he was lying, even to himself. And she could prove it when she had to. "For once, Rick," she said, "you're going to have to prove it to me. I want to leave, now. I want to leave everything."

Stapler took a step back. "You're joking." He felt she had to be kidding. She knew he couldn't. "What about J.J.?"

Heloise shook her head sadly. "J.J.?" she asked harshly. "What about him? He is a wonderful guy who married me because you wouldn't." She had never admitted that to anyone before. She had certainly never admitted to herself. J.J., of course, knew without anyone telling him. Maybe that was why he always looked so sad.

"Heloise!" he exclaimed appalled.

She glared at him, angry with his innocence. "J.J. is not an issue, but I'll tell you who is," she snapped. "Madelaine Jordan!"

With that Heloise stomped past him and out of the study. Rick did not turn to watch her exit. He was fuming at her. Madelaine Jordan? Where had that come from?

CHAPTER SEVENTEEN

Acting Chairman Francis DeJong called the meeting to order. The members of the Board of Directors reluctantly took their seats. The hum of conversation, the buzz of speculation died only with DeJong's exercise of the gavel. All eyes fixed on Madelaine Jordan's empty chair.

DeJong called for the reading of the minutes of the prior meeting and the Corporate Secretary read the report himself. The unusual procedure surprised no one, as the assistant secretary, Richmond Stapler, was expected to remain aloof from the conduct of the meeting. Stapler sat glumly in his chair, his eyes lost in deep shadows above pale cheeks. He did not acknowledge the reading of the minutes in any way.

Once the minutes were approved, DeJong turned the floor over to Josh Einberg. Einberg rose slowly from his seat, his long expression approaching sorrow. "Gentlemen and ladies," he began hoarsely. The sound of his cracking voice reminded him to clear his throat. "I have bad news for you again today. Madelaine Jordan is still too weak to attend the meeting."

The sophisticated gathering broke out into boisterous conversation like a group of astonished children. Einberg made no effort to quiet them. He just let the uproar subside on its own. "Mr. DeJong and I have decided that we must go ahead, in her absence," he stated, staring straight at Stapler. "J & T cannot continue in its current condition, without leadership. We will, therefore, act today to elect new officers and fill the vacancies on this board."

John Borov, president of Trans-Pacific Transport, a J & T subsidiary, objected. "Mr. Einberg. Without Miss Jordan, how can we pretend to proceed properly. She is the major figure here."

Fatigue clouded Josh Einberg's face. "John," he began, "It must be done. We cannot guess how long it will be before Madelaine can attend to business."

"Considering the divisions involved," Borov countered, "I think we should wait." Borov had long been Madelaine's only dependable ally on the J & T board. She was responsible for his elevation to the head of Trans-Pacific and he knew it. "I for one will not be a party to a rump board election."

Mopping his brow Einberg looked to DeJong for comment. DeJong quietly shrugged, and said, "I think we have to go ahead, John."

Rising from his seat, Borov growled, "In that case, I leave you to your work."

Before Borov could get to the door, it opened from the outside. George Bestral poked his head inside and then withdrew it. In the next instant, he wheeled Madelaine Jordan into the conference room, to the joint gasp of the directors.

Seated in the metal chair, the gaunt, languid Madelaine surveyed the room through half-open eyes. Her bowed head nodded a greeting, accompanied by a wan smile. Her hair was drawn off her face accenting the hollowness of her cheeks and the darkness around her eyes.

"I'm sorry to be late," she said weakly.

The directors sat frozen in their seats. Only Stapler was on his feet and he did not seem aware of it. The expression on his face betrayed his horror at her arrival. He glared at Tony Morex when he entered with a nurse.

"What are you trying to do, Tony?" he demanded.

Madelaine chortled as George took her around to her place at the table. "You needn't stand, Rick," she said. "I'm already seated."

Stapler shot a glance at her, trying to assess her condition. She opened her eyes fully for the first time since that nightmare and stared back. He sat down, fixing his eyes on his hands.

Turning to Einberg and DeJong, Madelaine asked softly, "Have I missed anything?"

Both men shook their heads.

"No elections yet?"

They shook their heads again.

Her voice barely carried through the acoustically perfect conference room. "Good, since I asked for these elections, I thought I should at least show up for them. Besides, I have my own slate of candidates to offer, as you probably know."

"Yes," Josh replied lifting a sheet of paper, "I was prepared to present them for you."

"Sit down, John," she said to Borov, suspended halfway to the door.

"I may want your vote." She paused to gather some breath as Borov assumed his chair. "I cannot stay long, I'm afraid. I want to express my views and leave. If I'm not quick about it, Tony will drag me away."

Morex nodded gravely.

Madelaine's head nodded with Morex's, unconsciously. "I have a good list of people here and I think they are better qualified than those Rick's Susan Hill will submit. If only because they will work better with me."

Susan Hill stiffened at the mention of her name and fingered the papers in front of her. She looked at Stapler, but received no indication from him. His eyes were glued to his fingernails.

Despite frequent pauses, Madelaine's voice became progressively weaker as she spoke. "I have plans for J & T," she continued. "Not all of them will be acceptable to you, but I think most will. Unfortunately, I don't have the strength to carry them out without your support. If that is not possible, I will concede the post of Chairman to Josh."

Madelaine motioned George to pour her some water. When she had taken several slow sips, she went on, her voice more faint still. "To assure some measure of harmony, I have petitioned this morning to have Mr. Stapler replaced as trustee of several trusts holding J & T stock. I also apologize to him for such surreptitious action, but it was necessary under present conditions."

Her announcement drew another round of gasps from the board and a whimper from Susan Hill. Stapler heaved a sigh and rubbed his damp forehead. The struggle, such as it was, had finally ended.

"Don't think that I..." she began again only to stop as her face went white and she faltered. She held up her shaking hand to stop Morex. "I don't think I can stay any longer," she gasped. "But don't think that I will not be back." She measured her words to insure that each one would be said. When she had finished, her head dropped slightly and as she passed Rick, a feeble smile returned to her lips. "Sorry, Rick," she whispered.

Stapler watched her the entire time Madelaine was being wheeled from the room. There was something odd about her, he had noticed, but not until he saw her frail left hand dangling over the armrest did he recognize what was missing. There was no ring on Madelaine's hand.

~ ~ ~

She was in his office before he returned from the debacle at J & T. Madelaine stood by the window staring out into rain when Rick entered. His only thought was that she had taken over his building at last, too.

If she heard him come in, she did not react. Her hands on the window sill for support, Madelaine remained stationary. Her tailored green suit flattered her back and narrow waist. Though she still could not hold herself completely erect, she seemed much taller than he felt.

"Good morning, Miss Jordan," he said, stepping up beside her.

The rain outside had had its effect on Madelaine's hair and her face still shone with moisture. With the damp hair clinging to her head, her eyes looked larger than usual, her cheekbones more pronounced. He assumed that the dew on her cheek had combined with her profound exhaustion to soften the normally harsh features.

She looked terribly tired and drawn as she turned slightly towards him. Tiny red lines showed on her eyelids. Through the weariness, Madelaine managed a smile. "Good morning, Counselor," she said, her chest straining for volume.

"No thanks to you, Maddy," he replied lightly. "I'll bet you've been smiling like a four year old ever since you got me canned."

She nodded, still smiling.

Stapler shook his head in amusement. "Madelaine, Madelaine, what is left for you to do to me."

Barely suppressing a laugh, Madelaine replied, "I'm going on vacation."

"Good," he said, "I need a break."

"Tony said I needed one," she explained. Madelaine's ashen cheeks then displayed their first blush of color. "I guess you'd be glad to get rid of me."

"I try to reciprocate your feelings," he retorted.

Gazing into the distance, she said almost sweetly, "I had to do it, Rick. For both of us. Surely you understand."

"Madelaine," he said sadly, "I don't begin to understand you."

Her high eyebrows went higher. "You may find it's possible."

Bemused, Stapler examined Madelaine's profile. Certainly the hard lines were still prominent, the mouth just as thin, the chin as sharply drawn. Something was missing. Stapler's eyes left her face and drifted down to the hands braced against the window sill. They were both unadorned. "What happened to your ring, Maddy?"

The smile grew wider, producing, of all things, tiny dimples at the ends. Madelaine half turned toward him and pulled on a chain around her neck. Out of the blouse came the thin silver band she had never been without. "This is where I used to wear it," she said. "My fingers were too thin when Father first gave it to me. It was my fourth birthday." Tucking it back where it belonged, she added gently, "It was the first thing of value I ever owned."

His voice barely dented the quiet pattern of the rain. "You've got it all now, Maddy."

She breathed in deeply and, then, let herself deflate. "I'm working on it, Rick."

Stapler wrenched himself away from her side and sat on his desk. "Who's going to take my place?"

"Does that matter?" she asked with a shrug.

"Sure, I'll have to cooperate with whoever it is."

Madelaine gave him an amused glance. "A committee. George. Myself, of course. I have also asked for Heloise Carpenter."

He almost struck her. The tantalizing way she had said the name infuriated him. Madelaine was no longer destroying him. She was playing with him.

"She knows the estate and she has agreed to accept," Madelaine went breezing on. "And the conditions attached. Obviously, she can't work here anymore."

Finally, he grabbed her by the shoulders. The only thought he had was to send her out the window. "What are you doing to me?" he roared. "What am I supposed to do without her?"

Madelaine half collapsed in his hands and he had to hold her up for a moment. Regaining her balance, she said unabashedly, smiling, "That is what I'd like to find out."

Had Madelaine gone mad? That experience she had had several nights before had weakened her physically, had it also ruined that special, intricate mind of hers? Stapler wondered. He released her and fell into his chair. He felt he should grab a seat while he still had one.

Madelaine put her hand on his stooped shoulder briefly as she went by. Then she was gone, without another word.

While Rick mulled over the end of his career, Heloise strolled into the office with his coffee. The cheery expression she wore angered Rick, to the point of rage,

"What are you doing here?" he asked politely.

She struggled with her warmest smile. "I still work here," she said. "Madelaine said that I could wrap up a few things here with you."

"Gee, that is really swell of Madelaine," he snapped, rising, "but I think you and I are pretty well wrapped up already."

Heloise's smile fell into a frown of regret. "Yes, I thought so, too, Rick."

Somehow her unhappiness pierced Stapler's anger. "It's all completely wrong, isn't it, Heloise?" he asked, confused.

Heloise had started to cry and, at his words, ran to him. Her arms around him, she sobbed for a moment. Rick stroked her head as he held her as firmly as he could.

"I'm sorry," she whispered against his jacket.

"You always were the sentimental one, Hel."

The tears running quickly down her face, she looked at him. "I'm going to miss you even more this time."

"Come on," he pleaded, embarrassed by her affection. "We'll still see each other, won't we?" Or, was that up to Madelaine, too?

She smiled a little, "Madelaine said J.J. and I should meet you in London," she said uncertainly. "I don't think she's afraid of me."

The comment went right over Rick's head. "London? What am I going to be doing in London?" he asked demurely.

Again, Heloise's face fell. "Didn't Madelaine tell you that you will be in London?" She seemed so surprised that she stopped crying. She also left the room.

Stapler watched her go incredulously. The world had gone mad without him. He seized a bottle of bourbon and poured himself two glasses. By the time Heloise returned, he had started on the second.

She presented him with a neatly typed itinerary with London circled in red. "See," she said, sniffling.

He nodded. "Sure," he agreed. "London." As she turned to leave, he demanded, "Heloise? What is going on here?"

Heloise's face reflected her confusion. "What do you mean?" she asked, "I was just afraid we'd miss you in London."

"I'm not going to London," he explained.

"But your vacation?"

"What vacation? This is forced retirement."

"With Madelaine."

"I'm going on a vacation with Madelaine," he stated as though he had known it all along. "How wonderful for me."

Heloise sighed sadly. "She thinks you'll be perfect company," Heloise said. "I guess she's right."

With that comment Heloise retired from the office. Rick left to his own devices went back to his favorite, the bourbon. He had taken care of his third glass when Madelaine came back. In her long white hand she held what looked like airline tickets.

"When do we leave?" he asked dryly.

Smiling as broadly as her narrow face would allow, Madelaine replied, "Thursday. We have to hire a new attorney for the estate work first."

"Shouldn't I have been told, at least, if not asked?" he wondered.

Madelaine swallowed before she said, "I didn't think you'd go."

"Maddy, Maddy," he replied, smiling in spite of himself. "Don't be silly. If I stay here, I'll have to do my own typing."

"There is this little English company I'd like to buy."

"Bully for you, old girl."

"And then, we both need a vacation," she insisted.

"I do now," he agreed. "Shuffleboard aside, Madelaine, are you really all right?"

Her silver eyes glimmered as they met his. "I think so. I'm not sure, but I feel better. Better than ever, I think. And, now, I need company."

Stapler pursed his lips. "And I'm it?"

"You are the company I want," she declared.

"What about that little British..."

"That, too." She smiled and then got serious. "Father always liked you. And I think I did, too. Not much, but a little."

"A little is more than zero, Maddy," he said.

"More than zero, yes," she concurred.

He shook his head in wonder. "Sometimes, you scare the hell out of me, Madelaine."

"I know," she said. "I'll be back at twelve. I have to see Josh about Tylton's reorganization. Will you have lunch with me?"

"If you go now," he replied. "So I can get myself organized just once more."

"Oh, and I brought a little light reading for you." Madelaine handed him two blue-backed documents.

"Am I 'served?'"

Her eyes lit up, but she only said, "One to think about, the other just to read."

"You did something legal that I won't like?"

Madelaine Jordan nodded firmly. She smiled again and turned to leave. He was convinced that it was not the same Madelaine Jordan he had known for so long. She did not stride or keep her back rigid. Her face no longer remained impassive, indifferent to expression. Had that part of Madelaine Jordan been sacrificed during a two-hour struggle with Carleton and his machines? He had little idea what Madelaine was like, now. He could tell she would be just as difficult, just as fascinating.

God forgive him, the way he wanted her.

He glanced at the documents she had given him. He did not intend to...

The first was an employment agreement, bearing Madelaine's signature: Richmond Stapler, Vice-President and General Counsel of Jordan & Talbot. If she wanted him... He nodded his head and signed it.

The second was entitled "Assignment and Settlement." Raymond Carleton's estate and his heirs were parties, his research was the subject matter.

Rick skimmed the instrument. It did not take him more than a few lines to grasp what she had done.

Carleton's machine...

He couldn't help but laugh.

Now, Madelaine owned that, too.

~

About the Author

Born in 1950, John Nicholas Datesh lived mostly in and around Pittsburgh, Pennsylvania until early 2009. At Brown University, he took many courses in writing as an institutionalized rationale for doing just that. Then, at Boston University School of Law, he learned to mix in words and phrases like *It Depends* and *Hereinafter.*

In Spring 2009, he moved cats Lila and Lucy Liu to a condominium one mile in from the east side of Naples Bay in Florida. He left his Pittsburgh career in law, business and product development in favor of concentrating on writing fiction, winging blogs and cultivating beach chairs, presumably in that order of dedication.

He began writing fiction with a pencil and published, on paper with actual ink, his first three novels, the SF/Mystery *The Nightmare Machine*; Soft-boiled Detective *The Janus Murder*; and International Suspense *The Moscow Tape.* All three novels are available in virtual ink at e-book stores on the Web and in trade paperback.

Also available are short stories *The Pro Station* (WWII), *The Final Equation* (SF), *Reruns ad Infinitum* (SF/Fantasy) and the Christmas short story, *You Could Call It a Christmas Story,* all published after the move to Naples.

He concocted a humorous and/or satiric blog at Empty-GlassFull.com shortly after moving. His Christmas Story started out as post to the blog, and he has e-published a collection its other early posts, grandly entitled The Very First Blog Posts of All Time. As novel writing began to take more of his time, he sent blogging on long vacation.

His 2013 novel, The Girl in the Coyote Coat, came to ignore the boundaries of mystery/suspense genre for which it was originally intended. No one would call it a romance, either. With a real estate and finance backdrop, the novel exposes how love, sex, money, scams, drugs, house-breaking and -shopping and fur coats can affect the lives of complex and intriguing characters and even kill a few.

November 2016's *The Body in the Bog* is a Sunset Noir mystery novel. It is the first in the author's planned Death by Condo series starring prematurely retired lawyer Ian Decker.

His screenplay *The Last Three Minutes* was the first piece written partly on the beach and entirely in the Naples Bay scenery, though it is not set there. *The Last Three Minutes* has been adapted as a novel, if not a movie, by the author and was published in December 2016.

Author's Note: The New Cover Art
for The Nightmare Machine

Special thanks to artist Julie Kimball whose wonderful painting *The Gates of Hell* is the basis for 2016's redesigned cover for *The Nightmare Machine*. I should add that Julie's vision was too cheery for the theme of the novel. I like to call my twist *The Gates of Hell as Seen from the Inside Out*.

Author's Note: The novel
The Girl in the Coyote Coat
and A Need Apart

That heading is not an error. They are the same novel. So, why? To double sales? Not likely.

The novel *The Girl in the Coyote Coat* had a long, tortuous road to its final form, right down to the cover and the very title. It was published under that title after some serious consideration. The novel had gone through any number of working titles, as time allowed, from the 1979 original *The Real Estate Novel*. *The Girl in the Coyote Coat* was always my favorite, inspired, as it was, by an actual coyote coat on an actual model. In the end, that was the title I chose, in a close call (if only to me) over number two, *A Need Apart*, but I did not use the photo that initially inspired the title.

In 2016, I decided to try a little Amazon Kindle advertising. Amazon would not accept the somewhat racy cover. That rejection got me thinking. The novel had grown into what I must loosely call a literary novel, if only because it does not fit into any genre. Why not try a different cover for an ad? Then, I thought, why not try a different, more literary-sounding title. The result is the identical novel with a different name, *A Need Apart*, and a different cover.

Ironically, the *A Need Apart*'s cover uses the shot that originally inspired the working title *The Girl in the Coyote Coat*. Fortunately, I love both titles and both covers, equally. Oh, and both the coat and model, too, if not quite so equally.

www.ingramcontent.com/pod-product-compliance
Lightning Source LLC
Chambersburg PA
CBHW020734250626
47155CB00003B/746